A SLOW CLIMB UP THE MOUNTAIN

A SLOW CLIMB UP THE MOUNTAIN

By Sue C. Dugan

This book is dedicated to my family – Ken, Doug, Kathleen, Steven, Dustin, Lindsey, Brady, Grace, and my parents, Clieve and Maxine

Acknowledgments and Heartfelt Thanks

During the metamorphosis of this book, when it went from cocoon to butterfly, it was touched by many talented writers and editors. I know I will leave someone out and if I did, I'm sorry. I appreciate everyone's input, large and small. For you see it takes a village to write book, much like rising a child. Launching a book can be painful and filled with emotion and trepidation like giving birth.

Here goes! A big thank you to Marti, Sunny, Amy, Sharyn, Gail, George (first editor that saw promise in my work), Holly, my family, and friends.

A Slow Climb up the Mountain

By Sue C. Dugan

School Bus Yellow

August

Chapter 1

"Hurry, Jotty! The bus is coming," Ma called. "You'll be late, and I have an early shift."

"Coming," Jotty said, surveying Rolling Stones and marine blue. They both had their redeeming qualities."Stick out your tongue, suck it" versus calm-blue, endless horizon.

Jotty wasn't one of those girls who cared what she looked like. She agonized between the soft, comfortable, second-skin feel of the Rolling Stones tee and the new shirt, still creased from the package.

"Jotty! The bus just stopped by the Crowders'!"

Jotty slipped on the Rolling Stones shirt, took her backpack, and headed for the front door.

Ma frowned. "You're not going to wear that, are you? What about the new shirt I got you?"

"I like this one." Jotty smoothed it over her stomach.

"It has burn holes and paint on it. I'm going to use it to dust the furniture."

"Don't do that!" Jotty hugged herself and settled her pack on her back lest Ma try to take the shirt from her. "I like this one," Jotty said, an old friend like Tanya or Sal.

Jotty heard the huff and squeak of the bus's brakes coming closer.

"Gotta go, Ma. Bus. See you later."

Jotty walked toward the bus stop at the end of the trailer park drive. Sal and Dee were already standing in a haze of cigarette smoke.

"I need a smoke this morning," Jotty said, taking Sal's cigarette without permission and sucking smoke in, immediately settling her brain chatter.

When Sal opened her mouth to speak, Jotty interrupted her. "I heard." Heck, it was the talk of the town.

"I'll miss Mr. Miller," Sal asked.

"I won't," Jotty said, adjusting her backpack to rest more comfortably on her shoulders.7"I wonder what she's like," Sal said, dropping her cigarette as the yellow bus turned the corner.

"That's a perfectly good butt," Jotty said, picking up Sal's cigarette and placing it in the side pocket of her pack.

A new principal might make Jotty's decision to attend or leave much easier.

With a heavy sigh, Jotty got on the bus, stowed her backpack under the seat, and sat next to her best friend, Tanya.

Tanya started to speak, and Jotty cut her off. "Already heard." Their thinking in sync.

Something ran by their feet.

"What was that?" Tanya asked, her voice edging up.

"It looked like a mouse," Jotty responded, before realizing some sort of disgusting rodent had indeed run by. As an afterthought, she jerked up her legs as another brown streak ran under the seats. Tanya did the same, snatched up her backpack, and held it to her chest.

"I found one in the cupboard once. Totally freaked me out," Jotty said.

Another brown streak, followed by a gray streak. Panic on the bus.

"My stepdad drowns them when he traps them. They're disgusting, but I think drowning would be terrible," Tanya said.

"Gross!" Sal said.

"Step on it!" Dee Dee said.

"No, the mice are for the snake," Roger said. Roger, valedictorian and the smartest boy in their class—now an expert on snakes—hurried by, peering intently at the aisle floor and beneath the seats.

"Snake!" A scream and a shriek.

2

Kids jumped around in the aisles, stomping and yelling"Sit down!" the bus driver commanded.

"There it is!"

More screams.

Jotty watched as the black-and-red snake slithered down the aisle, dodging feet. Thank goodness, they didn't jump. The screaming from the silly girls in the back grated and scraped on Jotty's nerves.

"Shut up!" Jotty said irritably.

"It's only a king snake!" Roger shouted. "It's harmless!"

Jotty didn't care what kind of snake it was; she didn't want it slithering up the leg of her jeans. The skin on her shin bristled, and she shook her leg.

And to think a place called Rattlesnake Mountain was Jotty's place for solitude. The king snake evoked the same shivery feeling as a rattler.

The driver pulled over and put on her emergency flashers. "Everyone remain calm." She opened the side door. The noise level increased and the bus rocked as the students jumped on the seats to get away from the invaders.

"Someone get the snake!"

"Don't let it get away! It belongs to the biology department," Roger said as he ran down the aisle after the reptile that was slithering for the front of the bus.

"I got it!" Roger held up the snake, wrapping itself around his arm. "Someone give me the cage."

Students passed the cage to the front of the bus.

"A mouse!" someone shrieked.

The mice headed for the open door. From the commotion on the bus, Jotty imagined there were hundreds of them.

The driver closed the door and turned to them. "Everyone sit down." She patted her chest as a way to steady herself. "Roger has the snake, and the mice are gone."

"How many mice did you see?" Roger asked.

"How many were there?" the driver asked, her eyes narrow with concern.

"Four."

"I think I saw that many."

Then came a shriek from a girl in the back.

Did that mean another mouse lurked under their feet?

"It's just a mouse," the driver said. "We can't go until everyone takes a seat."

Jotty slid down and propped her paint-splattered knees up on the back of the seat in front of them. She closed her eyes as her breathing returned to normal, only opening them when she felt the bus move again.

Tanya looked at her with wide eyes and gave her a wobbly grin. "I'd say that was a good start for our senior year."

"Ha!" Jotty said. A snake, mice, and a new principal—how could she be so lucky?

Sour Hurt-Your-Eyes Lemon Yellow

Chapter 2

The bus lurched to a stop in front of Sagebrush High School. Jotty stood and smoothed down her jeans and T-shirt. The shirt was moist and stuck to her back from the encounter on the bus and the August heat. The news channel said it would be ninety-five degrees. They left the bus and turned toward the air-conditioned school.

"Well, let's get this over with," Jotty said, pushing open the double metal doors.

"I'm sure it will be fine," Tanya said, hurrying after Jotty, always in her wake.

"Easy for you to say," Jotty said. "You like it here."

"It's better than being at home."

True, but not as good as going to the mountain. Jotty's heart sank and her feet dragged when she saw the shiny new lockers, fresh paint on the walls, and a bold Sagebrush Stallions sign over the library doors. Cinnamon, coffee, and chocolate smells from the cafeteria were the only familiar things.

"Wow," Tanya said. "Finally. New lockers."

What else had the principal changed? Jotty had painted a beautiful mural of Rattlesnake Mountain on the cement-block wall of the girls' restroom. She was particularly proud of that one and if the new principal had painted over that too… Jotty took off running, pushing aside those in her way.

"Jotty," Tanya called. "What's the matter? Slow down."

Nothing slowed her progress until she got to the girls' restroom where she stopped in the doorway and surveyed the interior slowly, critically. In her mind's eye she remembered her mural; in reality the walls were freshly painted in sunshine yellow. All the walls glowed with "sour hurt-your-eyes lemon."

Jotty felt the tears well, but she wasn't going to cry, the paint color stung her eyes—that's all.

Tanya came in, looking around the door to judge Jotty's reaction. "Oh no, they painted over your picture."

The paint wasn't the only difference; new gray metal walls replaced the dented and battered stalls. Her bathroom, the one she liked, had chipped tile, scarred countertops, and writing and pictures on the walls.

Jotty scowled at the hypnotizing yellow walls, secretly scared for the other changes. Why did the new principal have to go and spoil everything.

She felt the fight drain away and the urge to sag against the counter, but she didn't want Tanya to see her act that way. She squared her shoulders and took a deep breath.

Tanya stepped in and took out a bag of potato chips. "Want some?"

Jotty wrinkled her nose. Chips sounded gross right now. "Yuck. Is that your breakfast?"

"Nothing to eat at our place," Tanya said.

Jotty stood back from the wall with folded arms. "We'll have to do something about this. That's a terrible color. What am I supposed to do with yellow?"

Tanya nodded and ate her chips, wiping her greasy hands on her jeans. "A sunny day?"

Nevada was almost always sunny, but the sky was Pacific blue, not sunshine-puke yellow. Blue felt restful and hope-filled whereas yellow, happy and jagged.

Jotty licked her lips, took her colored pens from her bag. The pens had the traditional names of red, blue, yellow, green, etc. Ma had once given her a set of paints with names like misty emerald for green, mayflower blue, winter-sky gray, and sandcastle tan. She had loved those paints. She particularly liked their names.

"Yellow is a bad backdrop for my picture."

"Are you sure?" Tanya asked. "I like yellow."

"I like it too, but it's not a realistic color in a desert of blue, brown, lavender and green."

"Are you going to paint another one on the wall?" Tanya asked.

"Of course." That's what Jotty did. She painted, daydreamed, and cut class.

She drew the same picture in her notebooks and textbooks and on her bedroom walls: her signature picture of Rattlesnake Mountain behind their trailer—the one that loomed over Sagebrush. She drew it as if it would give her strength and fortitude, which it did, but it also kept her grounded and sane.

"This one will be bigger," Jotty said as she fished out a cigarette and lighter from her backpack, lit it and sucked in a lungful of smoke before handing the cigarette to Tanya.

Tanya shook her head and wrinkled her nose and patted her stomach. "I don't feel too good. I might be getting something."

Or it could be the greasy potato chips for breakfast.

"Good morning, Sagebrush High students," chirped Sue Ellen McCabe over the intercom.

"I wish she would shut up," Jotty said. "Reminds me of a bird." The finches darting in and out of trees and bushes, their endless chatter waking her up.

"I like Sue Ellen."

"I do too, even if she gets on my nerves with her happiness," Jotty said.

Lee Greenwood's "God Bless the USA" played softly in the background. "Welcome back to school! Don't forget tonight is soccer tryouts, and Friday is our first home football game against the Dayton Dust Devils. Go Stallions. Today we're on an abbreviated schedule, with classes letting out at noon for teacher in-service."

"That's the best news I've had all day," Jotty said. The day already felt endless, and she pinched the bridge of her nose; a headache threatened behind her eyes.

Sue Ellen continued, "Our new principal, Dr. Benninger, would like everyone to meet her at lunch before school is dismissed. She's excited to meet all of us! Have a great first day!"

Tanya blurted, "I've got to go."

"What's your hurry?" Jotty didn't want to go to class yet, but she didn't want to stay here, either. She had never had this dilemma before.

"I wanted…The bell." Tanya stopped and gave her a playful smile.

Jotty waved her hands. "Don't tell me—Buck. You want to see Buck."

"I knew you'd understand," Tanya said with a shrug and a toss of her head, her flaxen yellow hair briefly airborne before leaving in search of Buck.

Jotty closed her eyes and leaned against the counter, remembering how Tanya had met Buck. They had been cruising around one hot night and came upon Buck and his buddies, he had trouble written all over him when he waved around a beer can and jerked his head toward Tanya and then to his beat-up Impala. Tanya went with him.

Jotty leaned back against the counter and was envisioning her newest mural when Tanya returned.

"Jotty!"

"What? Did you forget something?"

Her friend stood in the doorway. "I saw the new principal, and she's headed this way," Tanya said.

"I expect so," Jotty said. Better get the confrontation over early; no use pretending to be someone she wasn't. Even so, she flipped the cigarette into the nearest toilet.

"Not bad," the woman commented as she stepped over the spilled powder and flushed the toilet.

"Can you do better?" Jotty didn't think a woman wearing a suit and white blouse with a little bow tie at the neck could be that coordinated.

"Probably not. I'm out of practice in butt flipping." The principal surveyed the room, even the ceiling, in a slow, methodical way and then wrote something on her clipboard. "I better tell Emmett to clean up this mess. Maybe we should lock the door for a while," the woman said.

Was that a threat?

The principal turned to Tanya. "Are you finished in here? I'll give you a pass for class."

Tanya scurried away with a backward glance at Jotty.

And what's your name?" the principal finally asked Jotty.

Jotty studied the woman as she moved closer. She had short dark hair and a neutral face. Neutral because everything fit together and was the right size. None of her features stood out one way or the other. Her eyes were neither friendly nor hostile, just neutral. A learned expression, Jotty thought. A face a principal had to acquire to deal with students like Jotty.

Should she tell this woman her real name or not? Heck, the school wasn't that big; it wouldn't take her long to find out who she was.

"Alpha," Jotty answered with a challenge in her voice. She was the alpha dog at this school.

"Unusual."

"I'm unusual," Jotty said, puffing out her chest. "And who are you?" she demanded.

The woman stopped, pursed her lips as if she was thinking, and said, "Clyde."

"Clyde?" Jotty shook her head. "You must be joking."

"If you can be Alpha, then I can be Clyde." She held out her hand. She had polish on her nails, rose-petal pink.

Jotty was familiar with that color from her paint palette.

"Nice to meet you, Alpha."

Jotty swallowed back the lump in her throat and reluctantly took the cool, smooth hand in hers. She had a sinking feeling this year would be anything but normal.

Chapter 3

"Well," Clyde said brightly, "you won't mind if I lock this bathroom while we get the mess cleaned up?"

"Yes, I would." Jotty looked sternly at Clyde, hoping to intimidate her, but Clyde's eyes didn't look into hers; she stared instead at the wall as if she hadn't heard Jotty speak.

"You can use the one by the gym," Clyde said absently. Jotty guessed she had heard but chose to ignore her.

"This one is mine. I spend all my time here," Jotty said.

"You own this bathroom?" Clyde asked, her brows pointing up in an exaggerated peak before her eyes finally locked onto Jotty's. "I thought the taxpayers did."

"You thought wrong." Jotty leaned back and folded her arms.

"You go to class, don't you?"

"Sometimes. I'm not into school," Jotty said.

"What does that mean?" Clyde asked, clutching her clipboard to her chest.

Jotty noticed Clyde's eyes were like a kaleidoscope, moving from blue to gray and to shades in between, depending on her mood. Ah, Jotty had struck a nerve! Cutting class was Clyde's thing. And it was her thing, too!

"Just what I said," Jotty retorted.

"Education is important." The neutral gray shade returned to Clyde's eyes.

"I knew you'd say something like that," Jotty said.

"If you're so good at reading my mind, what am I thinking?" Clyde asked.

"Go to class," Jotty replied dryly, another attempt at sarcastic humor.

"Exactly! It's a miracle." Clyde raised her arms to the ceiling. "What else am I thinking?"

Jotty shrugged. Clyde thought she was funny. Of course she was thinking go to class. She was the principal, wasn't she? That's all they cared about. They didn't care about feelings, boring teachers, or how worthless the classes were.

Clyde peered again at the freshly painted wall behind Jotty. "No more drawing on the walls."

"Why do you think it was me?" Jotty asked, pretending innocence.

"I don't know exactly who did the picture, but—"

It wasn't a picture. Pictures were for kids in elementary school. Hers was a painting. There was a big difference between coloring and painting.

Jotty cut her off. "I wouldn't say picture. I'd refer to it as a painting. It takes some talent to paint a scene like that. Pictures are in coloring books!"

Clyde's nostrils flared. "For someone who doesn't know about the painting," she emphasized the word, "you seem very passionate about it."

"It wasn't me," Jotty said, feeling her cheeks get hot. Damn, she was blushing.

Clyde studied her for a long time as if trying to see into her head. That would be tricky because Jotty didn't let many people know what she was feeling or thinking. She even hid most emotions from herself.

Clyde looked at the gold watch on her wrist. "But for now, I want you to go to class. Give me your name, and I'll write you a pass."

Nice try.

Clyde raised her brows. There was no exaggeration this time, just questioning, probing, and wondering. Jotty had seen that look from teachers before, unspoken questions about what made her act the way she did.

"Just make it out for Alpha."

"We have no such student at Sagebrush. That's not your real name. A nickname perhaps?"

No, she was Alpha here, top dog.

"And your real name is Clyde?" Jotty retorted.

"A college nickname." She chuckled as if it was funny, which it wasn't.

Jotty's mouth remained a firm line.

"I'm Dr. Benninger."

Jotty would never call her that. She would be Clyde or nothing.

"Everyone knows me," Jotty said.

"But I don't."

"You will." Jotty waved her hands around. "Just put down Alpha." It didn't matter anyway. She wasn't going to class. She needed another cigarette and couldn't wait for Clyde to leave.

Clyde wrote out a pass for Alpha and with a swish of her skirt, turned as if she was doing military maneuvers, and left. Jotty crumpled the pass and threw it on the floor.

Then Tanya was back.

"Why are you back?" Jotty asked.

"I told the teacher I felt sick."

Jotty looked at Tanya's pale, sort of greenish, complexion, compounded by the sour-lemon color of the walls. She couldn't recall the name of that green, a cross between olive and khaki. Olive drab—a name as uninspiring as the color. Even Tanya's flaxen hair had the green tinge.

"You don't want to make trouble already. She's smart. Mr. Miller was dumb and didn't care."

Mr. Miller seemed to hide in his office, afraid to confront students. He only dealt with Jotty when he had to, when her detention and misbehavior slips mounted. He gave her detention to keep the teachers off his back. He wasn't stupid exactly, more like tired.

"Mr. Miller didn't care. He was just waiting until retirement," Jotty said.

"That too."

"Why can't they ask us what we want?" Jotty said, more to herself than Tanya.

"Do they do that?" Tanya asked.

"No, but they should. We're the ones who have to attend." Jotty chuckled.

"What's so funny?"

"I told her my name was Alpha," Jotty said, smiling to herself in the mirror, examining her teeth for any food particles.

"She'll figure out there's no Alpha at Sagebrush."

"She already knows that. Probably Mrs. Nixon already blabbed to her." Mrs. Nixon was the school secretary, a woman who loved the goody-goody students.

Clyde would be a challenge for Jotty's last year, but Jotty had a surprise for her. She was dropping out at eighteen and going to work. "I want to keep her off my case."

Tanya shook her head slowly. "I don't think she'll be an easy one to get around."

Probably not, but she might make the year halfway interesting while she worked on Ma to let her quit school and help with the finances. It might be fun to play cat and mouse with Clyde. With the thought of mouse, she felt the involuntary shiver run up her leg.

Tanya wet a paper towel and dabbed at her face. "I don't feel so good." She went into a stall and Jotty could hear her gagging.

Jotty knocked on the door. "Hey! Are you OK? Do you need anything?"

"Maybe something to wipe my mouth."

Jotty wet a paper towel and handed it over to the top.

Tanya came out of the stall wiping her mouth. She took a handful of water from the faucet and rinsed her mouth.

"Do you feel better?" Jotty asked.

"A little." Tanya motioned with her head toward the door. "Are you going to class?"

Jotty stood with feet far apart, arms folded, as if deciding to leave or to stay. "I'm going to do what I want."

"You should at least go the first day to get the assignments." Tanya put the paper towel in the garbage can.

"I'll think about it." She stepped closer to the counter and away from the door.

"I've got a bad feeling about the new principal. She's going to be trouble," Tanya said, as she edged toward the exit.

13

"I can be trouble for her too." Jotty gave Tanya a little push in the direction of the door and settled herself back on the counter. She heard Tanya's footsteps retreat down the hall.

Chapter 4

With Tanya's departure, Jotty was alone again. The way she liked; she could think better when she studied the bare yellow wall and envisioned her newest painting. She'd draw her signature painting of Rattlesnake Mountain, of course. The new paint job on the concrete walls might be a problem. She liked the gray color they'd been before. Urban gray was easy to make the sky look stormy and ominous, which it rarely was. Sagebrush was usually clear and bright, a contrast to her dark moods.

Jotty took out her black marker, uncapped it with her teeth, and drew a mountain outline on the wall. The black ink looked like the tracks of a roller coaster. She took a blue marker and streaked it behind and around the mountain, the beginning of the sky. She had a start to her painting and could fill in the color and details later.

"Oh, Jotty," Emmett, the janitor, said apologetically, coming in and setting down a pail, mop, and broom. "Dr. Benninger told me to clean up the bathroom. She said it was closed to students."

"Not to me, Emmett," Jotty said.

Emmett, wrinkled and brown from the sun and hard living, rested his broom against the counter. He grinned, revealing a gap in his tobacco-stained teeth. "How come?" His calloused hand rubbed the stubble on his chin, making sandpaper-like noises.

Jotty liked Emmett. They talked a lot last year when he came to clean during class.

"She likes me," Jotty said with an uncharacteristic giggle. She usually didn't giggle. Tanya giggled, but Jotty usually omitted a gravely growl from deep in her throat.

Emmett smiled broadly, revealing another large gap at the side of his teeth where two or three were missing. Jotty wondered how many teeth he had left. "You're joshing me."

Jotty shrugged. "I've started on my latest creation."

"It's the mountain, right?" Emmett asked.

Of course, since she didn't paint anything else. "I'm making it bigger. What do you think?"

"Just like the last one, but…" Emmett's voice dropped to a whisper, "Dr. Benninger wants this place cleaned up and all the smoking stopped."

"I'm not smoking." Her cigarette butt, a fat slug, lay at the bottom of the sink.

He sniffed before shaking his head at the remainder of her cigarette. "You won't get to finish this." He used the broom handle to motion toward the lines on the wall.

"I will," Jotty said stubbornly, searching her backpack for her paints.

Emmett started sweeping the spilled soap into a pile. "That Dr. Benninger's a determined woman."

"So am I."

He chuckled. "Yes, ma'am, you are at that."

"Don't do anything with my picture," Jotty warned, adding a ridge to the mountain.

"If she tells me to paint over it, I'll have to. I need my job, what with my wife, Millie, on oxygen and all."

"Try not to. Avoid her."

He whistled through the space between his teeth. "There's no avoiding her; she's got a lot of spunk, always moving around. Checking on things. Talking to the teachers and students. I've never met a woman like her." He shook the broom at her. "You better get."

Reluctantly Jotty put away her pens, pulled out her class schedule, and stepped into the hallway, keeping a lookout for the navy suit. She squinted at her crumpled schedule; she had Mrs. Markley for English first period.

Chapter 5

The hall was deserted for as far as Jotty could see—only the imprints of sneakers on the new carpeting, oval shapes, and dusty outlines like a herd of cattle had stomped down the corridor. A crumpled piece of paper was the only occupant, looking lost and out of place. Even the lockers stood silent as she passed.

When Jotty got to class, Mrs. Markley frowned, grunted, and waved toward an empty desk.

"Your name?" Mrs. Markley asked.

"Alpha." She slid into the only available seat.

Someone said, "Her name is Jotty."

Jotty turned and shot daggers at whomever had said that, probably Carl, do-gooder Carlsen, always sucking up.

With an exaggerated motion, Mrs. Markley put a check on her book. "And why are you late, Jotty?"

"I got lost." She heard a snort from the back of the room and a laugh.

"I see. Don't make a habit of being late."

No, she wouldn't be late, but she probably wouldn't be here, either.

Jotty blinked at the bare eggshell-colored walls. The whiteness had a hypnotic effect on her. She felt sleepy and drugged.

After distributing the books and class outline, Mrs. Markley faced the class and said breathlessly, "This is senior English where you will prepare a research paper using the correct format. We will also be reading and analyzing world literature." Walking down the aisles seemed to have winded her, and she patted her ample chest, which held a pair of reading glasses suspended from around her neck. "I've taught at Sagebrush High School longer than any other teacher, and I'm proud of that fact. Thirty-three years!"

Ugh. How could anyone stand Sagebrush High School for thirty-three years? Jotty shook her head, trying to clear the lethargic feeling the eggshell color made her feel.

"Today we're going to review punctuation marks. You'll be writing your senior report, and I'm a stickler for detail. If you're missing a comma or a semicolon, it's an automatic point reduction."

Mrs. Markley's flat, monotone voice made Jotty think about sleep, white noise. Jotty yawned, jaw cracking in the effort. Soon Mrs. Markley's voice sounded faraway.

Jotty put her head down, resting her cheek on her folded hands. She could hear the clicks as Mrs. Markley wrote on the board. Click. Click. Click. The clicks lapsed into nothingness as she fell asleep.

"Young lady." Jotty felt someone shaking her arm. "This isn't nap time. Wake up."

Jotty licked her lips. She had drooled on the desk, and her face felt numb from resting on her hands. She shook her head and looked around as several students laughed.

"You march right down to the office. I'll not tolerate sleeping in class. Out with you!"

Jotty picked up her backpack but left the book on the desk. She wouldn't need that this year.

"You need your book," Mrs. Markley called. "You have an assignment tonight."

No, she wouldn't need the book. She'd use Tanya's or Sal's books to do her work. She heard more laughter as she finally escaped to the bathroom, which Emmett had left clean. She felt better here even though her heart raced wildly. She wasn't going back to Mrs. Markley's class anytime soon.

Emmett hadn't touched the start of her picture. Jotty took out a cigarette stub, lighting it while she contemplated what to draw next. She inhaled deeply; the acrid smoke calmed her nerves. The buzzing in her head cleared. She took out her black marker and added to the smaller hills. Jotty took three more drags from her cigarette and flicked the rest into the toilet as she shaded the sky a grayish-blue. Not a bright sunlit sky, but one overcast with pending thundershowers. Something they didn't see very often in Nevada. And the same color as...

"So it is you drawing on the walls."

Clyde's eyes.

Jotty jumped. She had been concentrating so hard that the voice startled her, and she dropped her pen. The sky was the same color as Clyde's eyes—harbor mist.

"I had a feeling it was you. I'm a pretty good judge of people."

"So now you know. It's me," Jotty said without turning around. She needed to brighten the sky; no way did she want to think of Clyde when she worked on her mural.

"That's kind of depressing, don't you think?" Clyde asked.

Yes, it reminded Jotty of school and jail and Clyde.

"If you went here, you'd be depressed too," Jotty replied.

"Come with me, Alpha."

Jotty squared her shoulders, gritted her teeth as she put her markers away, and followed Clyde's swaying navy hips to the office. Mrs. Nixon, the secretary, looked up when they entered, but when seeing it was Jotty, she went back to her work. Jotty had been an office regular the last three years, and apparently, this year would be no different.

"What will we do with you?" Clyde said, standing in her office and surveying the walls as if she had never seen them before.

She couldn't do anything with Jotty; they weren't destined to be friends. Jotty transmitted her thoughts via a stony stare and a grimaced mouth.

"I'm not doing detention." Jotty flung herself into the chair Clyde indicated.

She slumped down so her ribs and stomach scrunched together. She wasn't comfortable, but slouching made her look nonchalant and unconcerned. Inside was another thing; her stomach was in a tight knot, and she couldn't seem to get enough air.

"Did I say anything about detention?" Clyde smoothed down her skirt before she sat and then adjusted a picture of two blond-haired girls in a silver frame. Jotty noticed the loving look Clyde cast at the picture. Her children probably—perfect-looking little girls. Jotty bet they never got in trouble at school.

Clyde seemed intent on looking at something on her desk. Jotty let her eyes wander over the office. The same one Mr. Miller used to have only Clyde decorated it femininely with plants on the file cabinets and a wreath of dried pink-and-blue flowers on the wall. Jotty preferred Mr. Miller's clutter. He'd always thumb through papers and shake his head when he couldn't find what he was looking for. Jotty liked to watch him because half the time he never did find her detention slip or the note the teacher had sent on her. She had even brushed past, sliding a stack of notes into the garbage—forgotten. His disorganization had worked in her favor. Clyde had three colored file folders, a desk calendar, a cup of pencils, and the pictures on her desk. She picked up the top folder and opened it to reveal misconduct slips before closing it, folding her arms on the desk, and studying Jotty.

The silence was overwhelming. Why didn't Clyde say something? She hated to wait. She blurted, "I heard you were giving everyone detention!" She thrust out her chin as if to emphasize her point.

Clyde picked up the picture, looked at it with a smile on her face, and said, "Why are you so angry? I'm not angry at you. I just wish you had told me you were going to the bathroom instead of cutting class."

Tell the principal she was cutting? That was a new one. Jotty almost smiled as she imagined the scene. "Oh, Clyde, you won't mind while I go outside and smoke for a while?" That wasn't against the rules, was it?

Jotty forced herself to glare at Clyde, hoping her pursed mouth and hunched eyebrows would make her look mad. "I rarely go to class."

"I hope to change that, Jotty. Your name is Jotty, right?"

"Yeah, what about it?"

"I asked who painted the picture in the bathroom, and Emmett told me."

Darn Emmett. She liked him, but did he have to be so honest? Couldn't he act like he didn't know?

"Don't waste your time on me. I'm dropping out of school when I'm eighteen."

Clyde looked at her with a shocked expression on her face. "What about college?"

"I'm not going to college. No one goes to college around here."

"I'm afraid you're wrong. Quite a few Sagebrush students go on to college."

Kids whose parents were in management at the gravel pit maybe—or the ones on the ranches with horses or doublewide trailers. The smart ones. Jotty avoided them. Their lives were much different than hers. They wouldn't understand what it was like to live with Leroy. The mean, pig-eyed man who worked at the gravel pit and drank to drown his unhappiness every night. Jotty's mother stood by him. When he had a bad day, he hit Ma. Ma, who never helped herself, only others, defended him, saying he had a bad day. At the remembrance of Ma's black eye, Jotty clenched her fist.

Clyde continued looking at the misconduct report.

Jotty, Ma, and Leroy lived on the edge where life was rough. There was a fine line between eating and having a roof over their heads and being homeless and waiting for the food truck to distribute boxes of bread, peanut butter, and canned green peas. Her days were a constant blur of "bad days" on the precarious lip between mediocre and crappy.

Clyde tried again. "I hope you'll change your mind."

Jotty pulled her mind away from their current existence. "I don't like classes here. Why would I want to take more after this?"

"College classes are different. And we have a new teacher this year."

Her heart beat a quick one-two. More art classes would be great. She'd stay if that was the case.

"More art?"

"No, science."

She didn't like science. Another boring class. Although she did wonder about the names of the vegetation she saw on the mountain and why certain rocks had striations of different colors and why the clouds hung low on certain days but floated out of reach on others. Could a new teacher tell her those answers?

Instead she responded with, "Forget it. I've made up my mind."

"I can make you go to class here," Clyde said, settling back in her chair, which rocked slightly as she moved.

21

"No one can make me go to class." Jotty stood up and glared down at her, but Clyde looked around her office, pursing her lips.

"I can go with you," she said. "At my old school, that worked well for students who cut classes."

"What?" Jotty demanded. "Go with me? You mean you would sit through a class?" Clyde was willing to sit in a boring class with her?

"Of course."

"Mr. Miller never did that."

"Do I look like Mr. Miller?"

Hardly. "That's ridiculous. Why do you have time for that?" Mr. Miller never seemed to leave his messy desk. Why didn't Clyde have all those papers? What did she do all day? Sure, it was the first day of school, but still…

"I'd make time to see you succeed with your education."

Jotty let out a noisy huff.

"As principal, I can invoke my in loco parentis rights." Clyde looked at the clock. "Let's go, second period is about to start."

Jotty slammed her hands on the desk and faced Clyde eye to eye. "Why are you picking on me? I told you I was dropping out!"

"Because you're smart, talented, and a challenge to anyone who calls themselves an educator. You're the reason I'm here."

Jotty snorted. Bullshit! Clyde was here to make life miserable for her.

"OK, go to class with me," Jotty said. "But you can't stay with me forever."

Clyde nodded. "I won't have to."

She had a lot to learn. No one pushed Jotty Alfarnso around, no one, not Clyde or Leroy.

The bell sounded, and Jotty bolted out of the office, a bull from a chute, and careened toward Mr. Harrison's class. She pushed her way through, plowing ahead, shoving people aside in the packed halls. She didn't turn her head, but she sensed Clyde keeping pace with her.

Tanya was already there, looking at Buck in a sickeningly sweet, totally absorbed way when Jotty rushed through the door. Jotty blinked rapidly while deciding where to sit. The chairs were in a circle, not in the traditional rows.

Tanya waved to Jotty and said, "Sit by us." But dropped her hand and frowned when Clyde came in too. She turned back to Buck, pointing her finger in their direction.

To his credit, Buck leaned back in his chair, folding his arms, oblivious to the direction Tanya was pointing.

Jotty sat far away from Tanya and Buck, as close to the exit as she could get. Clyde took the seat next to her. Jotty rested her chin in her palm and tried to ignore Clyde by studying the stuff on the wall.

Mr. Harrison didn't have the normal things on the bulletin boards like hygiene or counseling posters or classroom rules and regulations. Instead, he covered the walls with a wagon wheel, arrows, hatchets, horseshoes, and an old black frypan. Dull gray silverware, some with prongs missing, dangled from a fishing line attached to the ceiling, giving them a floating appearance. She had never been in a classroom like this before.

"This is interesting, don't you think?" Clyde whispered.

Jotty didn't answer. Where did Mr. Harrison get all this old junk? She had heard about his classes but had never experienced them before.

She looked around further. Inside the circle of desks were electric logs and, instead of books, Mr. Harrison had rocks and minerals on the shelves.

Slowly the room filled with students, but Mr. Harrison hadn't arrived yet. Everyone sat quietly, waiting, craning their necks to take in all the objects. Because the room was so different, they didn't seem to notice Clyde, and if they did, they didn't say anything. Everyone was looking around, and a few were pointing at the things they saw.

Suddenly, the lights dimmed.

"Yippee!" Mr. Harrison jumped into the circle. Jotty saw his profile in the hazy darkness. What was he wearing? An Indian headdress? It looked like something she had seen in an old western movie–feathers around his head and hanging down his back.

He switched on the electric logs. A golden light illuminated the floor and the faces of the students. Flames danced off the walls and the dangling silverware. Mr. Harrison slowly surveyed the room.

"Welcome to Nevada History." He shook his head. "I'm wearing the headdress of my dear friend, Running Coyate, Plains Cree chief." He paused to let his statement sink in. "We'll be studying about our local Indians, the settlers who came for ranching and mining, our statehood, the military, and the railroads."

Jotty felt glued to her seat, her eyes never leaving Mr. Harrison in the dim light.

"We owe a great deal to our Indian breatheran. The Washoe, Paiute, and Western Shoshone lived around Lake Tahoe and the Sierra Nevadas. They fished and hunted and in some instances cultivated the land. Regrettably their language is lost with only a handful of native speakers left."

Mr. Harrison carefully took off his headdress and set it aside. Jotty wanted to study its composition, but Mr. Harrison continued. "I'm going to tell you about the white dragon," he said in a hushed, low voice.

The weirdness in the room kept Jotty rooted to her chair, hardly breathing.

"Imagine with me what it was like to be an Indian of the old West. For my people the pinto pony is special. Yes, I am an honorary member of the Washoe tribe."

He shaded his eyes and surveyed the room. "This is what happened to my people over one hundred and fifty years ago. One day on a hunting party, they noticed a cloud of dust in the desert. They were horrified to discover the dust was following them." He walked around the circle as he talked and gestured with his hands.

Jotty looked around at the faces of her classmates. Tanya, her mouth open slightly, stared at Mr. Harrison. For once, she wasn't looking at Buck. Even Buck had lost his disinterested and distracted look, his eyes following Mr. Harrison's words and actions.

"Panicked, they ran through the brush, but the cloud still followed them. By dusk, the cloud stopped. Look around. Do you see the dust?"

Jotty found herself looking around the dark room, searching for the imaginary dust. She could envision it in her mind and see it in her pictures. Swirls of ink black, brown sienna, and gray fog. A dust devil that whirled through the sagebrush. Her nostrils flared; her nose felt dry and full of grit as if she had been breathing in dust from the desert. Of course that couldn't be; they were in class. Maybe the shadows dancing on the walls from the logs made her think she was somewhere else. Whatever was happening seemed real.

"When the scout came back to camp, he reported that there were white ghosts walking around campfires. Ghosts with pale skin. Best of all, the ghosts had pinto ponies. Pinto ponies possessed magic. My people couldn't resist going to see the ponies."

Mr. Harrison cocked his head and pretended to listen. "I hear them. Over there." He pointed to the wall.

Jotty's glance followed where he pointed. The shadows became ponies silhouetted against the walls. She could hear something. A pony or someone shifting around in their chair? From behind her, she thought she heard a horse nicker.

He continued telling the story about the white man and the horses before stopping dramatically and turning in the circle, studying each of them.

Jotty was far away in the desert at Rattlesnake Mountain, surrounded by pintos.

Mr. Harrison finished his story about the ponies and the white man, and before she knew what was happening, he stopped and turned on the lights.

"If you hadn't guessed already, I'm Mr. Harrison." He chuckled. "I love the old tales, so most of this class will be stories, and I'll share my adventures in the desert. We'll probably even take a field trip or two to see what we can find." He waved his arm around the room. "I need more treasures for my walls." He patted his rounded belly. Jotty thought he looked like a brown-haired version of Santa Claus.

Jotty glanced at the clock; fifty minutes had passed. Class was finished, but she wanted to hear more.

"Tomorrow we'll talk about the Paiute Indians and their dealings with the white man. Some not so mystical." He shook his head sadly. "Many bad things happened to the Indians."

Buck snorted, signaling his interest or disinterest—she couldn't tell. Or maybe he agreed with Mr. Harrison.

The bell shrilled, but no one moved. He surveyed the room and smiled warmly. "Have you all met our new principal, Dr. Benninger? Ta'mo'mo'? That means woman."

Most students nodded, and a couple clapped.

Jotty eased out of her desk, ready to bolt before frowning at Tanya, who shrugged in return.

The question of what to do about Clyde this year hung over her like the silverware in the classroom.

Chapter 6

After school, Jotty went to Joe's Diner where Ma worked. If they were slow, maybe Ma would make her a sandwich, and they could talk about the first day of school. Jotty had walked down Main Street for as long as she could remember. A street with a log cabin grocery store, an antique store, three bars, a convenience mart/gas station, and of course, Joe's Diner.

The diner sat next to an antique store that hadn't seen much business by the looks of the layer of dust on the objects in the window. She imagined the old typewriter hammering away at the news of the day; the tooled saddle on the back of a cow horse, moving the great beasts to different pastures; and the frilly parasol covering the head of a bonneted woman.

Jotty stopped on the sidewalk and watched a man painting a picture on the diner's front window. He turned and smiled. "Hi."

She nodded. He turned back to his work.

"What kind of paint are you using?" she asked.

He kept working but said, "Acrylic."

"Why not watercolors?" Dumb question; of course acrylic.

"Too runny."

He turned to her again, his brush dripping paint onto the sidewalk. He had a nice face, longish brown hair that curled over his collar, and a handlebar mustache that drooped over his mouth. He was on the thin side with paint-splattered jeans. She liked his jeans and pointed to her own.

"A fellow artist! And a Stones fan," he said, nodding toward her T-shirt and giving her a quick smile before turning back to his work.

Why wouldn't the school let her do something like this? There were big, bare windows on either side of the front doors to the high school—a perfect place for her pictures. Or rather, her paintings. The thought made her heart race. If only.

She tilted her head to watch him. He outlined the figures and filled them in with color and details. He was painting a cowboy, holding a knife and fork, and looking eagerly at a waitress, holding a pie. The cowboy was leaning over with his boot on a saddle. The waitress, who had big hair and wore a red-and-white gingham apron, leaned toward the cowboy. Who were those people supposed to be? No one looked like that around here—certainly not Joe or Ma, the only regular workers in the diner.

The bell on the door chimed, and Ma came out, wiping her hands on her apron.

"Hi, Betty," Tomm said to Jotty's mother.

"Tomm, this is my daughter, Jotty."

He turned to her again. "Nice to meet you, Jotty." He held out a paint-stained hand. "I've never heard that name before. It's unusual."

"Long story," Betty said.

Jotty shook his hand.

"I was going to name her Jody, but thought I would be creative with two t's, not a d."

Mrs. Markley would like to know spelling mattered.

"I like it," Tomm said.

No one ever called her Jody. She wasn't a Jody; she was Jotty, and she liked her name.

Jotty held up her hand, which had fire-engine red paint from Tomm's handshake. He frowned at his hand and wiped it on his jeans. "Sorry."

"Nothing to be sorry about. I like paint." She too wiped her hand on her jeans.

"We've talked. She's an artist, a kindred spirit," he replied.

Ma frowned. "She should be studying, not doodling and drawing pictures."

"Sometimes, Betty, a body just has to draw and be creative!" he said.

Jotty liked him.

"What do you think of it so far?" he asked.

Ma nodded. "I like it. Jotty?"

"Who are those people?" Jotty asked.

28

Tomm stepped back and stroked his mustache. "I don't know; just made them up. Thought maybe there were still cowboys around here."

A few, but they didn't wear polished boots. Most of them, ranchers' kids, smelled faintly of manure, had hay and straw sticking to the bottom of their boots, and wore jeans with big belt buckles, souvenirs from rodeo competitions.

"Nobody around here looks like that," Jotty said, for once wishing she hadn't opened her mouth when she saw the doubt in Tomm's eyes.

Ma frowned.

"What do they look like?" he asked, cocking his head at the picture.

"Regular—like me and Ma." Jotty moved her head toward the diner's door. "And Joe."

"Oh," Tomm said. "Can you give me some ideas?"

"Maybe." She hitched her thumbs through her belt loops. "The cowboys around here don't have shiny boots, and no one wears big hair anymore."

"An easy fix," he said with a grin.

"Jotty nodded and watched him begin to change the hair and boots.

She and Ma watched silently until a customer came. Then Ma went back inside the diner. Jotty continued to watch, her fingers twitching to pick up a brush and help.

When Tomm finished, he began to clean his brushes and put away his paint. She watched him work in companionable silence. The painted picture held a secret truth, revealing as much about the artist as the subject.

When Ma returned, she said, "I'm done. Let's go home. I need a nap. It was a busy day." She took off her apron, they said goodbye to Tomm, and they went home.

Chapter 7

At their house trailer, Ma sank onto the lopsided couch and put her feet on the coffee table, moving her skinny legs around, her joints cracking.

"Do you need me to massage your feet?"

Ma laughed. "You've been doing that since you were little. Always trying to help."

"Only to make things easier for you, Ma."

"I'm responsible for some of this myself." Ma held up her red, chapped hands. Already arthritic from washing dishes and bussing tables. "And to think they were once smooth like yours."

It made Jotty angry to see Ma's hands. If Leroy didn't spend all their money at the bar, maybe Ma wouldn't have to work so hard.

Jotty took Ma's hands in hers and ran her thumb over the skin, moving in circular motions.

"That feels so good, honey. You are the best thing that has ever happened to me."

"I try, Ma. Have you given any thought about me helping out? Financially?"

"No, I want you to stay in school."

Their eyes met and held. Jotty sighed. "I just want to help."

"I know you do and I'm grateful, but we'll get by until graduation."

Jotty gave Ma's hand one final caress and reached for the cigarette pack. She lit one, inhaled, and offered it to Ma.

"How was your first day of school?" Ma asked after her initial puff of Jotty's cigarette.

Jotty wasn't sure what to think about school or Clyde or the changes. The only bright spot would be Mr. Harrison's class. She smiled in spite of herself, remembering his room, only frowning when she recalled Clyde sitting next to her.

Ma saw the smile. "I'm so glad you like your senior year."

"I wouldn't say I liked school. There are a lot of changes," Jotty said, mentally checking off: pushy principal, clean school, ugly paint, and an unconventional teacher.

"But you smiled…"

"I have an interesting Nevada history teacher."

The wind shook the flimsy trailer, rattling the door with an invisible hand. Ma stared at the window, shivered, and pulled her sweater closer. Already the warm summer nights were getting shorter and colder. "Change can be good, can't it?" When Jotty didn't respond, she leaned back, her face relaxing slightly as she settled against the couch and flexed her feet on the coffee table.

Jotty wasn't sure about change being good, unsettling perhaps. She sighed and flipped open her notebook. She chose her words carefully. "All the walls are painted, and we have new lockers." Jotty looked down at the picture of pintos and Indians she was drawing for Mr. Harrison, although she wasn't good with people.

"Paint's good, isn't it?" Ma asked.

"I liked the old color better."

"Ah, Jotty. There's change everywhere." Ma ran her hands over her scalp and thin, scraggly ponytail. "That's the only thing you can count on. Change. The diner has a new cook." Ma inhaled and held in the smoke for as long as she could before she released it.

"Who's the new cook?" Jotty asked, as she shaded in the background of her latest picture. She called it a picture, so why when Clyde called her work a "picture" did she get so upset?

"Jeff something." Ma waved her cigarette at Jotty. "He won't stay long; no one does, except me and Joe."

"Is he young?" Jotty asked, not looking up from her drawing.

"Everyone is."

"Good looking?" Jotty raised her right brow and gave Ma a glance.

"Jotty!" Ma said with a laugh. "You've never been interested before."

Jotty looked away. "Nothing to be interested in around here, Ma. Most of the guys are redneck chauvinists, cowboys who drink too much and beat their wives or girlfriends."

31

"I don't think that's entirely true. Tell me about the other changes at school," Ma said.

"We have a new principal." Jotty spat out the bad-tasting words. "And she'll stay, I'm sure."

"Mr. Miller finally retired?" Ma chuckled and flicked an ash into the overflowing dish; the ash tumbled off and landed on the coffee table. "It's about time. He couldn't keep you under control. Why, I think of the calls I used to get—"

Jotty cut her off. "Neither can she."

"A woman, huh?" Ma's face relaxed as she thought about Jotty's revelation. "I don't want any problems this year. You need to graduate. Are you studying?" Ma motioned toward her notebook.

Jotty shook her head. "Drawing."

"Oh, Jotty. Make an effort and stop drawing. If you try, you'll graduate."

"You didn't graduate, Ma. I don't want to, either. I need a job. I want to quit school and help out."

"You'd make me feel good if you graduated. Then I'd know that you could fend for yourself. It's too late for me."

"I want to help by earning money." Jotty rubbed the tips of her fingers together.

"Look at me. Working for fifteen years in a diner, waiting tables, no benefits." Ma held up her hands.

Jotty winced and looked down at her own hands, the tips stained with ink and paint from her pens and brushes; the nails, bitten off and jagged; but the skin was smooth and even. She didn't want to look at Ma's swollen fingers.

"You can still get your diploma," Jotty said.

"How?" Ma asked.

"Night classes?"

"I'm exhausted after work. How can I go to school?" Ma asked, a tinge of regret entwined with her question.

"If I had a job, you wouldn't have to work as hard," Jotty said. "Then you could finish."

"You were meant for better things than waiting tables and washing dishes. You're smart, Jotty. Look at what you've done."

Absolutely nothing. Jotty frowned at Ma.

Ma shook her head, her mouth set in a thin, determined line. "You always pass your classes even though you hardly study. You're smart. Imagine what you could do if you tried."

Jotty didn't want to try. School was boring and worthless. Even thinking about it bored her. In response, she yawned.

"I'm going to quit at eighteen, Ma. I can't stand that place. And our new principal—she and I don't get along."

"Why don't you give her a chance? You need to learn to get along with people, not fight all the time."

"No one's going to tell me what to do."

"There'll always be someone telling you what to do. The government, a boss, a husband."

"I'm not getting married." Jotty picked up her neglected sketch.

"You asked about the cook?"

"So. Maybe I'll live with someone. I'll only get married when I'm sure." She added a spot of color to one of the pintos.

"You can never be sure," Ma said sadly.

"I'll never marry a man like Dad who'd run out on me and the kids. Or Leroy..." The rest of the sentence hung between them.

"Your father and I were too young and stupid to get married. He was a good man; we just didn't love each other."

"Why did you have me?"

"Well..." Ma paused as if deciding what to say. "You were the reason we married young. I know it's not the best reason to get married, but..."

"So why did you marry Leroy? How can you love him?"

"It's hard to make it all by yourself," Ma said, looking over Jotty's head, her eyes misty and faraway. "He has his good points. He wanted a child of his own."

Not Jotty, a castoff from another man.

"He was disappointed when I couldn't have any more children," Ma said.

Jotty remembered Ma telling her she was a difficult birth.

"Don't you remember when we used to take you to the park when you were little?" Ma asked.

Jotty's thoughts skipped to that pudgy little girl on the swing, laughing and hanging back so her hair swung behind her. A long time ago when Ma's hands were smooth, and her eyes sparkled.

"I was disappointed I couldn't have any more children. Leroy too." Ma stood and stretched. "We better get dinner started."

Or, Jotty silently added, Leroy will beat the living daylights out of you. The very thought made Jotty clench her fists. Someday, Leroy, someday, Jotty silently vowed.

They both stopped, frozen in their tracks by the crunch of tires on the gravel outside. Leroy.

"Come on. Let's hurry. You never know what his mood will be."

Chapter 8

Jotty threw down her sketch pad and followed Ma into the kitchen to begin dinner. Leroy usually calmed down after a couple of beers and food.

"I hope he had a good day," Ma said as she opened the cupboard.

If Leroy had a good day, they could watch television, and he would share jokes he heard at work. But if he had words with his boss or one of his coworkers, there would be hell to pay.

"We'll make spaghetti. It's quick and easy and one of Leroy's favorites," Ma said.

Jotty got out the big pot for spaghetti, and Ma reached for the can of sauce as the door banged open.

"We're just getting supper ready now." Ma stirred the sauce, pretending she had been hard at work for a while. Ma could make canned sauce taste good by adding the right spices.

All the spice containers in the cupboard looked the same to Jotty. What was the difference between sage and tarragon? Oregano and thyme? Each was green, only their smells revealing their uniqueness, much like springtime on the mountain. Each variety of sage had a distinct smell and color.

"What are we having?" Leroy sniffed the air before dumping his lunch box and coat on the table.

"Spaghetti."

"I hate spaghetti," Leroy said, scratching his bulging stomach. "I want a thick steak and a beer."

"I'll fix it just the way you like it," Ma said in the soothing voice she would use on one of the feral cats that slinked around the edge of their trailer.

Jotty put the water on, ignoring Leroy, who rummaged through the refrigerator looking for the beer, slamming jars together willy-nilly.

"We're just about out of beer. Only two left. I need some," he ordered.

Ma nodded and answered in the same calm voice, "Tomorrow, Leroy. Tomorrow I'll get some."

He pounded his fist on the counter. "It was a hell of a day. I need more tonight!" Leroy's watery blue eyes glowed red from the jagged veins, giving him a wild-dog look, the telltale sign he had already stopped off at the Half-Moon Tavern for a drink or three with his work buddies.

"Jotty can go get the beer if you call Frank and let him know she's coming," Ma said.

Jotty glanced up from the stove. Leroy, with his spoiled-brat look, beady eyes scrunched together, and his mouth in a pout, pounded on the counter. He didn't move toward the telephone.

"OK, OK, I'll call," Ma said.

"I'll go. Dinner should be ready by the time I get back." Jotty held out her palm. "I need the keys to your truck and some money."

"Christ," Leroy snapped, the pout gone. He glared at her, revealing his yellow teeth. "Do I have to do everything around here? Am I the only one with money?"

"You want beer, you pay," Jotty said with a challenge in her voice. She hated him for beating Ma down, reducing her to a silent, scared woman. Jotty would never act scared around him, and he couldn't make her.

Leroy raised a pudgy hand as if he was going to slap her.

Jotty's heart pounded as she thrust out her chin, tensing, waiting for the blow. Go ahead, she thought as she made a fist; she'd punch him back.

"Don't, Leroy," Ma cried, stepping between them.

"Go ahead, Leroy." Jotty pushed Ma away. She wanted him to hit her. She dreamed of sinking her fist into his doughy stomach. "I'll call the cops, and you'll go back to prison," Jotty said in a low, deadly-serious voice.

Leroy had spent some time in prison for a break-in when he was younger.

He reached into the pocket of his sagging jeans and threw the keys and a twenty at her. "Just hurry, and don't give me any more lip."

Jotty slipped out into the chilly, still night. When her eyes adjusted to the darkness, she could see forever. Funny, how things were so clear at night; funny and sad at the same time.

Jotty breathed deeply, glad to be away from her stepfather. She got into Leroy's pickup, which was parked next to Ma's. His and hers dilapidated trucks. She slammed the warped door and squealed out, scattering gravel in her wake. It felt good to jerk the wheel around; she just wished Leroy was tied to the back bumper!

She turned on the radio and pushed down hard on the accelerator, making Leroy's truck lurch and bump down the dirt road as she listened to George Strait. She hummed and tapped her fingers against the wheel, wishing the sides of the truck would rattle off and even shake loose Leroy's last hubcap.

The grocery store was an old log cabin at the end of the rutted dirt road. It was simply named Woody's even though Frank owned it. Jotty slammed on the brakes and skidded to a stop before realizing Buck's low-riding Chevy Impala was parked nearby.

What rotten luck.

Jotty heaved the truck door closed with all her might. The side mirror, held by a single rusty bolt, wobbled and threatened to fall off.

"What are you doing here?" Tanya asked, coming out of the store.

"Getting beer for Leroy, that scumbag."

"Buck and me are taking a ride." She held up a bottle of Coke. "Buck's waiting in the car for me. Why don't you say hi to him?"

She'd rather talk to a snake. "I need to get home."

"Come on, just for a minute," Tanya pleaded.

Reluctantly, Jotty let Tanya pull her over to the camouflage-green Impala with deer horns for a hood ornament and the trunk only inches from the ground.

"Jotty," Buck said, nodding his head, but still looking straight ahead. His black eyes glittered in the darkness, and a thick braid with a feather stuck through the end hung down his shoulder.

"Buck. How you doin'?" Jotty said through gritted teeth. She smelled alcohol on him already.

Buck motioned with his head for Tanya to get in.

"Wanna come?" Buck asked, holding up a flask. "Rum and Coke."

Some of the kids from the reservation drank a lot. Heck so did most of the school population.

"Come with us, Jotty," Tanya begged, leaning over Buck to see out the window. "We'll have fun."

She doubted the fun part. "I told you, I can't." She took a step back. "Leroy…"

"Oh, I understand," Tanya said.

Buck looked at Tanya and nodded to Jotty before backing the car out of the parking lot. She watched them drive away. Buck's tailpipe dragged on the ground with each bump, sparking like a firefly. She watched the sparks until they were out of sight.

Jotty didn't like the way Buck treated Tanya. Sometimes he looked at her like she was a naughty child. Jotty wanted to shake her sometimes and urge her to dump the deadbeat.

Jotty went into the store; a jangle of bells announced her presence.

"Your mother called," Frank said.

Jotty nodded before hoisting the pack of beer onto the counter and handed over Leroy's money. She hated buying beer for the scumbag, but things went smoother at home when he drank a few cold ones.

Beer didn't fix anything for Leroy; even drunk he was angry. Jotty tossed the beer into the truck and drove home quietly, all her bravado gone.

Sunshine Yellow

October

Chapter 9

Saturday. Finally. Jotty hummed to herself as she ran the vacuum and dusted the trailer.

"You sound in good spirits today," Ma said. The smell of bleach wafted out of the tiny bathroom. Ma's idea of a weekend was to clean the trailer from top to bottom.

"It's Saturday, and I'm going hiking!"

Ma came out of the bathroom wearing blue plastic gloves and inspected the furniture.

"I dusted the way you wanted," Jotty said.

"I can see that." Even with only about five hundred square feet, it seemed to take hours before she could escape the stifling trailer, smelling of pine cleaner, and go to Rattlesnake Mountain.

"I'm leaving," Jotty called over her shoulder when she had finished with the list of things to do. She struggled into her sweatshirt, grabbed her smokes and backpack, and headed out before Ma could call her back for one more thing...

The mountain, called Rattlesnake by who knows who, had been her playground and haven since she could remember. As she walked along the dirt road that led to the hill, she mused about why Rattlesnake was so special to her. She didn't like snakes, and the idea of encountering one made her apprehensive and jumpy—not in a totally bad way, but rather something to be overcome. A complicated notion only she understood.

Rattlesnake Mountain wasn't really a mountain, more like a hill. The steep path that was carved though the sagebrush and rocks was challenging. She had only ever made it halfway up before sitting and leaning against the boulder to smoke, draw, and think.

Today was no exception. She climbed to the boulder. She could have gone farther, but there was nothing to rest against. She walked a few steps and looked back. She was higher than she had ever been before, and the back of her legs protested the incline. She went back to the boulder and slid down, resting her back against the side. The desert was shutting down for the approaching cold weather, she could tell; the chill poked through her sweatshirt. Fall. The temperature, always cooler on the hill, was a welcome change from the heat in their trailer.

She took out her cigarettes and lit one, letting the smoke curl through her body, calming her thoughts. So much had happened in one week, but when she examined the past five days, there really wasn't much to consider. Sure, there was Clyde, and Jotty would figure her out just like she had Mr. Miller. She had learned to feign innocence with him and frown when he read off her infractions from a teacher. Clyde would be trickier.

Jotty thought it best to ignore Clyde than verbally spar with her. Although not Jotty's nature to keep quiet, a fight was probably brewing. She ground out the cigarette against a rock. Yes, Clyde and the sour-lemon paint would be a problem this year even if she had to admit secretly it brightened up the dreary place.

She took out her sketch pad and continued drawing the wild ponies. Ma's voice echoed in her ears about change being good. The mountain was changing from the summer colors to fall foliage. From her vantage point, looking up at the mountain, she saw tuffs of sagebrush, losing their summer color and dimming to gray and brown; the birds flying in formation overhead, navigating to warmer climates; and the wild horses growing thicker, patchy coats. The horses spent the winter huddled against pines on the backside of Rattlesnake Mountain. But now, they stood away from her, the big male watching as the mares fed. She studied them as she added contours to their sketch on the pad.

Jotty looked down the hill toward their house trailer. It was small, but she could just see it through the trees. Ma's truck pulled away for her lunch and dinner shifts. Leroy's truck was gone.

With Leroy gone and Ma working, she could have had the trailer all to herself, but she preferred the solitude of the mountain.

She looked back down at her notebook and continued with the horses, listening for their approach, but they didn't come closer. The only sounds were the sagebrush rustling, dry bristles scraping; pine needles rattling against an insistent wind; and air brushing the sand, hushing and sighing, a melodramatic female—the desert's music.

A sunshine-yellow flowering plant Jotty had always wondered about was beautiful in the summer, but now the flowers had closed into themselves and would soon blow away. She picked the stem from the nearest plant, smelling it before putting it behind her ear. There was no fragrance in its death. She picked another stem and placed it between the pages of her notebook. She'd ask the new science teacher what he knew about the flower.

And to test his knowledge, she added several stalks of cheatgrass. Did he know cheatgrass from ordinary weeds? She doubted he would know. She had seen him around the school, an odd-looking man wearing a bow tie and light-pastel shirts. He stuck out against the somber browns, navies, and blacks. She was curious about him, but not enough to actually take his class. No, it was too late for that.

The wind intensified, ruffling the pages of her notebook, and her eyes felt sandy with grit; even the horses turned away, their backs to her. She put her notebook away in her backpack, trekked down, and walked along the two-track to their trailer.

Green with a Hint of Blue

Chapter 10

On Monday, Jotty went in search of the new biology teacher. The sign next to his door read Mr. Hornbeck. Mr. Hornbeck, hmm?

She opened the door, unsure of what to say.

"Hello," he said, turning from the blackboard to face her.

"Hi, I have a question," she said, taking a step into the classroom.

"Are you in one of my classes?" He frowned at her before taking off his glasses and using a cloth on his desk to polish them.

"No."

She stayed by the door, rooted in place as she studied him: round academic glasses, a lavender shirt, and a plaid bow tie.

"You're not from around here, are you," she said.

"Do you want to know where I'm from? Is that your question?"

"Um, no. I want to ask you what these plants are."

He motioned her closer. She drew out her notebook and placed the stems on the table for his inspection.

"Interesting," he said.

Interesting because it wasn't something he was familiar with or interesting because it was unusual, which it wasn't. Both plants grew in abundance on the hill.

He stroked his chin. "This one is a Chrysothamnus nauseosus, I believe."

A what? Was he using big words to make her feel stupid?

As if knowing she didn't understand, he said, "In simple English, rabbit brush."

"I see. And this one?" she pushed the small brown stalk toward him.

He didn't study it but said, "Plain and ordinary cheatgrass. Bromus tectorum." He folded his arms and waited for her reply. "So why the questions?" he asked after Jotty had replaced the stems in her notebook.

"Just wondering, that's all. I've been climbing Rattlesnake my entire life and wanted to know about the plants."

His face softened. "You're a hiker?"

"No, I like to go up there to sketch."

"Do you have anything I can see?"

"What do you want to see?" she asked.

"Your sketches."

She flipped her notebook to the first page, the one with her pencil drawing of the hill and pinto for Mr. Harrison.

He leaned closer, and she noticed his nose curved down, much like the hawks that flew lazy circles overhead—birds of prey. His name should be Hornbeak, not Hornbeck.

"You have wonderful detail," he said, pointing to the spruce-colored tree—green with a hint of blue. "Pinyon pine. Do you have any more?"

"At home."

"Bring them in." He paused as the bell sounded. "What was your name again?"

She hadn't told him.

"Jotty."

"And why aren't you in one of my classes?"

"I'm not into science."

"I'd say you are most definitely into science with your natural curiosity and artistic talent."

She backed away toward the door. "I'll bring more pictures tomorrow."

"Sign up for my class!"

"It's too late," she said.

"It's never too late."

It was for her, wasn't it?

Green with a Hint of Blue

Chapter 11

Later at the trailer, Jotty rummaged through the drawers in her bedroom looking for the folder holding her pictures. It shouldn't have been a daunting task; the room was tiny and only fit a twin bed, a dresser, and a minuscule closet.

"Jotty? I'm home," Ma called from the doorway.

"In here."

"What are you doing?"

"Looking for the folder with my sketches." She poked her head out her doorway.

"That's an odd thing to do," Ma said, taking off her sweater and hanging it up.

"Mr. Hornbeak wants to see them."

Ma frowned. "Is he a new teacher?"

"Yup. He's an odd bird with a nose like a hawk." Even though he was odd and out of place, he intrigued her. He asked her to be in his class. Her. He must not have gotten the memo. Jotty Alfarnso was a deadbeat who didn't go to class.

Ma raised her brows. "He sounds interesting."

"I wouldn't know. I'm not in his class."

"Don't you need to take science?"

"I've already taken two. Don't need any more." Uninspiring classes studying one-cell organisms in pond water.

"You could take another one," Ma said.

Jotty wrinkled her nose. "Science was boring."

"Suit yourself," Ma said, taking a package of hamburger from the refrigerator.

"What are we having tonight?"

"I feel like meatloaf."

Jotty liked meatloaf too. She went back to searching though her drawers for the collection of pictures. She heard Ma opening and closing cupboards while she fixed the meatloaf. Next Jotty went through the closet. On the top shelf was the folder. She took it down,

44

opened it, and studied what she had done in previous years. Each picture was similar, but the details got clearer and more pronounced as she went from freshman year to senior status. Jotty judged her talent was becoming more defined. Were these the type of pictures Mr. Hornbeak wanted?

Jotty heard the telephone ring in the background. Probably for Ma or Leroy. She continued flipping through her drawings.

"Jotty?" Ma said from the doorway.

"What is it, Ma?" Ma came into her bedroom with a look of confusion on her face—cheeks ashen, and eyes bright with tears.

Ma opened her mouth and said with a choked voice, "Leroy's in jail for disorderly conduct."

Jotty chuckled to herself. A good place for the no-good schmuck to be.

"What are you going to do?" Jotty asked.

"I don't know. His bail is five hundred dollars. I don't have that kind of money."

"Call his brother." Jotty remembered Leroy's brother had bailed him out before.

"I guess I could do that. Or I could use my truck as collateral."

Jotty doubted the truck was worth five hundred, at best half the needed amount.

Ma stood in the doorway contemplating her next move. "Right," she said, talking to herself. "I'll call Richard."

Chapter 12

"Richard promised to wire the money for the bail when he got paid," Ma said as she and Jotty sat at the small table for dinner.

Jotty helped herself to meatloaf and small white potatoes before commenting, "I hope it takes him awhile to wire the money."

"What a thing to say!" Ma said.

"Isn't it nice just the two of us?" Jotty asked. The atmosphere in their trailer was casual and light. The feeling of being off-kilter and guarding her words, gone. It felt nice to have Ma to herself.

They ate their meatloaf in companionable silence. Ma looked more relaxed, her forehead smoothed out and her mouth upturned. Jotty didn't have to watch what she said; any little thing that struck Leroy as stupid set him off in a tirade of complaints.

"So what did he do this time?" Jotty asked, contemplating a second slice of meatloaf.

"Started a fight at the Half-Moon."

The bar with the half-moon shape carved into its front door. A dark, smoky place that swallowed up patrons. Jotty had only been in the doorway when Ma sent her to look for Leroy. He usually magically appeared out of the haze of smoke from the far end of the bar, an apparition, a demon. Her vision of hell.

"Why don't they kick him out for good?"

"Why would they? He and his gravel pit buddies bring in a lot of money."

Yeah, money that could be used to fix up the trailer or buy a few steaks for a change. She liked Ma's spaghetti and meatloaf, but steak would be nice, and her mouth watered in response.

"True." Jotty helped Ma clean up the table and kitchen, washing and drying the few dishes and stacking them in the cupboard.

"Do you want to watch television?" Ma asked when they finished.

"No, I'll probably take a walk."

Ma moved the curtains. The night already the blackest of black. "It's pretty late."

The clock on the wall read six forty-five—not too late.

"Just a breath of fresh air, and then we'll watch something."

Jotty stepped out into the clear, cool night. She walked down the short gravel patch that was their driveway to the road connecting all the trailers. They were the fifth trailer from the end. Green and yellow eyes glowed in the dark; the feral cats prowled for their next meal of mice or rabbits.

She tucked her hands in her pockets and walked past the row of metal buildings many people called home. Most of them were occupied, and Jotty saw lights through the curtain-shrouded windows and an occasional shadow and outline of a person. She wondered what their lives were like.

Did they have a stepfather in jail? A tired, scared mother who needed help? Did they have a meddlesome new principal? Did money troubles prickle their every waking moment?

They probably had their own problems. Everyone had them. Jotty stopped at the end of their road where it intersected with the lane leading to Main Street. A lone coyote howled in the distance, calling for his canine buddies. She looked up at the stars and wondered about the brilliance of those hot-white twinkling reminders that they were part of a much bigger universe.

A light blinked on in the caretaker's trailer, and she turned back and joined Ma in front of the television.

"It's so nice—we get to watch what we want for a change," Ma said.

Jotty pulled at the collar of her shirt; the trailer seemed overly warm after the crisp night air. But Ma was right; tonight, there would be no Leroy to watch football and hog the television, drinking beer and swearing at the refs.

"What do you want to watch?" Jotty asked.

"Designing Women," Ma said.

One of Ma's favorite shows and one she only rarely got to watch.

Leroy hated the rich-bitch interior designers with their silly problems and usually changed the channel. But problems were problems, even for the rich.

Jotty turned on the television and immediately got into the plot. "They are so funny!" Ma replied.

They continued watching until the commercial break. "Shall I make some popcorn?" Ma asked.

"I'll make it, Ma. You worked all day."

Jotty took a bag from the cupboard and put it in the microwave. She waited for the popping to slow, the smell of the corn permeating the room.

She placed it in a bowl for them to share.

"Wouldn't it be nice to live in a place like that?" Ma asked, pointing to the television.

The girls and Anthony were decorating a palatial, stately house with many rooms; large windows overlooking manicured lawns; and long, wide hallways. Jotty could hardly imagine such a thing. She looked down at the threadbare couch that had been in the trailer when they moved in. It sagged in the middle from Leroy's weight. Then she glanced at the mismatched lamps, one with a chunk out of the side that Ma had turned toward the wall.

"It would be nice," she said.

"I bet all those girls went to college," Ma added.

Jotty felt her face warm and redden. "Ma, it's just a television show."

"I know, but I want something nice for you."

"I don't think I want that."

The designer girls unrolled a carpet that looked luxurious and soft, no scarred linoleum for them.

"But you could," Ma said, her hand hovering over the popcorn bowl.

Jotty didn't think it was possible for a girl from Sagebrush to have that much grandeur.

Chapter 13

The next morning, Jotty tucked the folder of her sketches into her backpack and went to Mr. Hornbeck's classroom.

Mr. Hornbeck was sitting at his desk, studying class papers, when she came in.

"Ah, Jotty! You're back."

She nodded as she drew out the folder. "I brought a few pictures to show you."

He eyed the stack. "I'd say there are more than just a few." He took them from her and began to look through the pages. Some were dog-eared from her backpack and the closet shelf.

He frowned. "How come you don't have any sage grouse in these?"

Jotty had seen the funny-looking birds that spread their tails like a turkey or peacock and puffed out their chests during mating season. They seemed to prefer the flat ground and sagebrush for cover. She didn't see them up on the hill so camouflaged by their brown and tan feathers they blended with the desert.

"I've seen them around, but I didn't think they were anything special."

"They are an endangered species. I've been studying them," Mr. Hornbeck said. "That's why I'm here."

"Really?" She couldn't imagine studying the chicken-size birds or moving to Sagebrush voluntarily.

"Yes, they are fascinating birds."

"Why?"

"They have a complex social order and follow rituals for mating and chick raising. If you look at them, you can see the structure to their lives. Something we humans need to learn."

"Interesting," Jotty said, making a mental note to watch the birds next time she went to Rattlesnake. "So why are you studying them?"

"They are being hunted to extinction," he said. "That's why I'd like you to draw some pictures for me, as illustrations for my pamphlets."

Mr. Hornbeck's door opened, and Clyde came in. Her face registered surprise at seeing Jotty.

"This young woman is a fabulous artist," Mr. Hornbeck said.

"I know all about her artistic talent," Clyde said dryly.

Mr. Hornbeck looked from Jotty to Clyde, clearly confused at the exchange.

"I like to draw on walls," Jotty said by way of an explanation. "Murals."

"As in the school walls?" he asked.

"Yup."

"Is it too late for her to enroll in my class?" he asked Clyde.

Clyde turned to look at Jotty and the pile of pictures on the desk. "Do you want to enroll in this class? Or will it be another one you cut?"

"It depends," Jotty said.

"On what?"

"What do you teach in here? I've already studied cells and didn't find it very interesting."

"We'll mainly be studying the flora and fauna in and around Sagebrush. The wild horses, which aren't native to the West, but they have evolved and thrived; the sage grouse, of course; and the plants you brought in yesterday. The desert marigolds and cheat-grasses and the different kinds of sagebrush."

How many kinds of sagebrush were there exactly? His class might be interesting…

"She tells me she's dropping out of school," Clyde said.

"Hogwash. You need to stay and finish your education," Mr. Hornbeck said.

Why did everyone have an opinion about what she should do? Couldn't she make up her own mind?

"I'd like to take your class; it sounds interesting," Jotty said, a little surprised at her answer. The words popping out with a mind of their own.

50

"Good!" Mr. Hornbeck said, slapping his thigh. "It's all settled! Even for a short time."

And just like that she got sucked into his class.

Sour Hurt-Your-Eyes Lemon Yellow

Chapter 14

"I'm back," Leroy announced as if Jotty didn't have eyes. They were alone together in the trailer.

Heaven help them. Leroy's brother wired the bail money.

"I can see that," Jotty said. Her heart picked up the tempo.

"Missed me, didn't you?" Leroy asked.

"Of course, like a mouse misses a snake."

His facial expression changed from teasing to disgust. "Shut up, and do something useful."

"Like you?" Jotty asked.

He raised his hand as if to slap her. Jotty took a step forward. "Do it, and I'll call the sheriff."

"Just shut up, and make me a sandwich. Where's your mother?"

"Doing a double shift."

"Christ," he snapped.

"She wouldn't have to work so hard if you didn't..." The slap stung her cheek, and she momentarily lost track of time and her thoughts, but only for a short second. Jotty charged toward him, head down, and rammed his stomach. He fell back with a grunt.

Leroy gingerly sat up and rubbed his elbow.

"Anything else you want?" Jotty asked, her breathing and heartbeat hammering in her ears, adrenaline at an all-time high, her hand on the telephone.

Leroy remained silent, but he didn't make a move toward her again.

Next time she'd call.

"Make your own damn sandwich!"

Chapter 15

"What is it with you?" Clyde asked when she found Jotty in her usual spot in the bathroom.

Jotty sat on the counter, her feet in the sink and back against the wall. Leroy was back home. Oh, how she wished him permanently gone.

"Nothing's with me," Jotty said, ignoring Clyde, her fingers itching for the cigarette but knowing smoking directly in front of the principal would probably get her suspended. Was that a bad thing? Even though she dreamed about leaving school, now wasn't the time. Her mother would freak, and it would only add to the stress in her life. No, Jotty wouldn't do that to Ma.

"How do I get you to go to class?"

"You can't 'get me to do anthing,'" Jotty said.

"Do I need to sit with you again?" Clyde leaned closer, a crease between her brows.

That day was downright embarrassing, having Clyde sit with her in Mr. Harrison's class.

"If you like," Jotty said.

"I don't like having to sit with students who should be old enough to monitor and control their own lives."

Was she in control of her own life? Ma still told her what to do. Sometimes.

"I want to drop out of school, but my mother won't let me. I'm not in control of my life, am I?"

"You took me too literally."

"Took you too literally?" Jotty asked with a snort. Some kind of adult bullshit to explain the unexplainable. "Just leave me alone, and we'll get along just fine this year."

"Sorry, not my way of running a school."

"Sorry, but that's my way to cope with this place," Jotty said.

"Suit yourself," Clyde said.

After school, instead of going home, Jotty went to Rattlesnake Mountain, but not to climb the winding path. No, she sat on a boulder and watched. The very boulder, with the flattened top, she had sat on as a child when she had been paralyzed by the mountain's steep slope.

Contemplating in her five-year-old brain why her father had left and brought the new man, Leroy into her mother's life. It was at that point she began climbing the mountain. Being scared pushed away the sad and confused feelings. She searched for snakes instead of answers to life's questions and dilemmas.

Today Jotty concentrated on the task at hand. She had seen the sage grouse in this area before, passing them by when she went up the hill to think. An uninteresting diversion, but today they would be her focus.

At first she didn't see anything, then a small movement. The female sage grouse moved her head. The hen blended in so completely, if Jotty hadn't been watching carefully, she could have mistaken the slight movement for the wind ruffling the shrubs.

Careful not to startle the hen, she drew out her sketch pad and began drawing. The hen weaved in and around the bushes, all the while blending with the desert bushes, rocks, and cheatgrass. When the hen disappeared from sight, Jotty eased off her rock and moved cautiously toward the bush where she had first seen the bird. The nest, tucked under the branches, was an indention in the ground filled with brown grasses, camouflaged from the unsuspecting eye. The chicks had been hatched months ago in the spring and summer months. Only the empty nest remained. A bird that nested on the ground would need to hide her eggs and chicks. Interesting. No wonder they were endangered; prowling feral cats and coyotes would find an easy meal. The birds needed to be masters of disguise, hiding in plain sight. Something Jotty thought she had perfected when Mr. Miller had been principal at Sagebrush High. She wasn't so sure now with Clyde at the helm.

Jotty crouched down and drew the nest. When finished, she stood and crept away so as not to startle the birds and went home.

Chapter 16

Jotty's schedule for school was: skip first period—English, attend second period—Nevada history, skip—math, attend—desert science, lunch, skip—PE, skip—career guidance. English, Nevada history, math, desert science, lunch, PE, and career guidance. She skipped everything except Nevada history, lunch, and desert science. She was pulling a sage grouse, hiding in plain sight.

And the scorecard for confrontations with Clyde was three for Jotty and zero for Clyde. Clyde probably thought she was winning the battle over Jotty, but she wasn't. As much as Jotty wanted this school year to be like the last three, nothing was going as planned.

"Jotty," Tanya said as she pushed open the bathroom door. "What are you doing in here?"

Jotty wanted to put one of Emmett's closed for cleaning signs on the door so she could be alone and concentrate on her sketches.

"It's third-period math. I don't like math," Jotty said.

"Don't you want to graduate with us?"

Did she? "No, not really."

Tanya paused, thinking, her eyes moving rapidly back and forth. "What are you drawing?" Tanya frowned when Jotty showed her what she was sketching. "A chicken?"

"Sage grouse for Mr. Hornbeak."

Tanya giggled. "Hornbeak?"

"Don't you think his nose looks like a beak?"

"I guess. He's weird, isn't he?" Tanya asked, turning Jotty's picture and studying what she had drawn.

"Yeah, he fits in here."

Tanya gave her a come on stare, fists on her hips and brows raised.

The entire school was made up of misfits, students like Jotty who didn't fit in: Clyde, who had weird notions; Mrs. Markley, wearing a dress each day with her hair in a bun; Mr. Harrison and his unusual ways of teaching Nevada history; and now Mr. Hornbeak with his pastel shirts, bow ties, and interest in birds. An odd assortment of people come together to run a school.

"This is really good," Tanya said, handing back the picture.

"Thanks." Jotty scanned the picture, deciding what else to add to the sagebrush, rocks, and the bird's nest concealed under the bush. A few of the delicate fall flowers, tiny blossoms scattered among the rocks and desert floor, the last holdouts before the ground became frosty and cold.

Tanya turned to the mirror and put on lip gloss, saying, "You seem different this year."

"How so?"

"I don't know," Tanya said. "Just different."

Almost eighteen, an adult. She considered Tanya's statement before shrugging. "Maybe a little, I guess."

"You're going to more classes this year."

Two. Just the interesting ones. She leapfrogged around her classes, attending only Mr. Hornbeck's and Mr. Harrison's classes regularly. She avoided Mrs. Markley like the plague...

Mary Sue's midmorning intercom announcements interrupted them. "Don't forget, next Friday is the homecoming dance. Tickets are on sale in the office."

"Are you going to the dance?" Tanya asked.

Jotty had never been to a dance. "No." She settled back and contemplated what to add to her drawing of the sage grouse. Mr. Hornbeck had given her a pamphlet he had written about the birds. She had never met anyone who had published anything before even if it was only a brochure.

"Me and Buck were thinking about going for something different to do."

"I don't want to go." A dance was probably more of the same stupid bullshit. Popular girls like Mary Sue hogging the limelight, with Jotty and the others slinking along the outskirts, watching and waiting from the shadows.

"If you change your mind..."

"Sure." Jotty continued with her sage grouse, adding Rattlesnake Mountain to the background, no longer the focal point of the picture, but rather a complement. Even though Rattlesnake was massive, it had its place in the background.

Jotty added another clump of sagebrush to the picture. The sage grouse would be in pencil or charcoal if she had any left, with the other features colored in. She first used brown and then green paint to make the broccoli-shaped sagebrush. Even the colors of the bush were uninspiring—terrapin and cedar.

"What are you going to put there?" Tanya pointed to a bare spot.

She had been thinking about desert marigold with the purple-brown cheatgrass in the background, casting a majestic hue over the landscape. Mr. Hornbeak had called it chrystotalist or something that.

"Jotty?"

"Hmm, thinking." Wishing Tanya would leave her in peace.

Jotty sighed, closed her paints, and wiped her hands on her worn jeans. She left a swatch of brown on her leg, but if she looked closely, she could see other faded colors. She couldn't concentrate with Tanya here.

"You're making a mess," Tanya said as she hoisted her skinny body up on the counter, looking like she was staying. "Are you going to class?"

"In a bit," Jotty said.

Jotty's cigarette, forgotten during her painting, had burned down to a long gray ash, a dirty avalanche against the white porcelain. Jotty picked it up and took a drag. The smoke burned her throat a bit. She coughed slightly, but felt calmer. Ma was always saying she should quit. What was the smoke doing to her lungs? It was probably bad when she saw the ash left behind. She figured her lungs were already covered in the residue. Did it matter?

She thought for a moment. Yes, it did matter. She wanted to help Ma. Maybe she'd think about quitting when she left this place for good.

"Let's go," Jotty said.

"To class?" Tanya asked.

"Of course, class," Jotty said.

"I told you, you're acting weird this year," Tanya said.

"Am not," Jotty said.

Tanya studied her.

"It's just that his class is interesting," Jotty said.

"The science teacher?"

"I'm helping him with his project."

"Hmm," Tanya said, but Jotty saw admiration in her eyes.

Camouflage Green

Chapter 17

"Jotty, is that you?" Ma called when Jotty arrived home from school, the wind banging the door behind her.

"It's me." Jotty struggled out of her backpack and put it on the nearest chair.

"Come in here."

Ma's simple statement meant something bad had or was about to happen. "What?"

Ma drew out an envelope from her pocket. "This came from the school."

Jotty stood before Ma and waited.

"You've missed most of your English and math classes this year." Ma didn't mention PE or Career Guidance. "And you've only been in school since the end of August."

"Yeah." No use denying it.

"If you don't start attending, you'll have to repeat those classes in summer school or next year."

No, she wouldn't. No more school after she turned eighteen.

"You forgot a couple," Jotty said.

Ma smoothed out the letter, squinting as she studied the small type before asking, "What exactly is Career Guidance?"

"We write resumes." And take tests to see what they were good at.

Jotty's test results was inconclusive. She could have predicted the outcome. She was artistic, equally left- and right-brained. A curse or a blessing, only time would tell.

"Oh, you have a resume?" Ma asked.

"Yeah. It's not very good," Jotty said. Student artist and master cutter of classes was hardly anything to write down.

"Can I see it?"

"It's in my locker," Jotty said.

"Oh." Ma stopped as if thinking. "You need to start attending those classes."

59

"I'll think about it, Ma."

"Do more than think about it. Now, help me get dinner started. Leroy should be home soon."

She could only hope Leroy stopped off at the bar and got home late.

Camouflage Green

October

Chapter 18

"I forgot to tell you, I've invited Tomm for dinner tonight," Ma said after seeing Leroy off to work, his lunch pail banging against the porch railing as he went to his truck. Jotty exhaled, the trailer felt less stifling and more open with Leroy gone.

Jotty frowned. "Who?" Did she know anyone named Tomm?

Seeing Jotty's confusion, Ma said, "You know the artist at the diner."

Oh, that Tomm.

"Why?" Somehow his presence in town had gotten crowded out by sage grouse and trying to remain off Clyde's radar.

"Just thought it would be nice," Ma said.

"What did Leroy say?"

"I haven't told him yet."

Leroy would either be on his best behavior or not. "When?"

"I said tonight."

"Oh, what are we having?" Jotty asked, pouring herself cereal and a huge mug of Ma's strongly-brewed coffee, adding a heaping spoonful of sugar to the bitter keep the truckers going blend.

"I thought chicken would be nice."

Jotty liked chicken.

"It should be interesting," Jotty said.

"I've already warned Tomm about Leroy's unpredictability," Ma said.

To put it mildly.

"Can anyone prepare for Leroy?" Jotty asked.

"I guess you might say that," Ma said.

"Tomm seemed like a nice guy," Jotty said. "Isn't the mural done yet?"

"It's been done for a while, but he's still hanging around. Even helped wash dishes the other day when we got slammed with customers."

Later that same day, at dinner, Leroy regarded Tomm with a sneer, eyeing his paint-splattered jeans and shirt, a swath of blue on one sleeve. Jotty stayed in the kitchen and watched the exchange. She knew from experience how hard it was to get paint out of clothes. "A painter, huh?" Leroy finally said.

"I like to think of myself as a commercial artist."

"Never heard of it," Leroy said, pushing past Jotty into the kitchen and taking a beer out of the refrigerator, turning his back to Tomm.

"Would you like something to drink? A beer?" Ma asked Tomm.

"Water is fine."

Jotty got him a glass of water and after he thanked her, he said, "Betty tells me you are drawing sketches of sage grouse for one of your teachers."

Jotty placed plates and napkins on the table. "Yes, our new science teacher is studying them, and I've been drawing sketches for his pamphlet."

"I used to do something similar," Tomm said, taking the silverware from her and putting it next to each plate.

"Do you want to see them?"

"Dinner is almost ready," Ma announced.

"How about after dinner?" he said, looking toward the table and back at her.

They finished meal preparation in companionable silence as Leroy helped himself to his second beer. The baked-chicken smells coming from the oven made Jotty's stomach rumble.

Tomm laughed. "Me too!"

"Chicken smells good, Ma," Jotty called over her shoulder for both her and Tomm's gurgling bellies.

"They're hiring at the pit," Leroy said, taking his beer, flipping on the television, and flopping on the couch. "You interested in a job?" he asked Tomm.

"I have a job. I'm an artist."

"A bullshit job, if you ask me," Leroy said.

No one had asked for his opinion.

"I'm working with the antiques store owner about doing some cleanup and maybe painting a sign on the front window," Tomm said as if validating his work.

"That place has needed a little TLC for a long time," Ma said, taking the chicken and potatoes from the oven.

"Who owns it?" Jotty asked, using a hot mitt to place the potatoes in a bowl.

Tomm laughed. "Joe's cousin."

"He does?" Ma asked, turning to them. "I didn't know that."

Jotty helped Ma put the chicken on a plate and take the food to the table.

"Dinner's served," Ma announced. "Tomm, you sit in that chair as our guest."

The only chair without a torn cushion—usually Leroy sat there.

Leroy took another beer and sat in the chair closest to the television, so he could watch the game. If Leroy got into the game, dinner should be uneventful. Leroy turned away from the table toward the television and shook his fist in the air. "Fumble fingers. Can't catch a friggin' thing!"

Dinner went by smoothly, with Leroy ignoring them and yelling at the television.

Jotty wondered what Tomm thought about their life, but he made no indication of his feelings one way or another. She guessed since he was living out of a travel trailer behind Joe's, he had some family issues of his own.

When the dinner dishes were cleaned and put away, Jotty took the sketches from her backpack and shared them with Tomm.

She chewed on her lip as she watched him study the half-finished drawings. She tried to look at each one as he would with a fresh eye and not judge herself too critically. They weren't completed after all.

Tomm used a stubby finger, the nail rimmed with blue paint—nautical blue—to move each picture this way and that. First lining

63

them up in a row, then switching them around on the table. Ma hovered in the background, watching, a surprised expression on her face. Jotty couldn't read Ma's thoughts, only her interest in Jotty's work.

"Ma?" Jotty asked. "What do you think?"

"Why...I don't know what to think. I guess I didn't know how good you were. I only remember the pictures you used to pin on the refrigerator."

Didn't Ma pay attention to her sketching?

"I still have them," Ma said.

"Tell me about these?" Tomm finally asked.

"Sage grouse?" Not sure what he meant.

"Sage grouse, sure, but what else?"

Jotty pointed to the picture with the nest, shadowed by the sagebrush. "This is what their nests look like."

"A picture should tell a story," Tomm said.

"It does. They nest on the ground, and according to Mr. Hornbeck, they're endangered."

"So you are telling a story."

"I guess I am," Jotty said.

"Besides nesting under bushes, what else do they do to hide?" he asked.

Ma, interest piqued even more, edged closer to see what Tomm was pointing at.

"Score!" Leroy yelled from the couch.

Jotty lost her train of thought momentarily. "Their coloring helps them blend in. See." Jotty pointed to the bird and the bush.

"So you want the viewer to look at this and have trouble distinguishing the bird from the surroundings?"

"Now that I think of it, I'm wondering if that would be good for Mr. Hornbeck's pamphlet?" Jotty asked.

"Maybe not, but you have a real talent painting the ordinary and making it seem as if the viewer is along for the ride." Tomm pushed the picture of just the sage grouse toward her. "This one for the pamphlet and this one with the bird, nest, and bush could be finished and displayed."

"Really?" Jotty rocked back on her heels.

"Libraries. City halls. All sorts of places want artwork for their walls."

"I guess I never thought about it that way," Jotty said, her mind pinging from one thought to another, colliding with possibilities and considerations. Would Clyde display her work at the school even? Probably not.

Leroy turned off the television and scratched his stomach. "You still here?" he said to Tomm.

"I guess I better go. Thank you for dinner, Betty." Then he added, "Leroy." Ma went with Tomm to the door. "And, Jotty, I'd like to see more of your work."

"Sure." And he was gone.

Sour Hurt-Your-Eyes Lemon Yellow

Chapter 19

Every morning when Jotty arrived at school, she half expected the picture of the mountain to be gone under a layer of yellow paint. This morning was no exception. She closed her eyes, pushed open the door, and sniffed. No telltale smell of industrial-grade fresh paint. She opened her eyes, and the mural was as she had left it, a work in progress. A story to tell. She wanted to share this picture with Tomm but wasn't sure Clyde would let him in the girls' restroom for a look.

Jotty settled herself into her favorite perch and contemplated what to do today. To go to class and get Ma off her back or to stay and work on the mural or sage grouse. Those were some of the many questions she asked herself every day. To graduate or not to graduate? What worn and stained T-shirt to wear with her paint-covered jeans? To steal cigarettes from Leroy's package or not. Decisions. Decisions.

Jotty slid off the counter when Tanya came in. "What are you doing?"

"Deciding what to do today."

"Class?" Tanya asked.

"Only the interesting ones," Jotty said.

"Which ones are those?" Tanya asked.

Need she ask?

"History and science."

"Tell me something. What's she like?" Tanya asked.

"Who?" Jotty asked, clearly confused; men taught both classes. Who was the she Tanya referred to?

They were usually telepathically in sync. "The principal," Tanya said.

Jotty stopped and formed a picture of Clyde in her mind's eye. A swirling dervish. A military sergeant. A busybody. She responded with, "A whirlwind. A dust storm. In two places at once."

Tanya appeared to contemplate her answer. "That's what I thought. What are you going to do this year?"

Make like a sage grouse and hide in plain sight. "Not sure, but I'll think of something."

"I want you, I mean us, to graduate together. Show my stepfather."

"You don't need to show him anything," Jotty said, chewing on her bottom lip, taking her sketch pad and paints from her backpack. Tanya's stepfather and Leroy were cut from the same cloth.

Jotty put the remainder of her cigarette in a side pocket for safekeeping. "I've got nothing to prove to Leroy."

"I know, but...my stepfather told me I was worthless."

The only differences in their lives was Tanya had little sisters to confide in and Jotty didn't.

As Jotty talked, she continued taking her painting supplies out of her backpack, including the pictures for Mr. Hornbeck. "You are not worthless. You help your mother with your sisters all the time. It's the booze talking. People say stupid things when they drink. Leroy talks trash every night."

"You think so? Buck told me he loved me."

"Whatever love means." Jotty stopped and faced Tanya, judging her response. Love was one of those words that meant something different, depending on the person. Jotty had one definition, and Tanya probably had another.

"Don't you think love is love?" Tanya asked.

A convoluted circular argument. "No, I think love means different things to different people. They say they love you, but their actions don't support it."

"I guess you're right. My mother loves me. And Buck...he's a hard one to figure out."

After school, Jotty decided to stop by the diner to see Tomm and share her progress on the sage grouse pictures. She replayed Mr. Hornbeck's response in her mind's eye.

"This is splendid," Mr. Hornbeck had exclaimed, clasping his hands together.

"They're not finished," she had said.

"Wonderful detail. This one definitely for my pamphlet!" The very picture she had shown Tomm at dinner last week.

"Would you like this one?" The more complete of the trio: the bird, nest, rocks, and scrubs.

"Can I have it?" Mr. Hornbeck asked, clearly surprised and pleased.

"Sure."

"Would you mind terribly if I hung it on my classroom wall?"

Would she mind? She laughed inwardly but gave him a wobbly emotion-filled smile, a feeling she didn't often experience.

Even though a week had gone by, the elated feeling hadn't left her. She passed the antique store, the window cleaned and display contents dusted. Tomm had started the black, rimmed with gold lettering. It was half-finished, and she was curious what he planned for the window.

"Jotty?" Ma asked, surprised when Jotty came through the door, the bells jingling.

"Yup!"

"What are you doing here?"

"Looking for Tomm." Jotty scanned the mostly empty restaurant. Three o'clock wasn't a particularly busy time between the lunch and dinner crowd.

"He's gone in to Reno to run some errands."

"I was going to show him my progress."

"Should I let him know you stopped by?"

"Sure."

Sour Hurt-Your-Eyes Lemon Yellow

Chapter 20

Jotty wasn't sure how the change happened. Her body tingled as if charged with electricity. A new feeling of having a direction to her life, a boat with a sail, and a good wind. The start of being a commercial artist, Tomm had called it. Something she had been preparing for all her short seventeen years. Jotty leaned back against the restroom counter and folded her arms. Her picture of sage grouse and their habitat hung on the science room wall. Would she sign her name with a flourish at the bottom? Jotty Alfarnso?

"You don't want to be caught in here," Tanya said, pulling Jotty from her daydream and back to reality.

"Hmm?"

"You know, Dr. Benninger..."

How could she forget the drill-sergeant principal who wore suits to school with matching shoes?

She turned to Tanya. "I hope Clyde expels me for good." Those words sounded false and hollow, from another year and another girl.

Tanya looked relieved at the response from the same old Jotty.

For emphasis, Jotty flicked the ash on the floor. "Do you really think I jump at her every command?" Jotty studied her reflection in the mirror, narrowing her eyes under her unruly bangs, brown irises under sometimes blond/brown hair, a hodgepodge of colors. Her hair sprang from her head, and strands danced in the dry Nevada climate. Maybe she should start wearing a bandanna around her head to keep the sweat from obscuring her vision while she worked as an artist, peeking around an easel, not a cinderblock bathroom wall.

No, you never jump," Tanya said. "Sal had to do Saturday school for smoking. She had to pick up cigarette butts all morning. Said it was gross. I'm worried about you, Jotty."

"Well, I'm not." She inhaled, then blew out a perfect round circle of smoke. "I'll never do Saturday school. She can't make me."

Jotty nodded her head and folded her arms like she had seen Jeannie do to get back into her bottle.

"What if she expels you?"

"Then she expels me. No big deal." More time to work, but would Mr. Hornbeck want her painting on his wall then? She frowned.

"If you leave, who'll I talk to? You're my best friend," Tanya said.

"Talk to Buck!"

"Buck doesn't talk much. He's..." Tanya paused. "The dark, silent type. But he will talk if he's relaxed and has a couple of drinks."

"Tanya, he's another drunk."

"Not always."

"Tell me one good thing he's done for you." Jotty leaned against the counter and folded her arms.

Tanya shrugged, her skinny shoulders going up and down like she couldn't make up her mind. "He loves me."

"Yeah," Jotty said with a snort. "Just for sex. Don't be a sucker and fall for that line."

Tanya was quiet as she slipped off the counter, signaling the end of their discussion. Her face paled to a shade of gray tinged with green. She looked like she was going to be sick. She probably had slept with him. Jotty turned and opened her paints. This was a mountain day, not sage grouse.

Tanya sniffled. Jotty turned to see what the sniffing was about. Her friend was crying, huge tears rolling down her cheeks. Tanya leaned over the counter, hunching her shoulders up as if she was going to get sick.

"What's the matter, Tanya?" Jotty asked, gulping back a lump in her throat. "I'm sorry I was short with you."

"Oh, Jotty!" she wailed. "I'm scared."

She hadn't meant to snap at Tanya like that. Now Tanya was upset with her.

"I've missed two periods," Tanya whispered so softly that Jotty wasn't sure she heard correctly.

Class periods? Heck, she missed two periods each day, but Jotty didn't think that's what Tanya meant. "Do you mean..."

"I think I'm pregnant," Tanya whispered.

Jotty's stomach clenched. "Have you taken a pregnancy test?" She eyed Tanya critically. If anything, Tanya looked too skinny. Most pregnant girls filled out, but Tanya was a walking scarecrow.

"I don't know where to get one, and I don't want my stepfather to find out."

"He'll know eventually when you start to show," Jotty said.

"I'm afraid to tell Buck too." Tanya grimaced. "I was on the pill, but I forgot to take them a couple of times. I think I'm pregnant." Tanya's words got fainter and fainter. Pregnant came out like a soft, almost nonexistent word, a puff of smoke on a windy day.

"Oh, Tanya." Jotty reached out and patted Tanya's heaving shoulders and gave her a hug. "It'll be all right. We'll think of something." Her words didn't ring true. Pregnancy meant terrible things for the girls in Sagebrush.

"What will I do?" Tanya looked at Jotty through watery, red eyes.

"I don't know, Tanya." Jotty rubbed her forefinger over her thumb and bit at her jagged nail. "We'll come up with a plan."

Images of other pregnant girls from school flashed before Jotty. They didn't fare too well; most lived on welfare in run-down trailers. What the heck; Jotty's family lived in a run-down trailer too.

"You could keep the baby and raise it?" Jotty said. Her words came out as a half question, half statement.

Tanya didn't answer and looked expectantly for Jotty to continue.

"Virginia managed," Jotty said, as brightly as she could, remembering Tanya's older sister. "She got her GED, didn't she?" She didn't wait for Tanya to answer. "And they seem happy in their doublewide trailer with their little girl."

"Yeah, but Dan loved her. He married her. I don't think Buck loves me enough to marry me."

Jotty doubted Buck loved Tanya at all. He wanted sex with her, but when that was finished, the love was gone as well, just like her own father and Leroy too. She didn't see Tanya living on the reservation with Buck, the lone blond female in a sea of dark-skinned people inhabiting a small tract of land in the middle of the desert.

"He probably just said he loved you, so you would have sex with him," Jotty said.

"I thought he meant it," Tanya said.

"Maybe for that moment he loved her, but not after.

"You're probably right," Tanya said after a pause.

"Can't you go to the public health nurse? The one who gave you the pill?"

"I guess…"

They stood silently side by side, Jotty thinking the worst, and Tanya…Jotty wasn't sure what she was thinking, probably regretting her decision to have sex with Buck. But it was too late for that now.

They jumped when Clyde, clipboard tucked under her arm, strode through the bathroom door.

"Why aren't you two in class?" she asked, glaring only at Jotty.

Jotty glared right back. "Can't you see Tanya's upset?"

"That's what we have a counselor for," Clyde said.

"No one talks to the counselor about real problems," Jotty said. Only pretend stuff to keep him busy and an excuse to get out of class. "Tanya wanted to talk to me," Jotty said.

"Talk at lunch. Your classes are more important. I told you, no more hanging around in the bathroom. Go to class." Clyde's eyes flashed stormy blue.

"No," Jotty said, stepping toward Clyde. "She's really upset."

"I have eyes. I also see another picture on the wall. Since you won't cooperate with me, why should I with you? Cooperation is a two-way street, you know." Clyde was tapping the clipboard, emphasizing each word.

"That's OK, Jotty." Tanya wiped her nose on her sleeve. "We'll talk at lunch."

"I'll take those," Clyde snatched up the paints before Jotty could stop her.

"Those are mine. They may be crappy paints, but they're all I've got!"

Clyde turned on her heel and marched out of the bathroom, the sound of her heels rapping against the tile floor.

"She doesn't like us," Tanya said, shaking her head.

"I don't like her, either," Jotty declared.

"She'd probably be nicer if you were."

"Maybe."

"What do you think she'll do?" Tanya whispered.

"I don't know, and I don't care. I just want my paints back." But sweat formed under her arms and in the center of her back. She didn't want Ma bothered at work. If Ma didn't work, she didn't get paid. "You go on ahead, Tanya. I'll see you in class later."

Jotty walked down a little-used corridor that led to the industrial arts classes out behind the school, pressed against the wall, and waited.

Soon Emmett walked by swinging a paint can. Jotty leaned out.

"Emmett, wait," she whispered.

He kept going and by the time she got to him, he was already in the bathroom.

"What are you doing?" Jotty seized his arm. Emmett recoiled from her look and the grasp on his arm. She tried to smooth the alarm from her face so as not to scare Emmett.

"I thought you were in class." He moved his arm, but she held fast.

"What are you doing with that paint?" She finally let go of his arm.

"Emmett hung his head and shuffled his black army boots back and forth. "Gosh, Jotty, don't make this hard on me. Dr. Benninger told me to paint over your picture. She told me to paint the wall each and every time. One mark and I've got to paint over it."

"She can't do that!"

"She's my boss," he said, moving his tongue around his mouth, dislodging a piece of chew from his cheek.

Jotty shoved Emmett aside, knocking him off-kilter. One oversize boot tangled up with the other, and he lost his balance and pitched forward, hitting his head on the counter. He slid to the floor, dropping the paint, where it rolled drunkenly around until the lid fell off and yellow paint gushed out, leaving a huge puddle on the tile.

"Oh, my head," Emmett moaned, clutching his cap.

Are you all right?" Jotty asked, kneeling down beside him and lightly touching the bump that was already turning purple on his forehead. She felt horrible. She liked Emmett. She didn't mean to push him so hard.

Emmett sat up and gingerly felt his head. A trickle of blood slid down his face. There wasn't a lot of blood, but he might need stitches.

Jotty helped him up and heard brisk footsteps approaching. Oh damn!

"What on earth!" Clyde demanded, stopping just short of the puddle of paint.

"I tripped," Emmett mumbled, shaking his head.

"Really?" Clyde asked, her eyes darting around before she frowned at Jotty.

"Certainly, ma'am. These clumsy feet of mine." He moved them back and forth in illustration and shot Jotty a look as if to say don't mess this up.

"Well, I hope you're not hurt. And you, Jotty, are cutting class again. So." Clyde pulled out her clipboard and began writing. "You'll report for Saturday school on October nine. Eight a.m. sharp."

Clyde handed her the green slip, but Jotty pushed it away.

"I'll send this to your parents, then." Clyde shook the slip like she was fanning herself.

Good luck with finding Jotty's father.

"You're wasting your time. I'm not going." Jotty's heart beat faster, and she folded her arms to keep her chest from exploding. "But send it if you want."

"I will." Clyde ordered, "Now get to class."

Jotty took one last look at her picture, knowing it would be gone when she returned.

In between classes, Jotty went back to the bathroom. Even before she walked through the door, she knew. Only a few faint hazy lines remained where the paint hadn't covered completely. Taped to the tile was the sign, Wet Paint. Jotty thought only an idiot could ignore the odor and the wet glossy paint. Several splotches had dried on the floor where it had dripped. The circle of paint in the middle of the floor was gone. The only evidence was between the tiles; the grout was stained yellow, golden mustard.

Jotty took out her cigarettes and smoked while she stared at the blank sour-lemon-yellow wall. After only a few short puffs, she stubbed out her cigarette in the sink and lunged for the wall, stopping herself with her hands. Now they were covered with wet paint too. Jotty flexed her hands under the gooey, thick, glue-like paint, mesmerized by the power she felt. She liked having the paint on her hands. She had the urge to laugh, but she didn't dare.

Jotty looked at her palms and hesitated for only a moment before putting them on the mirrors and tile, going back to the wall for more paint, again and again, until the bathroom was covered with her yellow handprints.

When she finished, Jotty stood back and studied the design her prints made on the wall. She liked the outstretched fingers going every which way. If only she had another color besides yellow, the effect would be perfect.

She smiled to herself in the mirror as she washed her hands. Clyde got more of a paint job than she bargained for this time. She tossed her hair over her shoulders and sauntered out into the hallway with a confident stride. Yes, indeed, more than she bargained for.

Sour Hurt-Your-Eyes Lemon Yellow

Chapter 20

During Mr. Harrison's class, Jotty was summoned to the office. "Jotty Alfarnso is needed in the office."

Damn, Mr. Harrison was in the middle of the story about the Donner party. Couldn't the office have waited until she had English or math?

Mr. Harrison nodded to her when she didn't respond. "Jotty?"

"I'm going," she said, picking up her backpack.

Several students rolled their eyes at her. Good ole Jotty, in trouble again. She didn't care what they thought and glared at them as she stomped out. Twitters and giggles followed her; flies on the carcass of life. Well, so be it.

She hadn't always gotten in trouble. It started gradually. The more Leroy drank and hit Ma, the more Jotty didn't care. When they couldn't pay their bills, she acted out. She built a fortress around her emotions, and as her frustration with life grew, the more she acted out. Ma wouldn't let Jotty fight for her, so she got in trouble at school. Anything was better than thinking about Ma's bruises.

Jotty squared her shoulders, pushed open the door, and walked confidently into Clyde's office.

"What's the big deal calling me here?" Jotty demanded of Clyde, who sat behind her big desk. "I thought you wanted me in class."

For once Clyde was silent, her mouth a grim line as she stared at the door behind Jotty and then moved her head so Jotty would look behind her.

Jotty turned and froze in place. "Ma! What are you doing here?"

Clyde moved her arm to the chairs. "Please, have a seat."

Ma shook her head and dabbed at her watery eyes with a crumpled tissue as she sat in the offered seat. "Oh, Jotty. Why?"

"I didn't do nothin'." Her insides melted and lapped at her stomach. They knew. Clyde knew about the paint.

"You won't attend class, and I think you pushed or tripped the janitor and vandalized the bathroom," Ma said sniffling, taking a tissue from the box Clyde slid toward her.

Ma looked worse than normal when she cried. Her eyes rimmed in red, her nose swollen and pink from blowing it. Jotty looked away.

"I had to take the time off without pay," Ma said in a small voice.

Oh, crap. She didn't want Ma called at work. Knives stabbed Jotty's stomach, and she wanted to hit something. "You can't prove anything," Jotty said to Clyde, directing her anger toward her nemesis. And then she turned to Ma and said in a low voice, "Don't believe her, Ma." Jotty leaned sideways, so they could see eye to eye.

"It's hard not to," Ma said with a sniff as she dabbed at her nose.

"Are you on her side?" Jotty asked.

"I'm not on any side. I want you to stay in school. I don't want you to drop out and live like me. If that's being on her side, then I guess I am, but I'm also on yours. I love you."

Jotty gulped. She loved Ma too, more than she could say.

"I won't let her drop out," Clyde said. "I want to see her go to art school or college."

What gave Clyde the right to decide her life choices? She'd go to college only if she wanted to. Secretly, in the far recesses of her brain, she'd thought about it. She didn't dare get her hopes up. School was expensive. And now Clyde was making her think about it even more.

Jotty pushed back her chair, stood, and looked down on Clyde. "All you care about is me not being in the bathroom. Well, that's where I like to draw. Just leave me alone. I wish you never came to Sagebrush."

"I'm sorry you feel that way. I'm glad I came to Sagebrush. I see many students with potential and no way for them to utilize it," Clyde said.

"I'm leaving," Jotty said. "You can talk all you want without me. Plan my life! I'll do what I want."

"Jotty…"

Neither Clyde nor Ma made any move to follow Jotty, as she picked up her backpack and rushed into the morning sunshine, instinctively turning toward Rattlesnake Mountain. She licked her lips and judged how long it would take her to walk there. It wasn't far. She had all day; eventually she'd get to the rock-strewn slopes and the ultimate solitude.

The October sun was warm, but the wind neutralized the heat, making the walk comfortable. Where had the first month of school gone? Had it slipped away like the animals she saw on the hill? One minute a long-eared jackrabbit was nibbling on a blade of grass and the next it was gone, vanished like everything else.

As she filled her lungs with fresh air, the tension slipped from her shoulders, and the vise around her head loosened. Her sneakers made soft swishing sounds against the overgrown weeds, and slowly the pulsing, racing thoughts in her head quieted.

The narrow road heading to the mountain was barely paved. Its sides crumbled into the sagebrush where tires had swerved to avoid a jackrabbit or the blowing tumbleweeds. People drove this way only if they were going hunting or sightseeing.

A pickup truck slowed and stopped. The driver held out his hand and waved. "Hey, Jotty. Need a ride?"

"Sure." Jotty opened the door and swung into his truck. "Haven't seen much of you, Matthew."

"Been working." He adjusted his cap and put the truck in gear; it protested by grinding and bucking slightly. "Where to?"

"Over there." She nodded toward the mountain.

"Aren't you still in school?"

"Yeah, but I'm taking the day off. What have you been up to?" Jotty asked, taking note of the lunchbox and thermos between the seats.

The truck rattled over the uneven, cracked road, littered with rabbit and bird carcasses. "Miller still bothering you?"

"Miller retired. We have a new principal." She balled her fists.

"Come to think of it, I heard that." Matthew pushed the bill of his cap down to keep the glare out of his eyes.

"What are you doing now?"

"Working with my dad at the gravel pit. Just got off my shift," Matthew said.

His hair and clothes were covered with fine gray dust.

"How's that going?" she asked.

"Hard work, but it's a job. See Leroy occasionally. Boy, does he have a temper," Matthew said, shaking his head. "Hair trigger. Everything sets him off!"

"We know."

The truck jerked off the pavement onto the dirt path.

"You don't need to take me all the way," Jotty said.

"I don't mind," he said. "Good to talk about something other than gravel. I'm sick of gravel. There's only so much to say."

"Why do you stay there?"

Matthew shrugged. "Luanne is going to have a baby. We'll have bills. I need to pay on my truck. The family's here."

"I wish I was in your place. I hate school. I want a job."

"I used to think the same thing. Now that I'm through, school doesn't seem so bad. Working isn't a piece of cake. I've been meaning to come to a football game. How're they doin'?"

Jotty grimaced. "I don't know. You know me. I'm not into that. I never pay attention to sports." Or dances, pep rallies or...anything else pertaining to school.

"The pit is hiring part-time office help. You could apply for that," Matthew said.

Office work. "What would I have to do?"

"Bring in your resume, and tell them how fast you type, I guess. Filing, maybe. I'm not sure."

She had a resume, but she couldn't type. The thought of sitting at a desk, typing, didn't sound appealing. Nothing creative about that. She could draw; that was it.

"I'll think about that," Jotty said.

"Still hanging out in the can?" He turned his attention to the road and spun the wheel quickly to avoid a huge pothole.

"It's getting impossible with the new principal always snooping around," Jotty said bitterly.

He was quiet as he reflected on her words. "The good ole days," he added quietly.

Hah! Maybe for him, but not for her.

The weeds pushing through the cracked concrete scratched and scraped along the underside of Matthew's truck. "I guess this is as far as I go," he said.

"This is better than I expected. Thanks, Matthew, and say hi to Luanne for me." Jotty hopped out and closed the door.

He tipped his sweat-stained hat to her, backed up into the weeds, and swung his truck around, honking when he got to the pavement. Jotty turned to the mountain and walked along the rough path. She had been afraid of this mountain when she was a little girl. Who wouldn't be with a name like Rattlesnake Mountain? Each year she had declared to herself that she'd make it to the top—rattlesnakes and all. But she hadn't made it yet.

Jotty calculated how long it would take to climb to the top, but it probably wouldn't happen today. She stood at the base of Rattlesnake and tipped her head back. The solitude helped clear her mind, and the mountain was her place to do that. She began to climb. The path to her favorite rock was almost flat at first, and then it steadily got steeper.

The wind whispered through her hair, tugging and floating past her ears. She heard Ma's voice around her, urging and begging. Stay. Stay, Jotty. Make me proud. She wished the insistent voice would go away and leave her in peace. That's what she liked about Rattlesnake, the solitude. She stopped and pushed her hair away from her eyes. There was as much going on in the sky as on the ground.

A hawk flew in lazy circles around a withered, wind-battered pine tree. The branches were skeletal bones and claws scratching at the clouds. Jotty sat down on a boulder to catch her breath and have a smoke. The predator glided on the air currents, wings outstretched, no worries except for the next meal. It was too bad people couldn't exist on life's wind currents and live on instinct alone. So many other things interfered.

Life was funny in a way. She had hated school with Mr. Miller, but now he didn't seem so bad with his bumbling, slow gait and his habit of saying the same things over and over in a tired, low voice. But he'd seemed to understand she needed to be alone and busted her only a few times for cutting class.

A long time ago, she had tried to like school, but her mind always wandered. She couldn't find meaning in the things they studied. When her fifth grade teacher told her she wouldn't amount to anything if she kept doodling and drawing on her papers, she gave up on school. She guessed the teacher was right. And then there was her father and behind him, Leroy. She remembered her father's face—a kind face with gentle brown eyes and a mouth that drooped, even when he smiled. Had he hidden the unhappiness reflected in his eyes? His potential squashed in Sagebrush too? She tried to like Leroy when he first moved in, but when he started drinking, she gave up on him too. Jotty didn't want to give up on herself or Ma.

The only nonjudgmental thing in her life was her drawing. Drawing never pushed or bullied her into doing what she didn't want to do. She didn't want to be pushed into anything; she wanted to make decisions herself.

Jotty shaded her eyes and looked toward the summit, hoping to see the horses. The hillside was dotted with boulders and sagebrush, but no horses. She had never seen pintos like Mr. Harrison described. The horses that inhabited Rattlesnake Mountain were stocky, usually single-color horses with scraggly manes and tails. Life must be hard on the mountain. She knew farther down was an arm of the Truckee River, a tributary that supplied the horses' water. She had walked there before, sometimes coming upon people fishing or making out. The horses had beaten a path through the rocks and brush to get to the water's edge.

All along the mountain trail were horse droppings. Jotty wrinkled her nose; not a bad smell really—like fermenting grass.

In the distance below her, she saw a vehicle approaching. A cloud of dust followed and enveloped it, so it wasn't possible to tell if it was a truck or car. A white dragon? Or in this case, a gray dragon? Was Matthew coming back?

Jotty watched a long sleek green sedan roll out of the dust and come to a stop. She recognized the woman the minute she got out of the passenger side of the car and began to make her way toward Jotty: the worn and food-stained work smock, the thin gray/brown hair tied back into a scraggly ponytail, and life's worry etched into the thin mouth.

Jotty stood up and started down the hill. They met halfway. "Ma, why did you come here? I want to be alone, to think."

Ma reached for Jotty's cigarette and took a drag as she watched the sky behind Jotty's head. "I need to talk to you."

"Who drove you? Whose car is that?" Jotty asked, leaning down to see who was at the steering wheel.

"Dr. Benninger."

Jotty snatched back her cigarette.

"I know you, Jotty. You did trash the bathroom, didn't you? Did you push the janitor too?"

"What if I did? What if it was an accident?" The wind picked up, and Jotty turned away from Ma to keep her cigarette lit.

"You need to pay the price," Ma said, touching Jotty's shoulder. "What has she done to you that's so bad?"

"She's in Sagebrush; that's enough," Jotty said stubbornly.

"She says you're the most talented student artist she's ever met."

Jotty whirled around, emotions swirling like a dust devil. "What makes her an expert?"

"Quit acting smart and listen to me. I'm trying to save your life!" Ma jerked at her sleeve.

Jotty frowned at her. "What do you mean, Ma?"

"I don't mean you're going to get killed, just that I want you to live your dreams. Mine died a long time ago. It's not too late for you."

"What did you want to do?" She had never heard Ma talk about dreams before.

"Help people. Be a nurse or a teacher. I do help the people who come into Joe's with their problems. Education gets you a job that pays the rent and buys groceries. Do you understand what I'm trying to say? I want things better for you, but you seem hell-bent on making them worse."

Both were silent for a long while. Jotty smoked and gazed off into the distance, not really seeing the scenery, her vision fogged, the images wavy and blurred.

"I just don't want to be pushed, Ma."

"That's just the way life is. Get pushed or get run over. She's pushing because she cares, not because she doesn't. Leroy pushes because he's mad at himself and can't see a way out. There's a difference."

Jotty knew Ma had a point, but she couldn't shift her thoughts from one gear to another that easily. Earning trust always took time, and Jotty didn't trust too many people.

"So what do you want me to do, Ma?"

"I want you to finish school and go to college. Follow your dreams."

"Ma." The old arguments seemed to have blown away, and she couldn't think of a response. "I don't know if I can do that."

"Save yourself, Jotty. Let her push you. Don't be stupid like me and drop out. Quit being pigheaded."

"Are you through?" Jotty asked, tired of the conversation and the feeling of being in a corner with no way out.

"Yes. I've said what I came to say, and now I'm leaving."

Jotty watched as Ma walked away, painfully hunched as she picked her way between the sagebrush and rocks. It seemed to take her forever to reach Clyde's car.

Did Ma think she'd just roll over and play dead? She didn't want to stay in Sagebrush; she couldn't wait to get away, but was college the only way? Could she bear being in high school for the three months after her eighteenth birthday?

Jotty walked back to her backpack, leaned against her favorite rock, and folded her arms. She could do Saturday school. It didn't mean anything to her, but it would mean the world to Ma, and Ma was the world to Jotty. She loved Ma and wished she could make things better and easier for her. Was that so bad? Maybe she could eventually. For now, it was as simple as Saturday school.

Camouflage Green

Chapter 21

Jotty remained against the rock, her thoughts swarming around her, a cacophony of hornets, until Ma and Clyde rolled away in the green sedan. She shook off the buzzing and leaned against the smooth side of the rock before sliding down, her back resting against it with her legs stretched out.

It was mid-afternoon and pleasant on the mountain, warm with a hint of pending cold weather in the coming weeks. The sun warmed her face, and the wind ruffled her hair in tiny puffs; otherwise, the hillside was still, but she knew that was a façade. She watched as an industrious line of ants ferried a piece of leaf along with efficient teamwork. A bird whistled nearby. Slowly she became attuned to the undertone of the mountain.

Jotty looked around and knew there was still enough time for some good sketch work before sundown. Once she took the sketch pad and pencil out of the backpack, she settled down in earnest. Ma had given her a lot to think about, and Jotty thought best when her hands were busy sketching.

What were her dreams besides leaving school? Ma didn't consider dropping out of school a dream, and if Jotty thought about it, neither did she. Wanting to help—was that so bad? Help with the finances? Make things easier for Ma? She ached for Ma. She loved Ma more than anything in the world.

Ma's dreams had been to help people. Jotty didn't know exactly what she wanted to do besides draw and paint. Could being an artist pay rent and buy food?

They had studied famous artists in art class. Mrs. Jackson told them that some artists earned a living by painting or giving lessons, while others became famous only after they had died. Jotty didn't want to be famous because she was gone. She wanted people to view her work and imagine they were on Rattlesnake Mountain.

Tomm was the only living artist Jotty had ever met. When he had come to the diner, he didn't say exactly what his background was or why he was traveling around painting storefronts. Leroy was a distraction with the television blaring in the background, making it difficult to converse. Jotty decided she would go to Joe's Diner and talk with Tomm privately.

She opened her notebook and began to sketch the clouds and the hawks. Where there had been one hawk before, now there were three. They pirouetted in the air like graceful gymnasts, sharp eyes open to mice and ground squirrels—their next meal. The sage grouse lived farther down the mountain.

She continued watching the hawks fly effortlessly on the air currents—dipping low, climbing higher, their shadows moving against the dirt and rocks. It seemed their only duties in life were to make baby hawks and find food and shelter—it all looked so easy for them.

What had she thought about doing with her life? In the recesses of her mind, she got to a closed door and wondered if it was merely closed or locked. The courage to try the door escaped her. So she remained on the other side, waiting and wondering.

Thinking again about art class, Jotty knew she didn't want to become a famous artist. People from Sagebrush never became famous. But she wanted to create pictures for people to enjoy.

And what had Mrs. Jackson said about careers in art? Jotty chewed on her lip, trying to remember while doodling a daisy and filling in the flower's center with a lattice pattern. Yes, they learned about jobs to care for and restore art; no, that wasn't for her. She wanted to make her own art. Commercial art was a possibility: creating and designing brochures and pamphlets. Other jobs included running an art museum or teaching art. But teaching was never on her dream list. How had Tomm gotten his start?

Jotty stood, dusted off her jeans, and started down the hill. Hiking down was much easier than climbing up. Once at the roadway, she walked along its worn tracks until she turned onto Main Street and headed to Joe's Diner at the corner of First and Main.

Joe looked up at Jotty, then at the watch on his beefy wrist. "What are you doing here?"

"Is Tomm around?" Jotty asked.

Joe wiped his hands on his already stained apron. "Tomm, yeah. He's staying in his camper in the back. Why?"

"Just wanted to talk to him," she said.

"Is that it?" Joe asked, cocking one brow up.

"Of course."

"My wife thinks he's hot."

That was too bad for Joe.

"About art," Jotty said, firmly.

"If you say so."

Jotty's face felt warmer than when she was in the sun. Tomm was nice looking, she remembered, but that wasn't the reason.

"Joe!"

"If you took your attention away from your sketchbook and looked in the mirror, you'd see yourself the way you really are. You've got a nice face, kid."

She hadn't noticed or really cared.

"Your ma went to the school today," he said.

"I know."

"So why aren't you in school?" he asked.

"I cut."

Joe shook his head. "You worry your mother all the time. Try going to school for a change."

"I know, I know. But school's boring," Jotty said.

"I'm telling you," Joe said. "Life can be boring, but eating and having a roof over your head ain't boring."

"Yeah, yeah."

"Don't 'yeah, yeah' me. So why exactly are you here?" he asked.

"To see Tomm," she said.

"And?"

"Find out about his background," she said.

"I think he said he was a graphic artist, whatever that is," Joe said with a short grunt.

"I just want to know how he got started."

"Between you and me and the street sign, he's not very successful. He lives in a trailer and moves from place to place," Joe said.

"Oh." Ma wouldn't want that for her. Jotty shifted her feet. "Can I just talk to him anyway?"

"Sure, around back. You can go through the kitchen."

The trailer was parked against the fence.

Jotty knocked on the aluminum door. "Anyone home?"

"Who wants to know?"

"Jotty Alfarnso."

The door swung open. "Nice to see you!" he said.

"Thanks. Nice to see you too."

He frowned. "Aren't you still in school?"

"Yes."

He paused, considering. "So what can I do for you?" He stood in the doorframe, hands on either side of the aluminum. He had on a clean T-shirt, but paint-splattered jeans. Tomm looked her up and down and smiled at the paint blotches on Jotty's jeans.

"I...I just wanted to know how you got your start." That sounded completely lame.

He frowned.

"How you got started as an artist?" she added.

"Oh," he said, nodding his head. "Thinking of college?"

"Not really."

"Trade school?"

"Maybe. Just thinking about options. Trying to find out the how and why."

"Come on in." He stepped away from the door and motioned for her.

The trailer was small. Jotty shook her head, but nodded toward the picnic table.

They sat there.

"I started at the community college in graphic arts," Tomm said.

College again.

"I didn't finish my degree because...long story...I needed a job. I worked my way up at a small company in Reno."

"What kind of things did you do? Murals?"

"No, we designed logos and signs for businesses."

"How was that?" Jotty took out her cigarettes and offered him one.

He waved them away. "The job was OK. It paid the bills."

She lit a cigarette, sucked in the smoke and exhaled before speaking, "Why are you living in your camper now?"

"Another long story," he said, holding his arms wide as if he didn't want to answer.

She leaned forward on her elbows. She had time for a long story and took another drag from her cigarette.

He saw her gesture and said, "I went through a messy divorce and lost my job." He added bitterly, "And my house...and my kids...everything gone..."

"Do you see your kids?"

The discouraged downturn of his mouth told her he didn't.

"Another long story."

Jotty chewed on her lip. All the hard-luck cases ended up in Sagebrush.

She was no closer to knowing what she wanted to do, but she also knew what she didn't want to do.

"Thanks, Tomm." Jotty eased out of the picnic bench, took a last pull from her cigarette, and ground it out.

"Anytime," he said.

The smells of hamburgers and bacon beckoned. Her stomach grumbled. She thought about begging a sandwich from Joe, but decided against it. Besides, the sun was sinking, pushing away the afternoon. Ma was probably home, waiting for her, wanting to talk. She might as well get it over with.

When she returned home, Leroy was there. What rotten luck.

"I see you're back," he said, as if he hadn't expected to see her.

"I could say the same about you."

"Miss me?" He grinned, revealing yellowed teeth, a jack-o'-lantern smile. Not friendly, but spooky. "You sure took your sweet time getting me out of jail."

"It was your brother, Richard," Jotty said.

Ma was in the kitchen. She looked at Jotty silently.

"The bum!" Leroy said with a snort.

"I'm sorry you had to take off this afternoon," Jotty said, going into the kitchen and putting her arm around Ma's shoulders.

"Were you cutting again?" Leroy growled.

"What if I was?"

"Your mother doesn't get paid if she's got to chase after you. You need to grow up."

Jotty stood straighter. "You can't tell me what to do."

"Like hell I can't. I'm your stepfather."

"Big deal. You're not much help for Ma." Jotty looked around the trailer and rested her eyes on the sagging lumpy couch and the lamp with a chunk out of the side. He followed her gaze.

"I bring home a paycheck, don't I?"

"What's left of it."

Leroy growled deep in his throat, and purple crept up from his collar. Ha! She had gotten under his skin.

Ma came out of the kitchen. "Now you two, quit fighting." She stepped between them. "I've made a special dinner for Leroy's homecoming."

Things were much better when he had been in jail.

They circled each other like dogs sizing up the competition. Jotty was Leroy's height, but his girth was bigger. His arms bulged from shoveling and moving gravel to the waiting trucks. He hadn't been drinking, but smelled of stale sweat and onions. She could probably get in a couple of punches before he flattened her. It was better when he was drunk and unsteady.

Leroy threw up his hands, gave her a look that said you're not worth the trouble, went to the television, and switched it on. So much for the fight.

Jotty helped Ma finish making the meal and set the table, cringing at the sound of the television football game. She wished Leroy was still in jail.

Nothing had changed. Home, sweet home.

Sour Hurt-Your-Eyes Lemon Yellow

Chapter 22

Jotty yanked the curtain back, hoping to see weather that would reflect her mood, but typically, the morning of her Saturday school was clear and bright. An endless aqua sky floated over Rattlesnake Mountain with only a smoke-like cloud to mar the hydrangea blue. Jotty sniffed—winter was coming. She could tell by the crisp bite of air pushing through the tiny crack in the ill-fitting trailer window.

She let the curtain drop back into place. The mountain couldn't help her this time; she was going to Saturday school, probably to pick up cigarette butts left by her and her friends. How depressing.

"You're up early," Ma said when Jotty emerged.

Jotty glared at her.

"I forgot," Ma said, going back to drinking her coffee and watching the local news.

Jotty went to the cupboard for a mug and poured herself a cup of Ma's super-duper black brew. If that didn't get her moving, nothing would.

Jotty left for school, driving Ma's truck and wearing her oldest jeans and a sweatshirt with holes at the elbows.

Sagebrush High was a ghost town on weekends, silent and uninhabited. Jotty stopped inside the entry, surrounded by picture frames encasing the earnest faces of past athletic stars and student body presidents. What were they doing now? Most had left Sagebrush. They were successful and far away from this godforsaken place. The only sign of life this early morning was a faint light glowing from the principal's office.

Clyde, wearing jeans, sneakers, and a Stallions sweatshirt came out of her office and without a word beckoned Jotty to follow.

The principal looked less formidable without her suit and heels. As they reached the bathroom door, Clyde unlocked it, took down the Closed for Repairs sign, opened the door, and turned to Jotty, pointing to a box of rags and spray cleaner.

The bathroom was exactly as Jotty had left it. Her cigarette butt was still in the sink.

Inside, the air was stagnant and cold and smelled faintly of paint, smoke, and disinfectant. Jotty's nose flared and she shivered; it was an unsettling combination to her senses this morning. Normally she enjoyed the smells.

"Your job is to scrape off all the handprints, wipe away the residue, and sweep the floor."

"That's Emmett's job," Jotty said, standing taller and facing Clyde.

"He doesn't have time." Clyde's eyes darted around the bathroom. "I save the worst jobs for the students on Saturday school. Besides, you put the paint all over the tile and mirrors. I think it's fitting you clean it off."

"I have to do this all by myself? You can't prove I did this, you know." Jotty put her hands on her hips.

"I bet your hand fits these prints perfectly." Clyde grabbed Jotty's hand and put it on one of the prints.

Jotty jerked her hand away.

"In addition to the mess, you were talking to Tanya when you should have been in class," Clyde said. "And then there's the matter of Emmett's trip or fall...He had stitches and had to take the day off work."

Poor Emmett. She hadn't meant for that to happen to him.

Clyde opened her mouth to speak again, but closed it. Was Clyde through with her list of Jotty's faults? Did she also have bad breath, dandruff, and poor taste in clothes? The clothes part was true. There was no money for Wrangler jeans or expensive boots.

"So here's a razor blade, some rags, and turpentine. Get to work. I'll be checking on you."

Jotty tipped an imaginary hat to Clyde, picked up the razor blade, and scraped at the nearest handprint, now hardened to a pale-yellow outline. It flaked off and she wiped the spot clean with turpentine and a rag. This was easy. Jotty went to the next one and did the same thing. This wasn't bad at all.

She studied the razor blade, it would be so easy to draw the blade against her skin and cut an artery, but what would that prove? She was stupid? She continued working.

After about an hour, Jotty stretched her arms up and then dusted off her jeans. The flecks from the wall had landed on her legs and the floor. With the toe of her shoe, she traced a line in the flakes, and then her initials, JA, before straightening and looking around, assessing what still needed to be done. A cigarette would help, but Jotty didn't know when Clyde would show up. Would a quick puff on the butt in the sink hurt?

Reluctantly she returned to her task. By now, she had a system. She'd scrape off four or five handprints and then wipe with turpentine. She wouldn't have to stoop down so much. Already her back felt as if a giant rubber band was wound tightly around it. Soon she'd walk hunched over like Ma.

Three hours later, weary and a lot more slowly, Jotty finished. Her back refused to straighten up. She arched and stretched. She was tired, sore, and hungry, and she couldn't leave for—Jotty squinted at the clock—another hour. She left the restroom and sat in the dark, silent cafeteria.

"All finished?" Clyde said, coming to sit by her. Jotty moved over slightly.

So much for peace and quiet.

"Uh huh."

"Was the time spent talking to Tanya worth spending Saturday at school?"

Jotty turned slowly and fixed Clyde with an unwavering stare. "Actually, it was."

Clyde's serious gray eyes were absolutely still. "Your friends are that important?"

"Tanya told me she might be pregnant." Jotty stopped; she wanted to clasp her hand over her mouth. She hadn't meant to let that slip. Not to Clyde, anyway.

"Pregnant?" Clyde asked.

Jotty folded her arms and waited for Clyde's next words. Would she suggest Tanya go see the school counselor, an elderly man

93

who had no clue—or had forgotten years ago—what was important to kids? College...blah...Grades...blah blah...Responsibilities...blah blah blah?

Clyde remained quiet before clearing her throat. "I thought you were gossiping. I didn't realize."

Jotty never gossiped. "I told you she had a problem." Girls who gossiped were on the cheer squad or the rodeo team, clustered around a locker, heads close together, whispering.

"I didn't believe you."

"Well, maybe you better start," Jotty said.

"I think you're right. If we're going to get through the year we need to trust each other," Clyde said.

Huh?

They sat in silence for a while longer. Was this another of Clyde's ploys? Pretend to be interested, but not really, to get on her good side? There weren't enough days in the school year to do that.

"What am I going to do with you this year?" Clyde asked.

"Nothing." Jotty moved her shoulders and rubbed the back of her neck. "I told you I'm dropping out."

"Is there any way we can use your talents? How about painting signs for the pep squad?"

Never.

Sensing her disgust, Clyde continued. "Have you taken all the art classes we offer?"

"Yup." There were only two: Art 1 and Art 2.

"Hmm, what if I could arrange for you to take a class at the college in Reno? Or Fallon?"

She was interested, but she responded with, "Maybe."

"Or..." Clyde said.

Jotty interrupted her, "A man named Tomm painted the diner window. Why can't we do something like that here?"

"What kind of painting?" Clyde asked.

"We could paint a Nevada scene with Mr. Harrison's pintos . And Rattlesnake Mountain. Add a few sage grouse to make Hornbeck happy."

"Where would we put it?" Clyde asked.

94

Jotty's eyes darted around. "The front windows? Or the library? Even in here." She pointed to the big blank wall in the cafeteria. It was cinder block so not the best place for a mural, but it would do with the right primer, oils, or acrylic paints.

Clyde drummed her fingers lightly on the table. "Let me think about that. You may have something there. Is the bathroom clean?"

"Yup."

They went into the bathroom, and Clyde inspected the walls and wiped away a small remaining smudge. "You can go now."

Jotty still had twenty-five minutes left. "No, I'll do my time. Every second."

Clyde stood, smoothed down her jeans, nodded, and headed for the office. "Suit yourself," she called over her shoulder.

She usually did. And it never got her very far.

Puce – Reddish Brown

November

Chapter 23

The trailer shook, rumbled, and squeaked—metal rubbing on metal, the foundation grating on the cement blocks holding it upright. An earthquake. They were having an earthquake. Jotty bolted out of her chair. Something crashed to the floor from the kitchen, and Ma screamed.

"My gosh!" Ma said, running from the kitchen, still holding a wooden spoon with gravy dripping off the end. "What was that?"

"Felt like an earthquake. We need to get under something heavy." Jotty started for the kitchen table, but the shaking stopped. Then the handle on the door jiggled.

"Let me in," Leroy cried. "It's cold out here. I'm freezing my ass off!"

Jotty bit back a sarcastic remark as she reached over to unfasten the door. Leroy stumbled in, tripped over the rug, and sprawled on the floor. "What the..." he exclaimed.

The pungent smell of liquor blew in with Leroy and the cold November night air. Crisp fall weather was being pushed out by the winter's frost and snow. Leroy lay spread-eagle on the floor.

With arms crossed, Jotty studied him. Maybe this is what falling-down drunk meant. Leroy's legs were tangled in the bunched-up rug.

Jotty slammed the door, and Leroy clutched his head in agony. Ma pushed aside the curtains and looked out the window.

"He drove or crashed the truck into the trailer." Ma turned to Jotty. "Will you go outside and check the damage?"

Jotty grabbed her jacket before stepping out onto the porch, trying to see the damage to the trailer. Only a sliver of light shone through the window, not offering much illumination. Leroy's truck was against the trailer, and she was sure he had dented the side, even if it was too dark to see.

"Well?" Ma called.

"A dent."

"Oh, Lord. Come in, it's freezing out there."

A thin layer of frost on the ground glittered in the light from the open door. The clock was ticking down on 1987.

Leroy had come home drunk before, but had never managed to hit the side of the trailer. Jotty pushed him with her toe.

Leroy rolled onto his side and tried to prop up his head. His shirt gaped open, revealing a blubbery stomach, and his red nose throbbed—puce. A red-brown color, one she didn't like. Pukey puce.

Laid off twenty people today. Some of my buddies lost their jobs—bad news. Drowned our sorrows," Leroy said breathlessly, his words garbled and incomplete. He moaned, closed his eyes, and fell back.

"Did you get laid off?" Ma whispered, but he didn't answer.

They watched him for a few minutes until he snored softly.

"We can't leave him here. Help me get him to the couch," Ma said.

The thought of touching him made Jotty's skin crawl, but Ma would never be able to move him herself. She shook herself to chase the creepy feeling away.

Ma grabbed his arms and Jotty his legs, half lifting, half dragging Leroy to the couch. He weighed a ton. Every time they jostled him, he whistled through his teeth. They finally rolled him onto the couch and covered him with a blanket. They barely spoke through dinner and made no sound when getting ready for bed. Leroy never woke or stirred.

The next morning, Leroy was still on the couch, his mouth hanging open, spittle running down his chin. There was a puddle of vomit on the floor. Jotty looked away; the whole trailer reeked of rotten undigested food and alcohol. She wanted to punch Leroy in his fat stomach.

"Should we wake him?" Ma whispered.

"I'll do it," Jotty said, shaking his arm. "Wake up!"

Leroy moaned and jerked his arm away from her touch.

"Do you still have a job?" Ma asked.

"Of course I do!" His eyes snapped open, but he was unfocused and clearly confused.

Ma tugged at his arm. "You have to go to work, then. Help me, Jotty. Bring him a cup of coffee."

Jotty got the coffee. She wanted to dump the hot liquid on his head.

"Let's prop him up." Ma got behind his head and pushed him up, his chin buried in his chest. Jotty held the cup to his mouth, but the coffee dribbled onto his chin. She gave him more.

"Damn, that burns!" Leroy said.

"You better drink this, or I'll dump it on your head."

"I'll give you the biggest whupping of your life!" he snapped. "Get away from me!"

He struggled off the couch and into the bathroom. Jotty could hear the shower.

After Jotty and Ma had waited a long time, Leroy came out of the bathroom, hair dripping, but he had changed for work. He staggered out the door without a word.

They watched Leroy's departure until Ma said, "You better hurry. You don't want to miss the bus."

It wouldn't be the end of the world if she missed it. She took the shortest shower imaginable and thirty minutes later, with hair not quite dry, Jotty stomped aboard the bus and slid into the seat next to her friend.

Tanya smiled shyly, not noticing Jotty's sour mood, and whispered, "I've got something to show you when we get to school."

Jotty nodded wearily, slumped down in the seat, and tried to shut out the undercurrent of voices and road noise. She let the sway of the bus lull her into a stupor, all thoughts of Leroy's drinking and escapades pushed away. When the bus came to a stop, she opened her eyes, yawned, stood, and stretched.

"Come on," Tanya said, tugging at her sleeve.

Once at school in the girls' restroom, Tanya said, "I want to show you my belly." She slowly unzipped her jacket. "See?"

Tanya's belly was rounded and full, but it wasn't any bigger than Jotty's stomach.

"I talked to my sister about what her pregnancy symptoms were. I've got all of them. I'm going to see the public health nurse after school."

Jotty wondered what other symptoms Tanya was experiencing besides a distended stomach. But she asked, "What will you do if you are?"

"I don't know. I have to tell Buck first."

Images of a sullen and unhappy Buck flashed before Jotty's eyes.

"I'm going to tell him now. I finally feel pregnant." She took a crumpled bag of corn chips from her backpack and shook them at Jotty.

"No thanks. Don't you think you should wait to tell him until you're sure?"

"I'm sure. I'm sick, my stomach is getting bigger, and I'm really tired."

"It could be your diet," Jotty said, moving her chin toward the chips.

Tanya wrinkled her nose at the chips but continued eating them, "I hope he wants to marry me. I'll get to wear a white dress and carry flowers. My sister was a pretty bride. Don't you think that would be neat?" Tanya brushed the chips from her sweatshirt.

Jotty remembered Tanya's sister as a bride. She wore a flowing dress that camouflaged her stomach, and everyone knew, but she had a healthy baby, and they seemed fine. Would Tanya fare as well?

"I didn't think you were happy about being pregnant."

"I'm not really, but I want to get out of our trailer." Tanya set aside the chips, fished out her brush, and smoothed down her flaxen-colored hair. Jotty had wondered about that description because the flax flower was violet, not yellowish-tan.

There had to be a better way to leave than to get married, but Jotty couldn't think of one.

"I'm going to find Buck now and tell him. Wish me luck."

Jotty couldn't imagine Buck being excited about parenthood. Heck, she couldn't remember him showing emotion about anything.

While Tanya went off in search of Buck, Jotty leaned against the restroom counter. It still smelled faintly of turpentine, even weeks later. She knew every inch of this bathroom—where the grout was uneven and which tiles stuck out more than others.

Her first cigarette had no calming effect this morning, and she ground it out on the counter, envisioning Leroy's lolling, slack mouth as she twisted and pushed. She wanted to hit something. Anything. Mostly she wanted to hit Leroy. Is that how he felt when he hit Ma?

The bell sounded, and she slowly eased off the counter and gathered her backpack. A test today in English. She wrinkled her nose in disgust. She hadn't studied. She had just scraped by on the last test in English with a D–.

She heard raised voices from the hall. Someone was angry and yelling.

Jotty pressed against the partial wall and listened. Tanya and Buck. Tanya was crying, and Buck was angry. Jotty concentrated on slowing her breathing, willing herself to take deep breaths, but her heart quickened, and a boiling madness spread over her.

"Please," Tanya said with a hiccup punctuating her words. "I'm scared. I don't know what to do." Hiccup. "I want you with me."

"I don't want to get married," Buck said.

"What am I supposed to do?" Tanya asked.

"I don't know," Buck replied.

"Please don't leave me."

Don't beg, Tanya. Let him slither back into his hole, Jotty urged silently. She knew in her heart of hearts this was the outcome she expected.

"Then you should have stayed on the pill. We're not old enough to have a kid," Buck said.

"My sister had a baby at seventeen."

"My brother too, but I don't want to be end up with a dead-end job with a kid sitting on the res," Buck said.

So he was abandoning Tanya too. Jotty ached for her friend; anger closed her vision.

Jotty stepped from around the corner, ready to do battle for Tanya. "Then why did you have sex with her?" she demanded.

Buck's face registered surprise and then annoyance as he looked down his nose at Jotty. "She said she was on the pill," he finally responded in a bored-sounding voice.

"Nothing is foolproof," Jotty snapped. "Didn't you use protection?"

Buck pulled his collar up and acted insulted by her suggestion. "I don't need to answer to you."

Jotty folded her arms. "Stay away from Tanya, you scum. Crawl back to the reservation where you came from!" She knew that wasn't fair; some nice kids lived on the reservation, but Buck wasn't in the nice category.

Buck's face went dark, and his eyes narrowed. He reached out and pushed Jotty's shoulder.

Wrong thing to do.

Jotty saw flashes of red as her fist lashed out and punched Buck in the mouth. Her knuckle hit his teeth, and her hand stung. She shook her hand, but she didn't care about the pain. That punch was for Tanya, and this one was for Leroy. She pulled her arm back again and hit Buck in the nose. She saw only Leroy's red bulbous nose, not the long curve of Buck's.

Buck fell against the wall with a stunned look on his face as blood squirted from his nose. Her punches were blindsiding him.

"Fight!" Someone yelled from a doorway as students spilled out of the classrooms.

The rumble in her ears stopped, and her head was calm as the crowd pressed in on them.

"Stop, Jotty," Tanya said, holding her stomach, looking sick. "He's not worth fighting over."

She was right about that. Jotty's breaths were ragged and deep, blood pounded away in her temples.

Buck pinched his nose together to stop the bleeding.

"Aren't you going to fight back?" someone taunted Buck.

"I don't hit no girls," he said. "Besides, she's not worth it!"

The students magically parted as Clyde arrived, looking first at Jotty and then at Buck.

"Take him to the nurse," Clyde told a nearby student. Roger, Buck's cousin and class genius, stepped forward.

Buck skulked down the hall, holding his head back, still pinching his nose, jerking away from Roger trying to guide him to the office.

"My problem child," Clyde said to no one in particular before looking at Jotty. "What happened?" She gestured after Buck.

"She punched him," Tanya said with a sniff. "For me." Sniff.

"I see," Clyde said. "Anything else?"

"Buck didn't have a chance. She nailed him good. Twice," an anonymous voice responded admiringly.

"OK. Fight's over. Everyone to class now," Clyde commanded. The crowd melted away.

"My office," Clyde said, nodding to Jotty and Tanya.

Once there, they walked past Buck, sitting in a chair by the nurse's station, holding a paper towel to his nose.

Clyde motioned for them to sit opposite her in straight-backed uncomfortable chairs reserved for visitors and misbehaving students.

"Please, Dr. Benninger, don't do anything to Jotty," Tanya said, wiping her nose on her sleeve. "She hit Buck for me."

Clyde focused her attention on Jotty while handing Tanya a tissue box. "Now you're her bodyguard? Why do you have to use violence?"

Tanya blew her nose loudly.

"I felt like it." Was she turning into a Leroy, using her fists to vent her frustration? Her thought process paused. Was she as bad as Leroy? Never. This was for Tanya.

Clyde turned back to Tanya. "Tell me about the fight."

"It wasn't really a fight." Tanya shook her head vigorously, before looking down at her lap.

"Let me guess." Clyde was serious, her blue-gray eyes unwavering and determined. "When he found out about the baby, he left you."

Oh damn. Clyde let it slip about the baby.

Tanya jerked her head up. "How did....Do I show that much?"

"No, I mean..."

"How did you know?" Tanya looked impressed, thinking Clyde could read minds.

"Jotty inadvertently told me at Saturday school."

"I'm sorry, Tanya. I didn't mean to tell her," Jotty said. "My mistake."

"I guess it doesn't matter," Tanya said. "Are you going to call my mom?"

"No, but I'll give you a couple of minutes to talk and sort things out. Do you need to see the nurse?"

"No, I'm seeing the nurse at the clinic today," Tanya said.

Last time they needed to talk, she sent Jotty to Saturday school, and now she willingly suggested it.

"Sure." Jotty's voice sounded as if she was talking through a tube, hollow and distant.

Clyde led them to the conference room and closed the door.

Tanya's face had cleared some; only her eyes were red and watery now. She searched Jotty's face, until Jotty looked away. "What am I going to do, Jotty? I thought he'd want to marry me. My stepdad will kick me out now that I'm showing."

"You're not showing." Tanya would look good with some meat on her bones.

"No? But my stomach…"

"Nope."

Tanya looked relieved. "I thought everyone could tell. When I look in the mirror, I feel bloated and had to try three times to snap my jeans."

'We've got a couple of months to figure something out," Jotty said, biting at her thumbnail and viciously ripping off a hangnail. A bubble of blood appeared.

"I don't know what to do. If I keep the baby, how will I live on my own?"

There didn't seem to be an answer for that. Jotty's mind suddenly went blank, all thoughts MIA.

Tanya continued, "There aren't any jobs in Sagebrush. I already love my baby, but I don't see how I can keep it." Tanya patted her stomach.

103

"Corrina Black had an abortion," Jotty said.

"That's gross. They suck out the baby. The thought makes me sick," Tanya said, sagging a bit.

Jotty paused, imagining such a terrible thing. "Me too."

Clyde knocked softly on the door and came in. "Did you get things worked out?"

Tanya shook her head sadly. "I don't know what to do. My stepdad will make me leave when he finds out, and I don't want an abortion."

"What about an adoption?" Clyde sat down in a chair and turned it to face them.

"I don't want just anyone to have my baby," Tanya said.

"There are a lot of couples who would love to have a baby. People have a hard time finding babies to adopt. You could even arrange to meet the prospective parents ahead of time."

Tanya chewed on her lip, mulling over Clyde's words.

Jotty was quiet. Would Tanya be a good mother? She was a kind, sweet person, but was that all there was to it? Could she make it on her own without a husband? Ma couldn't.

They sat quietly. Tanya seemed to study her shoes, Clyde stared at the grain of the fake-wood table, and Jotty moved her fingers restlessly against her jeans.

"Maybe our counselor has some better suggestions," Clyde said and then took out a book of passes and wrote one for Tanya. "Jotty, you need to stay. I'll be right back."

"Suspension, right?" She could only hope.

"Maybe," Clyde said.

Jotty rolled her eyes. Not another Saturday school. She was sure to get cigarette butt cleanup this time.

Ivory-Yellow, a Nothing Color

Chapter 24

Jotty stared impatiently at the lopsided clock on the conference room wall. Where was Clyde? The times Mr. Miller suspended her didn't take long. He stopped her suspensions when she told him she liked being home. She should have kept her big mouth shut. Someone had forgotten a pencil on the table. Jotty picked it up and twirled it between her fingers.

As she waited, she traced the pattern on the tabletop, the curved grain resembling the waves of the ocean or the wind pushing the sand in the desert into flowing lines.

Jotty sighed, put down the pencil and slid farther into her chair as Clyde came in waving a thick ivory-yellow folder. A nothing color, blending in with the surroundings. Everything about her time at school held in the nothing color folder.

"What's that?" Jotty struggled to sit up, her interest piqued.

Clyde frowned at the pencil marks on the table. "Your file."

Jotty raised a brow. "All that's about me?"

"The biggest one in the drawer."

"I think you should suspend me," Jotty said.

"All in good time." Clyde drummed her fingers on the table, contemplating what to do. "You have a pattern of behavior issues."

Yeah, the more she wanted to quit school, the more she acted out.

Hurry up, Jotty urged silently. She hated sitting here, waiting for the inevitable. Just get on with the suspension! I can sit at home and draw and smoke without the interruptions and hassle.

Finally, Clyde said, "I was thinking about in-house suspension."

What was in-house suspension? Another of Clyde's ploys to keep her in school? Convert her? Mold her into a model student?

"What's in-house suspension? We've never had that before." Jotty folded her arms.

"I used it successfully at my previous school," Clyde continued after a brief pause. "You would be suspended at school, sit in the office, and do your assignments where I can see you."

Ma would like that; she'd rather be home.

"I won't do the work," Jotty said, a hint of challenge in her voice.

"Suit yourself," Clyde said, with a shrug of her shoulders.

"I usually do."

"You know, Jotty, that attitude of yours won't get you far."

"I don't care. I'm me." She puffed out her chest and sat up straight.

"That you are." Clyde stood and motioned for Jotty to follow her out of the conference room and to a desk enclosed on three sides with walls. "Have a seat."

All Jotty could see was the desktop and plywood sides. Someone had scratched, "Shit happens," "Call 677-4591 for a good time," and "RJ luvs KC" on one wall.

"Let me know when you want to do your work," Clyde said.

No chance of that. Jotty leaned back with her legs stretched out, ankles crossed. This was nice. No one was yakking or telling her what to do. The only interruptions were the ringing of the office telephone and the secretaries' voices. Student office helpers walked in and out, delivering messages, the door swishing each time someone entered or exited.

Jotty's mind drifted, and she was in a trance, having a dream while she was awake. She even tuned out the voices and ringing telephone noises of the office. How could anyone think with that? She pushed it all away and willed herself to be relaxed and calm.

Gradually the fog lifted, and she wished she had brought her notebook and a pencil. The way her stomach grumbled meant it must be close to lunchtime. Jotty blinked, stretched, and craned her neck to see the clock—only ten o'clock. A long day stretched in front of her. She stifled a yawn. She would have welcomed a homework assignment at this point. She didn't usually do them, sometimes acing the tests to the surprise of teachers. She jerked awake when her chin slumped against her chest. She yawned widely and blinked at the clock that now read ten thirty.

At lunch, Clyde brought her a tray and set it down silently. Jotty wolfed down the cheeseburger, fries, and canned peaches and sucked noisily on the milk. She glanced into Clyde's office, but her slurping didn't seem to bother Clyde as she worked at her desk, eating her carton of yogurt.

When lunch finished, and Clyde had picked up her tray, she said, "Do you want me to get your assignments?"

Yes. Anything. But she responded, "No."

Clyde looked at her disapprovingly before leaving.

Well, that was OK. Jotty wasn't here to please Clyde. She had her principles, after all. What would the other students think?

Jotty stopped herself. Did she care what other students thought? She never did before.

The afternoon ticked by. The deafening, overwhelming silence pushed in, making her feel trapped. With a rising panic, she jumped up. She had to do something!

"Where are you going?" Clyde called from her office.

"To the bathroom."

"Use the one in the office, but make it quick; the nurse uses it for sick students."

She couldn't take another day of this. She washed her hands as slowly as possible. She'd do homework, anything to make the time go faster at the little desk with three walls.

Day two of Jotty's in-house suspension, and she was prepared with a backpack full of colored pencils and a notebook. She hoisted her backpack up and boarded the bus for school, sliding in next to Tanya.

"I've got good news," Tanya said.

Was she, or wasn't she? Jotty stowed her pack under the seat in front of her.

"I'm not pregnant, but the nurse wasn't sure what's wrong with me. She drew blood." Tanya pushed up the sleeve of her sweatshirt and showed Jotty the bandage on her arm. Jotty winced at the thought of a needle in her arm.

"Didn't that hurt?"

"Like hell, but I just kept thinking, I'm not, I'm not."

"When will the nurse tell you what's wrong?"

Tanya inclined her head. "I don't know. Could be a few days. I need to tell Buck."

"Tanya, you just got a 'get out of jail free' card. Don't go back to him. He's not there for you."

Tanya was quiet as she mulled over Jotty's words. "Who will there be for me, then?"

"I don't know, but not him. He's using you, Tanya." Like Leroy used Ma. Like Tanya's mother used Tanya as a built-in babysitter.

Jotty continued, "You can find happiness in other places."

"I know. I know all that, but it's nice to have someone to do stuff with."

"We can do stuff together," Jotty said.

"Not like we used to."

In their younger years, they played imaginary games and pretended to be explorers in the desert or went to the playground swinging and sliding until Jotty thought she would heave or pass out.

"You're into your art, and I watch my little sisters. Buck picked me up, and we cruised down Main Street. My mother let me go because she acted afraid of Buck."

Jotty understood. She sensed the same thing when she looked into Buck's smoldering eyes, no demarcation between the pupils and irises, pools of simmering unhappiness.

Driving around Sagebrush didn't sound particularly appealing to Jotty. "What's the point of driving around?"

"See people. Something to do. You have your art."

So true.

"We'll have to think of something," Jotty said.

Their conversation was interrupted by the bus pulling to a stop in front of the school to let students out.

Chapter 25

The next day, Jotty expected more of the same from in-house suspension. She came prepared with colored pencils and paper. When Clyde was out walking around, she could draw a picture.

"Good morning," Clyde said as Jotty slid into her chair by the three-sided desk and plopped her backpack on the floor. "Big announcement at the assembly. I want you there. A surprise!"

Clyde actually smiled at her. Why the change of heart?

Jotty didn't usually go to assemblies or pep rallies; they usually threw off the schedule for the day, and it was easier to get lost in the crowd and miss class.

While Jotty waited, Mr. Hornbeck hustled into the office. He always appeared to be in a hurry with something important to do. What it was, she couldn't imagine. Certainly not his birds he was so passionate about.

"Jotty! Just the person I needed to see," he said.

She liked Mr. Hornbeck, his odd appearance and all. His class was interesting—all about Nevada's animals and plants.

"I have a project for you."

A homework project? Or something else?

"You know I'm updating my brochure on the sage grouse and was hoping you could draw some better pictures of the chicks."

The sketches she had made so far were of the adult birds. She had missed baby chicks by six months. "I'm not sure what they look like," she said.

"I brought photos for you to look at."

Would Clyde allow her to work on Mr. Hornbeck's brochure? She was supposed to be doing her homework.

"I'm on suspension."

"Oh yes, we've already discussed the project. Dr. B's definitely on board."

He placed the photos on the desk. The downy brown chicks appeared about the size of a large cotton ball. The pictures were slightly blurry like someone moved the camera or the chicks were moving, which they probably were.

"I'd like you to draw and paint this picture adding more details."

"Like what?"

"Sagebrush, natural habitat, native grasses, and plants. All the elements you do so well."

She could do that.

He handed her paper, colored pencils, and a small packet of paints and brushes.

This was better than Christmas. She just wanted to look at the paint containers and drool. Her imagination could run wild with the colors of pine green, espresso brown, cerulean blue, and daisy yellow. She particularly liked cerulean blue, the name rolling around her mouth, whetting her creative desire.

"So, we're all set?" he asked.

"I'll get right on it!"

Clyde came in and turned on the intercom. "Attention students, we have an important assembly today and a big announcement. Please go directly to the gym."

Jotty followed the mass of students to the gymnasium with Tanya magically appearing at her side.

"What do you think the announcement will be?" she asked.

"I have no idea. Probably some stupid BS Clyde thought up." She was anxious to get started on the sage grouse chick picture for Mr. Hornbeck.

Tanya giggled. "Clyde?"

"Yeah, that's what I call her."

"That's new."

The year was new.

"How's suspension?" Tanya asked.

"OK."

"I'm sorry you got in trouble."

"It was nothing," she said with a wave of her hand. In truth, she was mad at Leroy, and Buck got the brunt of her wrath.

Tanya studied her. "Really?"

"Yeah. Hornbeak gave me a project to work on."

Tanya laughed. "Hornbeak!" Tanya's face had cleared and the dark circles under her eyes were gone.

"He reminds me of a hawk's beak."

"You're always so funny!"

Leroy didn't think so.

"I'm drawing pictures for his new brochure."

"Jotty! That's terrific. You're good."

That was debatable.

The pep band played the school song. She selected a seat as close to the door as she could get, Tanya beside her. If this was an assembly filled with cheerleaders and football players, she'd quietly slip away.

Tanya fished a slightly brown apple from her pack and studied it, wrinkling her nose. "This looks gross."

"Is your mother buying fruits and vegetables?"

"I think they were giving this one away." Tanya took a bite of the apple and wiped away the juice on her chin.

Tomm walked by with Clyde. Tomm, the artist from the diner? What was he doing here? Jotty lifted her arm in greeting, but dropped it, studying instead the scene unfolding before her.

Clyde tapped the microphone and it buzzed and squeaked. "Testing. Testing."

Clyde fiddled further with the microphone and whispered to Tomm. Was he the big surprise?

The echo from the speakers and microphone bounced around the gym, squealing in protest.

"Let me have your attention, students. I have a wonderful announcement to make. I've applied for and received a grant from the Arts Council, and we're to have a mural painted at Sagebrush High School in the cafeteria. It will depict the rich history of our town." Clyde turned to the pep band, raised her arm, and the cymbals clanged.

Clapping.

A mural. Clyde was taking her suggestion. But she didn't hear Clyde giving her any credit.

"The work will start immediately by an artist in residence, Mr. Tomm Claybanks." Clyde gestured for him to come forward. Again, the cymbals.

Tomm, the diner's artist, would be painting her idea, her mural. Instead of being excited, she felt confusion followed by anger. Her face burned like she had eaten red hot chili peppers.

He stood and nodded toward the students lining the bleachers.

Jotty liked him, but she was mad. Not at him, but at this whole situation.

The microphone echoed and squawked again. "And I want Jotty Alfarnso to work on the mural with Tomm."

She was to help Tomm, or was it the other way around?

A bigger round of applause. Tanya elbowed her. "She said you, Jotty."

Jotty blinked. Had she thanked Jotty for the idea?

"She wants you to help," Tanya said.

"I bet."

"Aren't you excited?"

"It was my idea, Tanya," Jotty said, folding her arms to hide her clenched fists.

"But she wants you to work on it."

"That's different than giving me credit," Jotty said. She wasn't going to let Clyde get away with this.

Tanya screwed up her face. "I don't see the big deal."

She wouldn't.

"I want her to say it was my idea."

This way Clyde came off as the hero. It wasn't fair. That was her mural.

"Are you at least going to help?" Tanya asked, fishing a bag of saltine crackers from her pocket.

"No." Her answer was definitive. "She stole my idea. Besides, I can't stand that woman."

Tanya's answer was muffled from the crackers. "She seems nice."

Clyde continued speaking from her position on the gym floor, "Mr. Harrison will help with finding the historical facts and old pictures of Sagebrush for our mural. Mr. Hornbeck..." Clyde talked, naming teachers and what their contributions would be. She even mentioned Mrs. Markley, the English teacher.

Clyde put a picture on an easel—a blown-up snapshot. The picture looked familiar. Jotty leaned closer for a better look. She was too far away to see it clearly. Was that her picture? Had Clyde taken a picture of the bathroom mural and enlarged it?

More clapping before the cheer squad took the floor and pumped their arms in the air while the band played "Onward and Upward, Sagebrush High." The drums beat, and trumpets blared. The assembly was over.

"See you later," Tanya said with a nod, her face still creased in a frown as she joined the throng exiting the doors. Jotty continued to sit with her arms folded and her eyes in slits, looking at the feet marching by. The click click of heels on the wooden floor made her stiffen.

"Jotty?" Clyde said.

Jotty recognized the sound of those determined tapping heels even before hearing the voice say her name.

"What?" Jotty said.

"Aren't you excited about the mural?" Clyde asked. "And your part in it?"

"No," Jotty said.

"It was your idea," she said.

Exactly. It was her mural.

"There's a stipend for you."

Money would be nice.

"Still not interested?" Clyde asked, raising her brows and leaning forward.

"I can't be bribed."

"This isn't a bribe," Clyde said.

"I'll think about it."

"I don't understand you," Clyde said.

And she never would.

Jotty went back into the office to the cubbyhole from hell, her mind blank. Black and blank. Black with thunderous emotions. Clyde

113

had stolen her idea. No adult had ever done such a thing to her before. They arrested people for stealing, didn't they? A kernel of a thought needled her. Sometimes she could quell those ideas, but not this one. The mural, bigger than life, flashed before her mind's eye. There would be a mural. Her mural in the school for all to see and enjoy. Did the means justify the end? Ma's voice whispered in her head, Get it done the easiest way possible. Was this truly the easiest way forward? The anger leaked away bit by bit. As much as she wanted to hold on to her indignation, she couldn't. The old Jotty would throw a fit, but this new, unfamiliar Jotty felt disconnected and off balance.

The picture she had started for Mr. Hornbeck stared back at her. She picked it up and studied what she had done before they were called to the assembly. She would draw the best damn sage grouse chicks he had ever seen. Jotty picked up a pencil and twirled it in her hands before adding feathers. She stopped when the jarring ring of the telephone momentarily threw her thoughts and ideas off track. As soon as one call ended another started. How could anyone work with the noise? Her rebellious side pushed to the forefront. She couldn't work and concentrate in the office. She hated sitting here, the telephone and voices rattling her head. She needed the solace of the restroom or her mountain. She put down the pencil and slipped from the office, quietly and unobtrusively, so on one would notice. No one followed her.

She stopped at the front doors of the school and waited. Nope, no one noticed she was gone. She opened and closed the doors quietly and again stopped, waiting for someone to say her name and call her back, but no one did. She turned toward the mountain. Like a flame attracting a moth, it drew her closer.

As she walked, she turned each piece of the morning over in her mind. She started with the pleasant part, Mr. Hornbeck's request. Someone asked her to draw a picture. Leaving school had nothing to do with his request. Clyde's underhandedness still hung over her. The mural would be painted with or without her. Which did she want? Not helping sent a message almost as great as helping. But would others see it that way? Did it matter? Should she wait until the process had started to make her decision? See how Tomm did things?

114

Ma's voice whispered in her ear. Don't be so stubborn. Take it as a compliment, not a threat. Listen to her. Jotty shook away Ma's words in her ears, but they wouldn't leave her alone.

At the mountain path, Jotty inched upward, taking one step after another. Before she knew it, she was at her favorite boulder. She hardly noticed the ache and pull on the back of her legs or her breath coming in quick gasps.

Surveying the school from this point put it in perspective. From here, the school was small and dollhouse-size.

Yes, she wanted to work on the mural with all her heart, but she wanted it to be her suggestion. Would anyone know it was her idea? Yes, Ma's voice whispered in her ear. Everyone already knows, and they're excited for you.

Was the need to fight with Clyde greater than the significance of the mural?

Chapter 26

The next morning, as Jotty boarded the bus, all the kids sitting around her bombarded her with questions.

She slipped into her seat next to Tanya, and already she felt a pounding tension between her eyes.

"When do you start on the mural?"

"Are you going to have people?"

"Can I be in the mural?"

The questions kept coming and Jotty remained silent, shrugging her shoulders instead of giving a snappy comeback. The fellow bus riders took her silence as agreement.

"Can't you tell us anything?" Sal asked.

"Nope, my lips are sealed!" Jotty finally said.

"Come on!" Dee Dee said.

"Is it the same as the one you painted last year?"

The blown-up snapshot of her picture Clyde took without her consent. Clyde said the school belonged to the taxpayers. Wasn't Ma one of those? Maybe she didn't need Jotty's permission in theory, but as a matter of courtesy?

While the comments strengthened her desire to help Tomm, they also strengthened her resolve not to help and show Clyde a thing or two about her fortitude. Ma had said her stubbornness wouldn't get her very far, but was turning off her unwieldiness the same as turning on and off a light switch? On. Off. On. Off?

The bus reached the school, and the questions stopped, but she was accosted in the hallways.

"Jotty! Who's the guy you'll be working with?"

They assumed she was working on the mural.

"Tomm," she said, an edge to her words while pushing aside students to get access to her locker.

"Do you know him well?"

"Nope."

"Is Mr. Harrison part of the project?"

"Why are you asking me these things? Ask our prin-ci-pal!" she said in exasperation, forgetting her locker combination in the process.

"What's the matter with you?" A girl from her English class asked.

"Nothing," Jotty snapped. "I haven't even said I'd help." She banged her fist against the metal in frustration.

The girl, slack-jawed, looked at Jotty like she had two heads. "I just assumed. We all did."

"Well, don't!"

"There you are," Clyde said from the packed hallway. "Just the person I need to see."

Damn.

"What did I do now?" Jotty said, irritation making her words short.

"It's what you didn't do," Clyde said, leading Jotty to the office.

"Huh?"

"You left after the assembly and never came back."

I had to think. It's too noisy in the office."

"Nope, you can't decide that."

It figured.

In Clyde's office, she handed Jotty the incomplete picture she had started for Mr. Hornbeck yesterday. Her mind drew a blank as she looked at the picture. What had she started? A pigeon?

"So what do you think of my announcement?" Clyde asked, putting her elbows on the desk and leaning toward Jotty. Clyde's eyes took on a stormy-gray hue in the glare of the overhead lights.

"I think it stinks."

Clyde straightened, looked at her, mouth open for a moment before she closed her lips into a thin line. She said nothing; she just stared.

Jotty glared back. They continued the stare down for several minutes, with Clyde finally breaking the silence.

"OK, tell me what's bugging you."

"Do you really want to know?"

117

"I do."

"You. You bug me, barging in here and running everyone's lives! Making changes, bossing everyone around. Stealing ideas."

"When have I ever stolen your ideas?"

"The mural. That was my idea. You never said anything about who suggested such a thing."

Clyde sat quietly, listening, moving her head a bit with each of Jotty's points.

"Everyone thinks I'm going to work on it, but I'm not! Tell them to leave me alone!"

"I'm afraid you'll have to explain that yourself," Clyde said. "In the meantime, you'll need to spend the day in the office for your absence yesterday."

And just like that, Jotty was back staring at the three walls of the suspension desk, heart racing and anger bubbling until slowly it wasn't, and she was alone with the picture. The way she liked it, right?

Tanya tapped on the glass separating the office from the main hallway and mouthed,

"Can you talk?"

Jotty nodded her head.

Tanya came into the office and sidled over to Jotty's desk. "I forgot to tell you something," she whispered.

"Hmm?"

"The results."

Jotty thoughts went off-track momentarily.

"I have a thyroid problem." When Jotty didn't immediately reply, Tanya continued, "You know the weight gain, nausea, and tiredness? My thyroid!" Tanya pointed to her neck. "It's right here!"

"Can I help you, Tanya?" Clyde asked.

What could the interfering biddy want now, Jotty wondered. Wasn't it enough to keep her stuck in here and away from the bathroom?

"Oh, no, just had to tell Jotty something."

"How are you feeling?" Clyde asked, giving Tanya's shoulders a squeeze.

"OK, I guess."

Clyde waited.

"My thyroid."

"What do you mean?" Clyde asked.

"I'm not pregnant."

"Good, now run along. Jotty can't talk to anyone. She's suspended."

"Oh." Tanya backed up toward the door and left.

Clyde turned to Jotty, fixed her with her storm-cloud gray eyes, frowned, marched back to her office, and closed the door.

At the end of the long, uneventful day on in-house suspension, Tanya waited by the door for Jotty.

Jotty struggled to her feet, her legs numb from sitting all day. She gathered her backpack and pictures for Mr. Hornbeck and staggered to the door on her wobbly legs.

"Gosh, I've missed talking to you. How many more days do you need to stay in the office?" Tanya asked.

"I have no idea, but I'm tired of it. It's sooo boring." Jotty leaned against the wall and moved one foot and then the other to get the circulation flowing again. "I fell asleep sitting there. And my legs." She shook each leg for emphasis. "Feel like pins and needles. And the telephone rings nonstop!"

Tanya smiled in sympathy.

"So you have a medical problem?" Jotty asked.

"Yeah, my thyroid. I'm supposed to be on medication."

"Have you started it?" They were briefly interrupted by students going out the front door to their cars or the bus. Several said hello, but most were intent on leaving the school, not staying to chat with Jotty and Tanya.

"Anyway, my mom says it's too expensive."

"Did you tell her you need it?"

"She still says we can't afford it."

"That's rough."

"I know."

"Is there some way to get what you need?" Jotty eased away from the wall, but Tanya remained by the office entrance, oblivious to the exiting students. The throng of students became smaller and smaller until they were alone.

"I'm worried," Tanya said.

"What could happen if you don't get your medicine?" Jotty asked.

"It sounds terrible, but I could get the shakes, have heart problems, and my hair might fall out."

"That sounds bad."

"I know." Tanya stopped talking and looked around. "Gosh, did we miss the bus?"

They exited the school. The bus was gone, and the parking lot was nearly empty.

"I think we did." It wouldn't be the end of the world. Jotty could walk to the diner and hitch a ride with Ma. But Tanya's family lived off a gravel road on the other side of Sagebrush.

"Can you call your mother for a ride?" They turned back to the school and went inside to the office.

"I can try, but she never has any gas in the car."

"Problem, girls?" Clyde asked when she noticed Jotty was back.

"We missed the bus," Tanya said.

"How did that happen?"

"I wanted to talk to Jotty."

Jotty stayed silent, watching the exchange between Tanya and Clyde.

"Do you need a ride home? I'd be happy to take you."

"That would be great," Tanya said.

"I can walk," Jotty said.

"Ride along!" Tanya said, tugging at Jotty's sleeve.

Jotty guessed it wouldn't hurt, although the thought of spending more time with Clyde in close proximity didn't sound like fun. She reminded herself she was doing it to help Tanya. She set her feelings aside and followed them out into the parking lot to Clyde's green sedan.

Tanya gave Clyde directions to their trailer, while Jotty sat in the back seat and listened to their conversation. Clyde's green sedan was clean with no torn seat upholstery, and the seat belts worked. She buckled herself in as they rolled out of the school parking lot.

Clyde repeated her question from this morning. "How are you feeling, Tanya?"

"OK, I guess. Apparently, my thyroid makes too much of something."

"Hormones. The thyroid is small but controls so much in the body," Clyde said.

Clyde was a walking, talking encyclopedia. If that's what college did to you, Jotty would pass; thank you very much.

"I'm happy I'm not pregnant. Oh, turn here," Tanya said, pointing to a gravel road.

Clyde turned and slowed her car as they bumped over the stones lining the road. The conversation paused as Clyde maneuvered around the ruts, weeds scraping the underside of the vehicle.

"Thyroid issues are easily treated," Clyde said.

"If you take the medicine," Tanya said.

"Why wouldn't you take the medicine?" There was a dip in the road, a small gully. Jotty watched the scenery as they inched along. The scenery—brown, tan, and gray this time of year—the shut-off valves closed for the impending snow and cold weather.

Tanya continued talking. Jotty saw the outline of Tanya's trailer in the distance. A solitary rectangle with several vehicles parked nearby. Where the gravel road ended, they would turn right.

"My mom can't afford it now; she's saving for Christmas. But she said we could get it after the holidays."

Christmas was almost two months away.

"Hmm."

Tanya pointed to the sign leading to their trailer. "We live down there."

Gas line road. Not a real road but access for the gas company. Jotty had often wondered how Tanya's family managed to continue living there. Did the gas company mind them living on their property?

Clyde slowed the car as they moved along the bumpy road and stopped by Tanya's family travel trailer. "Is this it?" Clyde asked.

Jotty scanned the horizon. Nothing for many miles except rocks and a few spindly fir trees, gnarled from the wind, sand, and heat.

"Yes, this is our place. Thanks for the ride."

"I'll see if I can find some resources to help with your medication."

Tanya opened the door and exited. "That would be great! And thanks for the ride!" With that she slammed the door, leaving Jotty alone in the car with Clyde.

What rotten luck, stuck in a small car with Clyde.

"Do you want to sit in the front?" Clyde asked.

"Nope, just drop me off at the diner."

Clyde turned the car around, and they drove back over the uneven tracks toward Main Street. Neither talked. Once at the diner, Clyde stopped, and Jotty got out.

"You're welcome," Clyde said as Jotty slammed the door and turned toward the front door.

She had only accepted the ride for Tanya. You're welcome indeed!

Chapter 27

Inside the diner, Jotty first spotted Tomm sitting in a booth, drinking coffee. He was doodling or drawing on the placemat.

"When do we get started?" he asked, motioning for her to sit opposite him and putting down the pencil he was using.

"Not we, you," Jotty said, sitting across from Tomm, and she motioned toward his placemat.

He frowned. "I thought we were working on this together, that's what Dr. Benninger said. It's the reason I agreed to do it."

Jotty chewed on her lip, her decision waffling between pride over Clyde's duplicity and the need to be expressive and better understand Tomm and what he did. A chance for her to see if that was the life for her. A tug of war.

"I'm mad at her."

"She seems like a nice person," he said.

"She's not."

"Why do you say that?"

"She's making my life miserable."

He half laughed and snorted. "I see."

"No, you don't. I had everything figured out, and she came in and ruined it."

"Life changes on a dime," he said, fingering his coffee cup with a finger rimmed with paint, the bluish-purple Jotty liked, sometimes called cobalt or azure.

"What does that mean?" Jotty demanded.

"It means life takes some unexpected detours. Mine did. Yours will too."

"Oh?"

"Tomm," Ma said, stopping when she saw Jotty in the booth. "What are you doing here?" Ma held the coffee container and poured some into Tomm's cup when he nodded.

"Talking."

"Did you walk here?"

"No, I got a ride."

Ma waited, the coffee pot hovering over the table.

"Clyde."

"Clyde?" Ma asked. "Who's that?"

"The principal."

Tomm laughed at the dramatic way she said "principal."

"They don't get along," he said as an explanation.

Ma's mouth moved into a tight line. "Are you in trouble again?"

Always, but she responded with, "No, she gave Tanya a ride home, and I tagged along."

Ma's shoulders visibly relaxed. "That's good. Do you want coffee?"

"Sure." Jotty turned over the cup by the placemat so Ma could pour the coffee.

Ma continued to stand by the table until the door jingled, signaling another customer, and she went to greet them.

Tomm said, "Don't run out on me now."

His words pricked at her subconscious. Scummy people ran out or avoided the unavoidable—her father for starters. He had left them many years ago, leaving her angry and resentful. Is that how Tomm felt? She knew abandonment all too well.

"Let me think about it." Her resolve wavered.

"Don't take too long. I start next week," Tomm said.

Next week was four days away. Four days to decide. Four days sometimes went by fast or excruciatingly slow. Jotty had the feeling the days would whip by, and she'd have to decide.

Sour Hurt-Your-Eyes Lemon Yellow

Chapter 28

"Oh goodie," Tanya said the next morning when she saw Jotty in the bathroom between classes.

Tanya's presence made all Jotty's thoughts of the mural and what her decision would be fly out the door.

Oh goodie? Tanya's little sisters were having an effect on Tanya's vocabulary as well as the tight Micky Mouse T-shirt she was wearing. Oh, goodie, indeed.

"Everything's back to normal," Tanya said, slumping against the counter and giving Jotty a big grin.

"Hardly," Jotty replied, taking out her sketch pad of the incomplete sage grouse. "What really is normal?"

Tanya frowned. "You're taking in riddles. What's up?"

"Nothing."

"I can tell."

It might make the decision easier if Jotty told someone.

"Tomm wants me to help with the mural, and I have to decide."

"What's so terrible about that?" Tanya asked, finding her lip gloss, unscrewing the top, and putting pale-pink "rose petal" on her lips.

"And give in to her?"

"Who?" Tanya pursed her lips before turning from the mirror.

"Clyde."

"You're not giving in."

"Like hell I'm not. I told her I didn't want to help."

"So, change your mind," Tanya said. "I do it all the time."

"That makes me sound wishy-washy." It wasn't as easy as that. But could it be?

"Does not!"

"I really don't like her." Jotty stopped when the bell announced the start of second period.

"That's obvious, but she seems nice enough. She gave us a ride, didn't she?" Tanya shifted toward the door to leave.

Jotty had no desire to go to math.

"Mr. Miller probably would have done the same thing."

Jotty watched as Tanya's eyes rolled up, and in slow motion she fell to the floor. It happened so quickly, Jotty remained rooted in her spot watching Tanya's fall like she was viewing a movie.

"Tanya!" Jotty jumped off the counter and knelt by her friend. "What's wrong?"

Tanya's eyes fluttered open. "I suddenly felt dizzy."

"Did you eat breakfast?"

"All the crackers in the cupboard."

"That doesn't sound like a good breakfast."

"I left the cereal for my sisters. That's all that was left."

Jotty helped Tanya sit up. "Do you need some water?"

"Yes, that would be good."

"I'll go get some," she said after helping Tanya move to the wall to support her back.

Where to get water? The nurse? The nurse always had little cups hanging in a dispenser by the sink.

Jotty ran to the office. Second class period had started, so the hallways were deserted. Once in the office, she burst through the door. "I need a cup of water. My friend fainted."

Clyde jumped up. "Tanya?"

"Yes, she's in the bathroom."

Clyde grabbed a cup and filled it with water, and together they hurried back to the bathroom and Tanya.

Once back in the bathroom, Clyde knelt next to Tanya and handed her the cup, while Jotty wet a paper towel for her face.

"Let's get you to the nurse," Clyde said, brushing Tanya's bangs from her eyes.

Jotty wiped Tanya's face as she drank the water.

"What happened?" Clyde asked.

"All of a sudden, the room went dark, and that was it," Tanya said.

"She didn't eat breakfast this morning," Jotty offered.

"You didn't?"

"Some crackers," Tanya said.

126

"Do you get breakfast at school?" Clyde asked.

"Sometimes when my mom has leftover money, I do."

"I'll get you a breakfast card," Clyde said, holding Tanya's right arm; Jotty held the left. Together they helped Tanya stand.

"I...I think I'll be OK," Tanya stammered.

"I'd still like the nurse to check you out."

"I'm sorry to cause a fuss."

"No fuss. That's what we're here for."

Jotty listened, and all snide remarks escaped. After all, Clyde was helping her friend. Did a bad person do that?

Chapter 29

"Where could he be?" Ma asked, peeking out the curtains and then looking at the clock. "It's almost seven thirty. Our dinner is ready."

Jotty's stomach rumbled in protest. Ma had kept the casserole in the over on low for an hour, the smells filling the trailer. She put down her sketch for Mr. Hornbeck and asked,

"Do you want me to check the Half-Moon Bar?

"Would you?"

Ma handed her the truck keys. It had been a while since she had visited the bar looking for Leroy. After she parked and went in, the same atmosphere greeted her. She waved away the smoke that stung her eyes. Nothing had changed. Smoky interior, loud cowboy music, broken furniture, and an undercurrent of voices talking over and around each other and the jukebox.

The bartender nodded for her to come in. She was underage, after all. "Leroy?"

Who else.

"Sheriff took them away. Broke a chair and smashed some glasses."

"Oh."

"People laid off at the pit today, I understand," The barkeeper said with a knowledgeable nod.

Was Leroy one of those laid off?

"You'll find him at the jail. Drunk and disorderly. Those guys owe me two hundred bucks for the things they broke."

He could stay there.

"Thanks, I'll let Ma know."

"You do that." He turned away toward someone wanting a beer.

Jotty drove home and delivered the news to Ma.

"Did he get laid off? Do you know?"

"I don't," Jotty said. The table was set for the three of them. Jotty put Leroy's plate back in the cupboard, and she and Ma ate the tuna casserole that had been warming in the oven for hours. The casserole was dry, but it filled Jotty's stomach.

"I wonder what bail will be?" Answering her own question, she said, "We don't have that kind of money anyway. I guess we could call Richard again," Ma said, putting down her fork and shifting her weight to stand.

Jotty put up her arm to stop Ma. "You don't need to do it now."

"He'll be upset if he has to stay too long."

"Too bad," Jotty said, adding, "I bet Richard is getting tired of bailing his no-good brother out of jail."

"Possibly," Ma said, moving her food from one side of the plate to the other, finally stabbing a piece of tuna.

They ate silently. Jotty's mind was flitting from one thing to the other, but mainly thinking of the mural. Did she want to work on it? Or didn't she? Why the big decision? Yes or no? Her principles or the principal's? She liked that. Ha! Would Mrs. Markley, the old biddy, like her play on words? Principles, principals? Probably wouldn't see the humor in it.

"What happened at school today?" Ma asked, taking a drink of water to help swallow the food. Jotty followed with a drink from her own glass.

"Tanya fainted today."

"Oh, my goodness. Why?" Ma put down her fork.

"She has a thyroid problem and not eating very much. Saving it for her sisters. She's supposed to be on medicine, but her mother says they'll have to wait until they can afford it."

Ma was silent, eyeing the pile of noodles, celery, and tuna on her plate. "I was thinking this is much too dry and that I should throw it away, but I hate to waste food when Tanya is doing without."

"The principal got her a breakfast card, so she can eat at school."

"Things are certainly shaping up now that the new principal has started."

Jotty had been thinking just the opposite.

129

"Jotty?"

"Hmm."

"Don't you agree?"

"Maybe."

Ma laughed. "That sounds like the Jotty I know."

Richard bailed Leroy out of jail, and he came home, quietly and a bit meekly. The two days sitting in the cell had done him good. Even though he was unusually quiet, Jotty was still wary around him. When Ma went to work and Jotty finished her Saturday chores, she left for Rattlesnake. No way did she want to be alone with Leroy in the trailer.

It had been several weeks since she had been here, and the mountain was shedding fall and preparing for winter. Everything was brown or varying shades of gray, camouflage green, and tan. The color names of chestnut, burnt umber, and iron oxide came to Jotty's mind. She especially liked burnt umber. Somehow brown didn't cut it, not like burnt umber.

All around her, leaves had closed and stalks dried, conserving energy for the winter months until they would burst forth with their spring foliage.

The ponies had grown thick shaggy fur. When Jotty reached her rock and sat, they remained standing on the far side, watching her. She hadn't brought carrots or apples, only a peanut butter sandwich for herself.

The horses munched on the brittle grasses, nosing around for anything tasty. There wasn't much. Jotty watched the mares jerk their heads up, searching. The stallion watched and didn't eat. On high alert. They kept moving to get more to eat.

The sage grouse were gone. Jotty wondered where they went for the winter. Did they fly south? She'd have to ask Mr. Hornbeck.

Chapter 30

When Jotty got to school on Monday, both Tomm and Clyde were waiting by the door. They stood motionless, waiting. Jotty turned and walked the opposite way.

"Jotty! We need to talk to you," Tomm called.

She didn't want to talk to them. She knew it was silly, but she wanted to be alone. To think. She headed for her sanctuary and breathed a sigh of relief in finding it empty. A thin haze of cigarette smoke hung in the air, left by someone sneaking a quick one before classes started.

The door to the bathroom opened slowly, and she heard tap tap tap on the tile.

"Why did you run off?" Clyde asked.

"I didn't."

"You saw us waiting and turned the other way."

Jotty kept her back to Clyde. "I didn't want to talk to you."

"Why are you making such a big deal out of this?"

She wasn't, was she? Who was she kidding? Of course she was. Pride.

"Are you upset Tomm is to be paid and you're not?"

"No."

She couldn't tackle a project of that magnitude on her own. There weren't enough months left in the school year for that and besides, she was thinking about dropping out in March. Five months was too short to start and finish a mural of this size.

Money hadn't entered her mind, only Clyde's duplicity in making it sound like it was her idea, not Jotty's.

"I can arrange for a small stipend for you too."

Clyde still didn't get it, did she?

"It's not money or wanting to work alone."

"So what is it?"

"I just don't want to do it." The words stuck in her throat much like the dry tuna casserole had.

"OK, I'll see if Brenda Rosenthal will help."

Jotty whirled around. "Brenda?" Brenda would be all wrong. She clamped her mouth shut.

"Yes, Brenda."

"Ask her," Jotty said, her heart sinking as she said the words. The mural would be all wrong, and it would be her fault for not helping.

Clyde turned, heels tapping as she marched away.

Jotty waited several beats and followed. Tomm stood waiting for her at the opposite wall.

"Jotty? Will you tell me what's wrong? Did I say something to offend you?"

She turned away from the hurt in his eyes. Yes, hurt. She could see the brightness in his eyes and went back into the bathroom, climbed up on the counter, and rested her forehead against her knees. Damn. Damn. Damn. She wanted to cry, but her throat was closed, and nothing came out.

"Hello," Mr. Hornbeck greeted her when Jotty arrived at his class after spending an hour in the bathroom. "I've been meaning to speak to you."

Did she flunk her last test?

"Me too." The sage grouse in winter.

He motioned her toward his desk. "What did you want to see me about?"

She took in a gulp of air. "The sage grouse. What happens to them in winter?"

"They stay and hide in the sagebrush. If you look closely, you might be able to see them. Contrary to other bird species, they like the snow. Some even make snow igloos to live in."

"Really? I'll have to look. I assumed they flew south."

"Nope, they need the sagebrush to survive. You have to look closely, but you'll see them hidden in the branches when there's snow."

"Oh," Jotty said. "And er, what did you want to see me about? Was my last assignment bad?"

"Oh, no, nothing like that." He waved his hands before taking off his glasses and cleaning them on a cloth he took from his pocket. "Dr. Benninger says you're not helping with the mural."

"That's right."

"Why ever not? I was hoping for some sage grouse."

"Brenda can paint those for you." Although secretly she doubted Brenda could do that.

"Who's Brenda?" Mr. Hornbeck demanded.

"She's helping Tomm."

"Tomm doesn't know the first thing about how to paint grouse properly in their natural habitat. I'm so disappointed to hear you're not helping. A waste of your talent, if you ask me."

Jotty shifted feet, unsure of what to say.

"I thought I heard your name mentioned at the assembly," he said, clearly confused and disappointed.

"She assumed I'd help."

"I think we all did."

"Never assume, my mother told me."

He chuckled. "I've heard somewhat the same thing." He paused and studied her. She wanted to look away, but couldn't. "There's something else going on here that I don't understand," he said. "You don't like the principal, I gather."

All that was written on her features?

"Something like that."

"So you're going to let this opportunity to showcase your talent go by because you don't like her?"

Put that way, it seemed silly and stupid. She studied the toe of her shoe, suddenly more important than facing up to her stupidity.

"My mother always said you get more flies with honey than vinegar." It was hard to imagine Mr. Hornbeck having a mother. Everyone had a mother though. "Just think about your decision," he said as the classroom began filling with students. Fourth period had started. The rest of her day was filled with thoughts about how to change her mind and help. She desperately wanted Clyde to beg her to help, get down on her knees and say, "pretty please, with sugar and a candy-red cherry on top," but she didn't, so Jotty suffered.

Nondescript Gray

Chapter 31

The days following the start of the mural went by in a haze for Jotty. She watched the progress unfold in the cafeteria, stopping to watch at every opportunity. Her schedule had changed from sitting in the bathroom to watching the production, the smell of paint pulling her forward.

Tarps covered the floor, the scaffolding erected, and the frame for the picture taped off and painted with primer, a nondescript gray color. The mural would be huge. Tomm was hard at work, his back to the cafeteria.

"Jotty?" Tanya came into the cafeteria for breakfast. "Hi, what'cha ya doing?"

"Watching." She followed the progression of the work, step by step. Tomm methodically completed each task before moving on to the next. Jotty rather liked doing everything at once, only cleaning at the end when the paint had dried or her brush bristles hardened, making more work for herself. Tomm always cleaned his brushes and put away the paint at the end of each session. She guessed that was the mark of a true artist—cleaning up the mess afterward. Unfortunately, the mess she had created for herself couldn't be cleared away with turpentine and a rag.

"Jotty?" Tanya said, tugging on her sleeve, pulling her back to the present.

"Sorry, thinking," Jotty said, rubbing the bridge of her nose before letting Tanya pull her over to the table.

"I bet you wish you could help."

Tanya didn't know the half of it.

"Maybe."

Sal Scott joined them. Breakfast service had started in the cafeteria, and students were eating and watching the mural's progress.

"So what's going there?" Sal pointed to the left corner. "What's he doing now?"

Jotty shrugged. "Why ask me?" She wished she could remember his sketches on the diner placemat, but she couldn't.

"It's your picture, right?" Sal asked.

"No." Pause. "I'm not helping with it."

Sal scowled. "Why is that?"

Jotty shook her head.

"But Dr. Benninger said…"

"I know what she said. I turned her down."

Sal elbowed her. "Girl! He's cute too!"

"I didn't notice," Jotty said. She saw Tomm turn and scan the crowd, searching. She leaned back. The shift in her posture wasn't lost on Tanya, who had a knowing look on her face.

"Everyone knows it's your picture," Sal said.

"Maybe," Jotty said. Why couldn't Clyde have said that? "Do you think it's wrong to steal someone's ideas?"

"Like plagiarism?" Something they had learned in English.

"It sure is."

"The principal plagiarized my idea," Jotty said, liking the comparison.

"I heard her say something about you at the assembly, but it was hard to hear."

Jotty had heard every word and no mention of it being her idea, only Clyde wanted her to help. Clyde stole her idea and made it sound like it was hers. Wrong, wrong, wrong.

Sal and Tanya got in line for cereal and yogurt, leaving Jotty alone.

How would she lay out such a project, just a bigger version of the original? No, the cafeteria mural had room for a lot more than the mountain: different animals, people, Mr. Hornbeck's blasted sage grouse, and part of the town of Sagebrush. She wasn't good at drawing people. She'd probably screw up the people part if she helped. But Tomm drew the cowboy and waitress. They looked lifelike and not just stick figures. A partnership could work—her landscapes and his people. Yet, here she was, stubborn Jotty, watching, not participating. Brenda the center of attention.

Jotty had conquered part of her fear of the mountain and snakes by sheer stubborn will, one step after another. Walk, stop, swallow her fear of the coiled shaking rattlers before taking another step. Why couldn't she swallow her fear, face Clyde, and say she had changed her mind? Somehow encountering a snake seemed easier to deal with.

The mural looked terrible. At least that was Jotty's opinion. The other students commented on the huge buildings and small view of the mountain. Jotty would have made the town smaller and the mountain, well, bigger. After all, it was the focal point of the community, wasn't it?

She had to admit it wasn't terrible bad, just terrible different. Although she couldn't define the difference between bad and different. Nope, she would have done things differently. Her mother had warned her that such stubbornness would get her in a fix someday. That day had come.

Tomm stooped to stir the paint. The pungent antiseptic smell permeated the room, beckoning her. She remained hidden. He turned once, searching. She stepped closer to the wall. Did he know she was there? Could he feel her disapproval?

Jotty studied what Tomm had done so far. There was so much she would have included in the picture. The buildings as sketched blocked the desert. She would have smaller buildings and made a desert scene of ranches, the mountain, and mining the point of interest. Brenda should have known that from art class or in studying the surrounding countryside.

"I wish you'd reconsider working on the mural," Clyde said, coming into the cafeteria and stopping behind Jotty. "I liked your picture better."

Jotty was so lost in thought that she didn't hear Clyde coming in her noisy heels. Damn.

"Then why have Emmett paint over it?" The retort came out, blunt, Jotty style.

"There is a time and place for everything," Clyde said.

Jotty folded her arms. "So the perfect place for the mural is the cafeteria wall?"

"I thought you'd be pleased. It was your suggestion, after all."

Secretly she was.

"Do I look pleased?" Jotty asked, making her eyes scrunch together.

"No, you look unhappy, and I don't know why." Now it was Clyde's turn to look unhappy and confused.

"This was my idea," Jotty said. "And you used my picture without asking."

Clyde gave a strangled gasp. "This is public property. You don't own the bathroom walls—the taxpayers do."

They stared at each other, neither blinking or looking away. Clyde's blue eyes, stormy- sea gray.

"I would have felt better if you had asked to enlarge my picture."

"Is that what this is all about?"

"Could be."

Clyde frowned. "I assumed everyone would know it was your idea."

"No, they didn't."

"Of course they did. Is that why you're upset? Because I didn't say outright it was your idea?" Clyde folded her arms. "It was your idea, but I had a part too. I had to call the Arts Council, write the grant, and find Tomm."

Tomm lived in a travel trailer behind the diner close to the school, so he was easy to find. How hard was it to write a grant?

Tomm, hearing a conversation behind him, turned, climbed off the scaffolding, and came toward them.

"I thought that was you," he said to Jotty. "I was hoping you'd be my assistant or better, I could be your assistant. What do you think so far?" he asked with a smile.

"Good start," Clyde said with a squint, a diplomatic thing to say at this point.

"Jotty?" They both turned to her.

She moved her lips as she pondered his question. So far, she wasn't impressed, but she replied, "It's big."

"Come on," he said. "You can do better than that. You told me how to fix the diner picture. What do you really think?"

"The mountain isn't right." Her eyes scanned the work in progress before looking at his face to see how serious he was. "Rattlesnake is rounded, almost flat at the top, but that one is too pointed."

Clyde raised her brows, her eyes wide with understanding. She cleared her throat "I think you're correct, Jotty."

Clyde was siding with her? And the earth didn't open to swallow them with that revelation?

Just then, Clyde was called to the office, leaving Jotty and Tomm alone for the first time since the project began.

"Brenda told me more about you," Tomm said. "She said you were the best artist in the school. This is your baby, you know."

"Not anymore," she said.

"Oh, I get it." He shifted his gaze toward the office. "You still don't like her," he said.

That obvious?

"She painted over my picture and stole my idea," Jotty said.

"Hmm. Is that important to you?"

"Of course," she said.

He paused as if considering his words. "I don't think the process trumps the end result."

Jotty frowned.

"She may have made some mistakes and stepped on your toes a bit, but does it really matter in the end? At the end, the school will have a magnificent mural that will endure for as long as the school is standing. Do you know how special that is?"

"I guess I didn't think of it that way," Jotty said.

"You have a cult following around here. Since I started, all I hear the kids say is 'Jotty this' and 'Jotty that.' 'Jotty would paint it this way.'" He waved his arm behind him. "That's your picture whether I paint it or not."

That consideration hadn't crossed her mind.

"I guess you could be right." A weight lifted from her shoulders.

"I need your help."

"How do I do that?" she whispered.

He motioned toward the office door. "You'll have to let her know."

Jotty gulped back her fear. She wanted to help. She itched to get her hands on the paint and have it on her fingers and under her short, bitten nails. Everything about painting a mural would be exciting, even if it would be hard work. She had ideas. Her forefinger twitched, having a life of its own.

She pictured cowboys riding horses, chasing cattle over the desert; the mountain ponies on Rattlesnake, with the wind ruffling their manes and tails. The puffed-up sage grouse in their feathery finery frolicking at the bottom. The wall was huge. The cafeteria picture could have so much more than the one on the bathroom wall.

With leaden feet, she started to the office.

Once inside the office, she wasn't sure what to say.

Clyde saw her and said, "Come in," motioning for her to sit. "What's up?"

She wasn't going to make this easy for Jotty. Clyde's nautical-blue eyes, calm and still, the stormy seas gone.

"I've been talking to Tomm."

"And?"

Jotty moved the toe of her sneaker back and forth as she searched for the right words. "You made a lot of changes around here that I didn't like."

"I see. Is that the reason for the animosity?"

That obvious?

"I had things figured out before." Lame. Lame when she voiced it in those terms.

"Hmm. Did you come in here to tell me about your feelings about me?"

"No, not exactly."

Clyde waited, tapping a pencil against her desk calendar.

After taking a big gulp of air, Jotty plunged ahead. "I want to help with the mural." There, she said it, and her head didn't explore or anything.

"Why the change of heart?"

"People have been talking to me."

139

Again, the silence.

Jotty continued, "Everyone knows it was my idea, even if you didn't say it."

No reaction from Clyde.

"And Tomm wants my help." She began ticking off the reasons on her fingers. "I can draw scenery."

They each waited for the other.

"And sage grouse."

Jotty sucked at her bottom lip as she considered what to say next. "He made me understand you didn't say it was my idea because you wanted to take credit. You thought I knew what the others thought, and I was wrong."

Clyde took the pencil and studied the sharpened point. "I guess I owe you an apology for not making it clearer at the assembly. Would you like me to make an announcement?"

"No, not necessary. Can I start working with Tomm?"

"Of course..."

There was always a way.

"Your grades."

Now Jotty was at a loss for words. Working on the mural meant she would have to attend classes and bring up her grades.

"You can start tomorrow if you wish."

If you wish...Three little words that meant a shift in Jotty's thinking and then in action.

All major decisions in Jotty's life involved going to the mountain. And deciding about school and the mural was no different. After school, instead of staying at the trailer, she hitched her backpack over her shoulders and trekked toward Rattlesnake. The dirt, hard packed under her feet, unyielding like Clyde's ultimatum. The frost from the previous night hadn't completely melted.

With each footstep, her mind cleared, and she considered her choices. They were easy really. Attend classes and help Tomm or not attend classes and have Tomm work alone or with Brenda? The bitter with the sweet. A sticker after a shot at the health nurse's office.

She reached the path and began the climb to her favorite rock. Why was she so turned off to classes? She yawned at the thought. Of course, the classes were boring and didn't have any real-life connection.

She remembered taking her driver's test and answering questions that had no relevance to her life. Questions about pulling a trailer or having a baby in the car. Neither applied, but still she had to know the answers. Were there similarities to her current dilemma? Learn nonsense before she could get to the important stuff?

Jotty pushed herself the last bit and collapsed heavily against her rock. The sharp air pierced her lungs. Was the same true for English and math? Might she someday need to know how to write an essay? Or figure out percentages or fractions?

She fished in her backpack for a cigarette and came up with a half-smoked butt. It would have to do. The smoke warmed her as she looked toward the sky—an icy pale blue, bleached and still.

With her cigarette finished, she pushed away from the rock. Her decision made.

A Multi-hued Decision

Chapter 32

The next morning when Jotty stepped through the door, the secretary frowned at her and looked at the slips of paper on her desk. "Did I call you to the office?"

"No, I want to see Cl…er…the principal."

"She's with a parent. Can you wait?"

Jotty paced back and forth in front of the row of chairs too anxious to sit. She stopped her restless steps at the three-sided in-house suspension desk and breathed deeply. No, that wasn't her place today. She continued her pacing. If she were to paint her quandary, would it be dark and emotional like Munch's The Scream? Or soft and reflective—a Monet landscape? Neither quite fit. A decision was all those things—multihued.

The parent left, and Clyde beckoned Jotty into her private office.

"Ah, you've made a decision?" Clyde asked.

"I guess I have to play the game to get a goal," Jotty said.

A football or soccer analogy even though she had no interest in either sport.

Jotty continued, "I've been painting Rattlesnake for so long, I know how to paint the mountain, so people can feel its power and beauty."

Clyde stared at her for several beats before saying, "Even I could feel your passion. You'll need to keep your grades up though."

"I figured as much." That was the stipulation for everything at school. Grades, grades, grades.

"And only work on the mural before or after school. No cutting class."

"I understand."

"Then it's settled?" Clyde asked, giving her knees a slap, signaling the deal had been struck.

Jotty held Clyde's eyes. Did they understand each other? They sure did.

Glossy Brown and Gold Shimmer

Chapter 33

During classes—yes, classes—she attended every one of them, her mind off and away, high up on the mountain, her mountain and the work involved to get the mural to look like the image she had in her head and under her feet. Ideas bubbled around her brain, a kettle on boil. Nothing terrible had happened since telling Clyde her decision. No drum rolls or clapping, but she knew, and that was all that counted.

Bells sounded, and she walked from one class to another, in a trance of sorts.

"Hey!" Tanya said, "what's up?"

Jotty looked at Tanya, confused. "Huh?"

"You're a zombie today."

"I guess I am." It was good to be a zombie. At the end of day, she realized she had attended every class, the boring and the interesting; each got equal attention from her. Tomorrow she started work on the mural.

Before she left school, she stopped by the cafeteria. "Tomm!"

He turned. "Jotty."

"See you tomorrow!"

"Tomorrow." He grinned.

The next morning, she arrived at school early, having begged Ma to let her drive her truck to school.

She hadn't beaten Tomm. He was hard at work brandishing a paintbrush with a dark-chocolate-brown hue. She couldn't wait to get to the scaffolding and see the exact color he was using. Hopefully it wasn't one of those with only numbers. Four-six-two-nine didn't have the same significance as suede or sienna.

"Hey!" he said.

Her throat felt choked with emotion, and she just grinned.

"OK, tell me about your mountain," he said, using a paint stir stick to point to the outline on the wall.

Where to start? Her words rushed forward. "Rattlesnake isn't really a mountain, even if it's called a mountain." She took a few steps closer to the wall, looking up to the painting. "You experience a feeling of knowing when you're there." She couldn't describe her feelings in words—only colors swirling around her head—the artist Matisse stating he dreamed of art as purity and peace. A perfect description for this situation.

"Tell me more."

"I almost feel like a god. It's just me, the hill, the rocks, sagebrush, the horses and jackrabbits. I can hear myself think."

"An important distinction," Tomm said. "The difference," he said slowly, "is the feeling of the mountain. You've been there, and I haven't. In your picture I felt I was there and in this one." He swept his arm to the image again much as a conductor would an orchestra. "I can't picture myself being there."

"I hadn't thought about that," Jotty said, never taking her eyes off the wall.

"An artist must make people feel part of the picture. How do I fix it?"

"Are you really asking? Or do you already know?"

"I guess a bit of both," he said.

"Take a hike," she said with a laugh.

"Pardon?" Tomm asked.

"Up the hill."

"So do I need to climb it?" he asked.

She looked at him. "Do you want to?"

"Only if you'll go with me," Tomm said.

"I will."

They were interrupted by Brenda exclaiming, "Oh good, you're taking my place." She waved away the paintbrush Tomm held out.

Word sure traveled fast.

"My boyfriend doesn't want me spending all my time working on the mural," Brenda said, backing away toward the hall.

"Bye!" She called over her shoulder as she was swallowed up by the students in the hallway.

"I guess it's just the two of us," Jotty said as they watched Brenda's retreat.

"I think we'll work well together," Tomm said. "To Rattlesnake mountain and our joint venture. When can we go?"

"Tomorrow after school."

"Perfect," he said.

She went to the mountain at least once a week. Did she want to share her sanctuary with someone else? She guessed Tomm was OK. After all, it was for the mountain they were going to the mountain. A bit of convoluted thinking that made sense.

"Oh. What color are you using?" she asked.

He shrugged and looked down at the can of paint. "Why is that important?"

"It just is. To me."

"Fair enough, it's sable."

She turned over the image of sable in her mind—a glossy brown and gold glimmer, shimmering color, not flat and stagnant.

Chapter 34

"What shall we watch tonight?" Ma asked when they had cleaned the kitchen after dinner. Leroy slumped on the couch, his feet on the coffee table, drinking his fourth, no, fifth beer. With each sip, he sagged down deeper into the sofa.

Jotty shrugged as she hung up the dish towel.

"Leroy? Football?"

Jotty hoped they didn't have to watch football.

"Christ!" he snapped. "That's been over for weeks!"

"That's right," Ma said, in her flat, monotone, nondescript voice—white noise to keep the peace.

Leroy stood and went to the television and turned it on. Reruns of Welcome Back Kotter.

Jotty liked the show. Why couldn't they have teachers like Mr. Kotter at Sagebrush High? Sure, she liked Mr. Harrison's and Mr. Hornbeck's classes, but they weren't funny. She guessed a television show wasn't exactly like real life. The women from Designing Women seemed remote and fanciful to her.

"They're all a bunch of screw-ups!" Leroy declared, motioning with his beer can toward the television.

Jotty glared at him. "I like this show."

"You would."

"What does that mean?" She felt the hair on the back of her neck bristle.

"The show's about a bunch of dumb-ass kids."

"Are you saying I'm a dumb ass?"

"If the shoe fits…"

It didn't.

"How close did you get to finishing high school, Leroy?" Jotty asked, knowing he never went past the tenth grade.

"What does that have to do with anything?"

"What grade were you in when you dropped out?" she asked again.

"I was a sophomore. Who cares!"

She cared.

"I've made it to my senior year," she said.

"Only because your mother is always bailing you out at school."

"Like Richard does for you?" Jotty asked.

"Shut up!"

"I don't have to shut up. I live here too," Jotty said, turning on him in her fighting stance, legs apart and fists clenched.

"Christ," he snapped. "I can't wait to throw you out when you're eighteen."

"Now, Leroy," Ma said with her smoothing-the-ruffled-feathers voice. "When she graduates."

"Don't 'now, Leroy' me," he said. "Your daughter won't amount to nothing."

"She will, won't you, Jotty?"

"I don't think I can wait that long!" He turned his back to them, picked up his beer, and selected a new channel. The conversation over. Jotty and Ma sat at the small kitchen table.

Ma and Jotty whispered quietly to each other.

"What if I graduate? What then?" She didn't wait for Ma's response. "What about graphic arts?" The admission slipped out, surprising both.

Ma clasped her hands together like she was praying. "Jotty!" Her face glowed.

"It'll never happen," Leroy said, brushing past them to reach the refrigerator and another can of beer. "You'll end up at Joe's with your mother."

Ma turned to her. "You make me so happy!"

She'd show the pig-faced Leroy a thing or two. She could be as stubborn and hardheaded as he was.

Black, Brown, and Roan

Chapter 35

The next day, they all—Jotty, Tomm, and Clyde—got into Clyde's car and headed for Rattlesnake. Clyde insisted on coming. What did she think they were going to do on the wind-swept mountain full of rocks, prickly bushes, sage, and dirt? Besides, it was almost December—cold days with colder, black nights. The wind was biting and freezing. Did she think they would make mad passionate love in the dirt? Hardly. The plant needles, cruel little stickers, sometimes bore themselves into the soles of her shoes. Even then, they hurt her feet. She couldn't imagine them on other parts of her body. No, sir, they didn't need a chaperone, but Clyde came anyway.

Clyde had traded her suit for a coat and jeans for their trip.

Jotty sat in the back seat. Even from there, she could smell Tomm's cologne mixed with paint and turpentine—a pleasant smell, she decided as she settled back, looking out the window. Clyde knew the way. She had driven Ma before.

A few wispy clouds floated effortlessly in the dim ice-blue horizon.

They bumped over the jagged two-track road leading to the mountain, parked, and got out. The difference between the heated interior and the winter chill made Jotty burrow her hands deeper in her pockets for warmth.

"I'll just watch," Clyde said, rubbing her arms before getting back in the car.

"You ready?" Jotty asked and Tomm nodded. They began their ascent.

The climb was easy at first, only a slight incline. Even though it was cold, Jotty felt prickles of perspiration bead on her forehead. They climbed without talking. Jotty fixed her sights on the big rock ahead, her favorite place to sit and smoke. No smoking today. The rock, her rock, was about a third of the way up. Usually she had to stop several times along the way to catch her breath. Tomm seemed to climb effortlessly, swinging his arms, never slowing or pausing. He wasn't breathing hard at all. She tried to keep up by taking big gulps. Her shortness of breath must have something to do with her smoking; maybe she should cut down.

Finally, they stopped at the boulder. Jotty collapsed against it, holding her stomach.

"You OK?" he asked. "Are we going to the top?"

She shook her head, unable to speak.

"I guess this is a good vantage point." Tomm turned slowly and surveyed the landscape and the valley below. "Is there a reason it's called Rattlesnake Mountain?" He frowned at her.

"There are probably snakes here."

"Yikes," Tomm said but grinned. "Snakes don't really bother me."

They did her, but she responded with, "I've never really seen any. Besides, it's too cold now. In the summer, I always look. I've been scared of them forever. I guess that's one of the reasons I come here."

He nodded as if understanding, but she didn't think he did. She needed to confront things that scared her. Was that the way with everyone?

They stood quietly watching the surrounding hills as a lone hawk circled lazily and effortlessly in the air.

Jotty stiffened and turned to Tomm. "Shhh, look behind you," she whispered.

There, descending the summit, were the wild horses. They made their way toward them, zigzagged back and forth—black, brown, and roan colors blending as they stopped to nibble on sagebrush and dried grass here and there. Sometimes Jotty brought them treats of carrots or apples. They didn't seem afraid of her.

"Isn't that something," he whispered back.

The horses continued their slow descent and stood away from them, the big stallion eyeing them as the mares grazed.

"Do they always get this close?" Tomm asked.

"Sometimes closer." She pointed to a petite roan mare. "She comes up and smells my sleeves and will take treats from my hands."

"Shame we didn't bring anything for them to eat," Tomm said.

As if she knew they were talking about her, the roan daintily stepped away from the herd and made her way to Jotty. She stopped a couple of yards away and moved her head up and down as if assessing Jotty's presence and food potential.

Jotty held out her arms and shrugged apologetically. "I didn't bring anything today. Sorry, girl."

Sensing there weren't any treats, the roan retreated reluctantly and made her way back up the hill before bending her head to eat.

Tomm was shaking his head. "That is truly amazing."

"So, what do you think of my mountain?" Jotty asked.

"It's really a thing of beauty, even if it's only dirt, rocks, and sagebrush."

It was more than just dirt, rocks, and vegetation. There was hidden life to be observed if a person sat quietly and watched.

Jotty looked up and shaded her eyes as she watched a long-legged jackrabbit hop on the path, his ears moving around—listening. She wasn't sure she would use beautiful to describe what she saw, but nothing better came to her.

"I'm glad we came today. I want to climb farther, but I think I get the feeling now. This is more than just sagebrush and rocks; there's life up here." He paused, and the jackrabbit darted into the sagebrush as if chased by an invisible predator. "The mural needs to reflect all these elements."

Slowly they made their way down the hill and drove back to the school to fix the mountain's peak and cover over the too-large buildings.

Corduroy-Tan and Sienna

Chapter 36

"I think we should start with…" Tomm said after several days of working together in compatible silence.

And Jotty finished with, "the mountain." They had fixed the summit of the mountain to reflect the real one with a flat top and corduroy-tan-and-sienna-colored path winding through the rocks and bushes. Bushes the hue of olive, gray, and terra cotta.

"That's what I was going to suggest," Tomm said.

"And work from the mountain to the…"

"Town. My thoughts too. Then the desert, buildings, and …" He laughed. "We're finishing each other's sentences!"

"People…I'm not good at people," she said.

Jotty had never known anyone she was so in touch with, not even Tanya. It was as if she and Tomm shared the same artistic brain.

They calculated that they would complete the mural by April or May. Jotty was in charge of the mountain, but she would help Tomm with the rest. But Jotty secretly hoped the work on the mural would never end; she had never felt better or this motivated.

Green, Gold, and Burgundy Plaid

Chapter 37

Jotty, Ma, and Leroy were to spend Thanksgiving at Joe's. Joe
hosted it at the diner for anyone unfortunate or fortunate enough not to
have family in the area, but she guessed that depended on your
perspective. It would be an odd assortment this year: Jotty, Ma, Leroy,
Tomm, Mr. Hornbeck, and Sam, the deputy. Jotty tried to imagine how
Mr. Hornbeck and Leroy would interact.

When they arrived at the diner, Mr. Hornbeck stood inside the
door at Joe's looking at the pictures on the walls—old mining pictures
from a bygone era. The diner was an old wooden building with
roughhewn boards for walls; faded linoleum, curling in the corners;
and tables and booths out of a '50s cafe.

"Jotty!" Mr. Hornbeck greeted her with a smile.

She greeted him and said, "Ma, this is Mr. Hornbeck." She
looked at Leroy. "And this is my stepfather, Leroy," her voice
dropping an octave when she said Leroy's name. Mr. Hornbeck was
dressed for the occasion in a brown tweed jacket, orange shirt, and
bow tie.

Ma shook his hand, whereas Leroy looked him up and down
before going into the kitchen, probably to see if Joe had some alcohol
he used for cooking. The contrast between Leroy's sagging jeans and
Mr. Hornbeck's jaunty attire wasn't lost on her.

"I've heard so much about you," Ma said. "I couldn't believe
you got my stubborn daughter to take another class."

"She really is quite a remarkable student." He tapped his
temple to make his point.

Ma's mouth hung open, having never heard Jotty was
"remarkable" from a teacher. Jotty chuckled inwardly. "Oh my, that's
good to know." She looked pointedly at Jotty.

"Yes, she's helping me with my research on sage grouse."

"She mentioned something about that," Ma said.

"Drawing new pictures for my brochure. They are quite
fascinating birds," Mr. Hornbeck continued.

152

"I'm sure they are," Ma said, edging toward the kitchen. "I promised Joe I would help. I'm so sorry. Please excuse me."

"Nothing to be sorry for," Mr. Hornbeck said.

"I like your bow tie today," Jotty said.

"Why, thank you. One of my favorites." He fingered the green, gold, and burgundy plaid.

Tomm came into the seating area from the kitchen, and Mr. Hornbeck headed toward fresh ears for tales of the grouse. Jotty reluctantly followed along, not because she wanted to hear more about the birds, but she wanted to talk to Tomm. The bells chimed and Sam, the sheriff's deputy, came in.

Sam nodded toward Jotty. "Hey!"

"Hey, yourself," she said. "Do you know Mr. Hornbeck or Tomm Claybanks?"

He probably didn't; both were upstanding citizens.

Jotty introduced them to each other before Mr. Hornbeck could begin telling Sam about the nesting habits of the sage grouse.

Leroy came out of the kitchen with a coffee cup that didn't look like it held hot coffee because he guzzled it, spilling some on his shirt. Probably Joe's cooking wine. Leroy saw Sam and sneered. Ma came out carrying a covered dish she put on the long table set up for the occasion.

"No one said the pigs would be here," Leroy complained. "I'm going over to the Half-Moon."

Ma smiled. "Oh course."

"You coming?" Leroy asked.

"Nope, I'm helping Joe," Ma responded.

Jotty watched the exchange. Ma rarely stood up to Leroy unless Jotty was involved. Leroy wouldn't do anything to hurt Ma with Sam watching.

"Suit yourself." He pushed through the front door, bells tinkling in response.

All was quiet before Joe said, "Dinner's served." He placed the turkey in the middle of the table. They all sat, but Joe frowned at the empty seat. "Are we missing someone?"

"Leroy went to have refreshments," Ma explained.

A nice way to say "get his drunk on."

"Hmm," Joe responded.

Joe and Ma cooked all the Thanksgiving favorites. Jotty ate as fast as she could without looking like she was cramming it in. She loved Thanksgiving, Easter, and Christmas. Joe always had a great spread. Tomm talked about the mural, and Mr. Hornbeck continued to tell the group about the habitat needed for his endangered birds. Between bites, Joe grunted, which Mr. Hornbeck assumed was interest.

"Who has room for pie?" Ma asked when there was a lull in the conversation and plates were pushed back.

No one answered aloud, but everyone nodded. The bells chimed, and Tanya came in.

"You're just in time for pie," Joe said.

"Good, I'm starving."

She took the vacant seat and Jotty asked, "What are you doing here? Didn't your mother make dinner?"

"Sort of," Tanya said, taking a roll and butter from the table.

"What does that mean?"

"Our oven is broken and my stepdad…" Tanya's words were hard to decipher with the roll in her mouth.

Joe brought out a plate for Tanya from the kitchen piled with turkey and all the side dishes and she dug in while everyone else ate pumpkin pie.

Leroy stumbled in waving a Bud Lite beer bottle. "Happy New Year!"

Indeed.

Cinderblock Gray

Chapter 38

"Hey!" Tomm said with a laugh when Jotty got to school and joined them at a cafeteria table where Tomm, Mr. Hornbeck, and Mr. Harrison were sitting. "About time you got here!"

"Sorry," she mumbled. "I walked to school."

Ma had taken the truck to work, and Jotty had somehow missed the bus.

Tomm grinned. "Come on, we're looking at old photos."

The usual suspects were huddled around a cafeteria table looking at old photos and the rough sketches Tomm and Jotty had drawn as a working guide.

Jotty sat down and studied the sketches. They were to have lots of detail for Rattlesnake and the town with historical buildings in the background.

Although the cafeteria and breakfast were in full swing, Jotty was only marginally aware there were others in the room.

Tanya sloshed over, her shoes making squishing sounds on the cafeteria floor, wet from the light dusting of snow during the night.

"Hi, you weren't on the bus this morning," she said.

Jotty leaned back, studying her friend. They hadn't spent much time together since Jotty started on the mural and went to classes. Dull as some of them were, a bargain was a bargain.

"Missed the bus. Leroy didn't wake me in time." The scumbag.

"You having breakfast?" Tanya asked.

Jotty hadn't given food much thought. She had gobbled her cereal before trekking to school.

"No, we're looking at ideas."

Tanya backed up. "Sorry to interrupt. I better eat while I can."

It took a moment or two for Tanya's comment to sink in. "What did you say?"

"They're laying off at the pit. My mom will be out of a job for a few months."

The pit regularly laid off workers in the winter when business was slow.

"Oh." Would Leroy get laid off too?

"You better eat," Jotty said, turning her attention back to the sketches and the low talk from the group.

Purple and Yellow

Chapter 39

No light came from the trailer when Jotty arrived home, but strangely the door was open. Had Ma forgotten to latch it? It must be freezing inside. She had to be home; her truck was parked in the drive. Jotty hesitated before going inside.

"Ma?" Jotty closed the door and turned on the hall light.

No answer. Then Jotty spied Ma huddled on the coach, her chin resting on her knees.

"Where's Leroy?" Ma had her sweater wrapped tightly around her, grasping the edges, her head bowed. "Ma?"

Ma looked up. Her limp hair partially hid a black eye. Jotty saw the purple-and-yellow bruise on her eye and cheekbone. She stepped toward Ma. "Where did that come from? Is that from him?" She balled her hand into a fist...if Leroy was here...She'd...smash his nose. See if he enjoyed being a punching bag.

"Now, Jotty, don't get in a dither about this. It's nothing. Leroy lost his job today and is in a state."

"I don't care what he's in. Why is he always picking on you?" She was a boiling pot of water, bubbles of fury roiling around and onto themselves.

Jotty ached to get her hands on his pudgy neck and throttle him. She stood up to him and didn't cower. She'd never submit to Leroy's brutality. She forced her arms to her side and unclenched her fists. "What was it this time?"

"He came to Joe's wanting money, but things are slow, and I didn't have hardly any tips to give him."

"You gave him your hard-earned money to spend on booze?"

Ma shrugged and gingerly touched her eye.

"Does it hurt much?" Jotty asked.

"No. He's just frustrated."

"Did Joe see him hit you?" Jotty went into the kitchen and put some ice into a baggie for Ma's eye.

"No, Joe was in the kitchen, but he called the sheriff," Ma said.

"A lot of good that will do. We've called the law before, and nothing ever happens!" Jotty said.

"They're looking for him."

Sure they were, she thought bitterly. Even in a town of a few hundred people, they never find him. The sheriff is lazy. True, there isn't much crime in Sagebrush, but how hard can it be to find Leroy and his battered truck? There are only three bars in town. Too bad Clyde wasn't the sheriff; she'd shape up the town—detention and Saturday school for everyone!

Good riddance to Leroy. She hoped he never came back!

"Has he been home yet?" Jotty asked.

Ma shook her head sadly. "I hope he gets unemployment. Otherwise…"

"I can always get a job," Jotty said.

"No, we'll manage. I have a little bit stashed here and there."

Jotty saw flashes of light from outside the trailer; the rotating light from the police cruiser turning around. "The sheriff's here, Ma."

"Oh?" She patted her hair. "They must be looking for Leroy."

Who else? Jotty heard heavy boots on the steps and opened the door for Sagebrush's finest.

"Hi there, Jotty. Your mom home?"

Jotty opened the door and nodded for him to come in. Ma stood and came forward.

"Hi, Betty. You know why I'm here?" He peered closely at her face. "Leroy do that?"

Ma hung her head.

"Yes, he did," Jotty said. "Have you found him yet?"

"Nope, hoping you folks knew where he was."

"He…he hasn't been home yet," Ma whispered.

"There's been some vandalism at the gravel pit, and the foreman said Leroy was real sore at losing his job and threatened the supervisors."

"Oh my," Ma said. Her mouth sagged open.

"Will you call us if he returns?" the sheriff asked.

"Of course," Ma said.

"Any idea where he'd go?" he asked.

158

"Probably in the desert," Jotty said. "Or the bars."

"There's hundreds of acres of desert around here," the sheriff said.

Like he might need to leave his office and drive around more, Jotty thought grimly.

"I'm sorry we can't be of more help," Ma said.

Jotty showed him out. She wanted to get Leroy. Put him back in prison where he belonged, so they could get on with their lives. If only he'd show his weasel face...

She closed the door and locked it behind the sheriff. And just to be sure Leroy didn't barge in later, she pushed the table against it. He'd have to break his way in and cause a ruckus. She helped Ma into her nightgown and tucked her into bed. Then she remembered something important and reached under the bed for Leroy's rifle.

When Jotty was little, she was warned against touching it, but she had secretly taken it up in the hills and practiced shooting cans and bottles left behind by the hikers and hunters. She cocked it and looked inside: loaded and ready. Leroy would want this back—his one prize possession. She tucked it under her own bed. If he broke in tonight, she'd be ready for him.

Even with the reassuring rifle under the bed, she slept very little. Each sound and creak of the wind against the trailer woke her, heart hammering. She listened and breathed slowly, telling herself she heard only the wind. She reached down to feel the cool steel barrel. It was a long, restless night.

Cinderblock Gray

Chapter 40

"Jotty," Tanya said the next morning at school. "I need to tell you something important."

She had been so distracted by the mural and now Leroy on the run, she hadn't paid much attention to Tanya. Tanya, gaunt and hollow-eyed, carried her breakfast to the cafeteria table.

Jotty was preparing to help Tomm, but her feet dragged; tiredness from her sleepless night weighed her down.

"What?"

"Leroy came to our trailer last night."

"He did?" Jotty didn't know he was friends with Tanya's parents.

"Yes, he borrowed a tent and a sleeping bag."

Jotty processed the information. From the sound of it, Leroy was going to hide out somewhere, probably in the desert.

"Did he say where he was going?"

"Nope." Tanya put down her tray and began to eat.

"Are you getting enough to eat at home?" Jotty asked.

"Yeah, but my mom still hasn't got my medicine."

"I thought she said she would?"

"That was before. Before the layoffs."

"They fired Leroy, and he busted up the place," Jotty said.

"I heard." Tanya began eating her cereal. "My mom's just laid off. She'll get her job back when they get busy, and then she said she would get my medicine."

"Can you wait that long?"

"I'll have to. What else can I do?"

Jotty?" Tomm called. "Are you working today?"

"Yup. Sorry. Had to catch up." She eased away from Tanya as Sal and Dee Dee sat down. "I'll talk to you later."

It was all she could do to concentrate on her work today.

Cinderblock Gray

Chapter 41

The information about Leroy hiding in the desert churned around inside Jotty until school was over. She wished she hadn't promised to attend classes; she wanted go to the sheriff's office.

"I can't work after school," she told Tomm. "I have something I need to do."

He looked disappointed but nodded. She was torn between catching Leroy and working on the picture. Finding Leroy won.

Having wheedled Ma out of the truck this morning, she drove to the sheriff's office, a cinderblock building in the middle of town, next to the public clinic where Tanya saw the nurse.
Jotty had been to the sheriff's office before and always went away frustrated and angry.

A lone black-and-white police cruiser parked in the drive. There were only two officers—the sheriff and his deputy.

Sam, the deputy, was on duty this afternoon. She had known him all her life. He was a nice man with crooked teeth and seemed genuinely happy to see her. He reminded Jotty of the bumbling Barney on The Andy Griffith Show reruns.

"Hi there, Jotty. What brings you in?"

"Leroy's been causing trouble again," she said.

"Yup, heard that. Sheriff went looking for him last night," Sam said. "I thought I'd check around and see if I can spot him."

Probably the most action Sagebrush's finest had had since a drunk ran his car into the Half-Moon Tavern.

"Try Power Company Road. My friend said he came to her trailer and borrowed a sleeping bag and tent. Then he headed into the desert," Jotty said.

"I know that trailer," Sam said.

Tanya's stepfather had run-ins with the law too.

"That's a good piece of information. I'll take a drive out that way and see if I can find him."

He opened a file from the desk and thumbed through some pages. "I've got his truck description right here." He pointed his finger at the information.

Will you call us with any news?" Jotty asked.

"I'll let you know what I find, but he's one slippery devil."

She bit back a retort about "the incompetent sheriff," responding with, "Thank you," as she closed the door behind her. She guessed she was finally learning to keep her mouth shut at inopportune moments.

Blackest of Black

Chapter 42

Strangely, the front door of the trailer was open again. Flashes of Ma on the couch, battered and bruised flashed through Jotty's head. If Leroy did something to Ma again, why she'd...why she'd punch him. In response, Jotty balled her fist.

But Ma was working the dinner shift, she remembered. Jotty had stayed longer than usual to work on the wild ponies images. The night was already the blackest of black, the cold jabbing and piercing.

She sat in their drive and looked at the silent, dark trailer, its door swinging back and forth in the wind. She winced each time it banged against the metal siding. She needed to go inside. Carefully and quietly she crept up the steps, the small hairs on the nape of her neck charged with electricity. In the threshold, she took a deep breath and called, "Ma?" Jotty flipped on the light and heard a pop and the sound of sizzling from the bulb. Her nostrils flared. She smelled sour pickles and...eggs? She breathed in through her mouth as she groped along the wall for another switch. The hall light came on, illuminating the wreckage of the living room.

The TV, lamps, and overturned chair were in a smashed pile. The cushions on the couch were sliced open, revealing yellow foam. Jotty stepped over a broken lamp and went to the kitchen. The refrigerator door hung open and all the contents had been dumped on the floor. The cupboard door hung askew and the shelves were stripped of bread, cereal, tuna, soup, beans, and peanut butter—only a few stale saltines left.

Had Leroy found the rifle she had stashed under her bed? She stepped around the mess and into her bedroom. The bastard had dumped her paints on the floor, but the rifle was still hidden under the mattress. She took the rifle, propped it up, and began cleanup.

She had the urge to laugh at the pickles lying forlornly in a puddle of egg yolk, but she put her fist to her lips instead. Even in the cold weather she could smell the spoilage and Leroy's rank body odor—not an appealing combination.

Jotty went into Ma's bedroom. The room was turned upside down. All the drawers pulled out, clothes dumped on the floor, the blankets gone from the bed. Had he discovered his gun missing, or was he looking for warm clothing? Ha! She bet he was surprised to find his rifle gone.

The telephone rang. She hesitated for only a second before reaching for it. If it was Leroy, she'd let him have it. "Hello?"

"Jotty," Ma said. "We had a big party of hunters come in, and I'm still at work. I should be another hour or so.

"Sure." She'd have time to clean up most of the mess. No use worrying Ma about this. They needed the extra money now that they didn't have the remnants of Leroy's paycheck.

She got out a garbage bag, wiped up the eggs, and threw away the pickles. Ma had bleach under the sink. She ran water in the sink, added the bleach, cleaned the floor, and wiped down the refrigerator. It smelled overwhelmingly of bleach, but better than eggs and pickles. All traces of Leroy's stench, whisked away.

Next, she started on the living room, righting the chair and sweeping up glass from the TV and lamps. She then stood in Ma's bedroom doorway and looked at the mess. She stepped over the pile of clothes on the floor and inserted the drawers back into the dresser. She carefully hung up the garments until the door rattled. She froze briefly before leaping over the clothes and reaching for the rifle she had left propped up against the wall.

"Jotty? What happened?" Ma called from the door.

"We had a visit from Leroy."

Jotty met her in the kitchen where Ma sniffed the air. "Bleach?"

"Yes, I used it to clean up the mess. He broke the eggs and smashed the pickle jar."

Ma looked first in the refrigerator and then in the cupboard. "He cleaned us out. I'll have to make a grocery run."

"We need to call the sheriff again."

"I don't think they'll come around for missing food," Ma said.

No, Jotty thought bitterly, but if this were the gravel pit, they'd be all over it.

Jotty followed Ma down the hall to her bedroom. "I started to put away the clothes."

Ma frowned and chewed her lip. "Did he take my socks?"

Jotty shrugged. An odd question. "I don't know. I don't see any socks."

Ma crawled over a pile of clothes and began pawing through the layers, tossing things out of the way. She held up a sock ball. "Oh good."

Jotty frowned. Socks? What was so special about socks? Most of Ma's socks had holes and were worn thin, hers too.

"Help me move this stuff so I can find my other socks."

Jotty knelt and began pawing through the shirts, underwear, and pajamas on the floor. "I found one." She moved her hands around grabbing anything that felt lumpy and round. "Here's another."

"Good. Keep looking," Ma said.

"Ma? Why are you so worried about socks?"

Jotty pushed herself up and sat on the bed. Ma tossed another ball next to her.

"It's what's in the socks that's important," Ma said, her voice muffled.

Jotty picked up blue socks, turned them over in her hands, and unpeeled them. She felt something crinkle in the toe—paper? She put her hand in and pulled out a ten-dollar bill. Money.

"Do all of them have money?"

"Most," Ma said.

Jotty sat on the bed and unrolled a pair of brown socks. A twenty-dollar bill. All the socks were threadbare with holes, but each one held money. Leroy hadn't thought to look at Ma's socks. Ingenious.

Jotty inhaled sharply. "Did Leroy know about this?"

"I don't think so. Otherwise, he'd have taken them."

Together they found all the money, almost $500. How had Ma managed to squirrel away this much money?

As if reading her mind, Ma said, "I've been putting money away from my tips every week. I never told Leroy. I was hoping to give it to you when you graduated."

165

"Ma…" Jotty's voice was heavy with emotion.

"I'm sorry, but we'll probably have to use some of it now to buy food and pay bills."

Jotty put her arms around Ma's shoulders. "Thank you."

Ma amazed her sometimes. Jotty wished she could do more to help her.

Leaving Ma's bedroom for her own, Jotty returned with Leroy's rifle. She showed it at Ma. "If he comes near you, I'll use this."

"Oh no." Ma put her hand up in surrender. "He'll be back for sure."

"I know how to use it." Jotty thrust the cold steel shaft toward Ma for emphasis.

Ma moved away from the rifle and shielded her face. "How did you learn to shoot?" Ma asked.

"I practiced when you were at work."

Ma rolled her eyes. "You amaze me sometimes."

She amazed herself as well. "I'm keeping it under by my bed." Jotty picked up the rifle. "And if he dares try anything," she put her finger on the trigger and pulled, making the chamber click softly, "he's history.

Now they waited. Waited for Leroy's next move. In some ways, waiting was worse, wondering. Expecting. Two sleepless nights had passed.

Jotty sat up in bed, her eyes straining in the dark to see something. Anything. She didn't know exactly what woke her. The sound of a car backfiring? A lonely coyote howling? The night was so deathly quiet; she could hear the rapid hammering of her heart in her ears.

She knew this was coming. She felt it inside and out. Leroy wasn't through with them. There would be no peace until he was apprehended.

Slowly the inky darkness became transparent and Jotty saw furniture shapes. She wasn't afraid of the dark. In some ways, she saw more clearly at night. She could focus with nothing to distract her—no people, no sounds, nothing.

Outside, the wind rattled the sides of the trailer, shaking it with giant invisible hands.

There, she heard it again. The tinkle of breaking glass.

Jotty jumped from bed, grabbed the loaded deer rifle, and ran into the living room. The curtains blew straight up. The glass was gone from the front window, and cold air pushed out the warmth and surrounded her with bone-chilling frigidness. Jotty pushed the gun barrel out the window and took aim at two glowing lights by the side of the trailer. Taillights.

She fired. The gun slammed into her shoulder. She didn't care and took aim again.

"Jotty?" Ma called, her voice higher and faster than usual.

She pulled the trigger twice, hitting the vehicle with the second bullet. The lights moved toward the road. She aimed for the tires and fired again and again, but the red lights kept going, getting smaller and smaller until they disappeared. Click. Click. She was out of bullets. Damn, she missed him. She lowered the rifle and moved her bruised shoulder up and down.

"Jotty! What's going on? Are you all right?" Ma called.

"I'm fine. We have a broken window, though."

The lights flashed on and Ma stood in the hall clutching a blanket around her shoulders with a shocked, uncomprehending look on her face.

"Who were you shooting at?" Ma said, her bewildered eyes pushing her forehead into a mass of wrinkles.

Need she ask? It had to be Leroy.

"Dumb question, I know," Ma said.

"We should call the sheriff," Jotty said.

Ma waved her hands before taking a step back. "He'll do something worse next time."

What could be worse than a cold winter night and no window? Or stealing their food?

Tanya had told her there were more broken windows at the gravel pit. And someone had turned on a water valve and tried to flood the pit. The law was closing in on Leroy; only trouble was he kept moving.

We need everything we can get on him." Jotty stepped around the glass with her stocking feet.

"I'm just worried…" Ma said.

The rock was sitting in the middle of the floor. An innocent hunk of gray. The source of the broken window. Jotty grabbed it with one hand, but needed both to place it on the table. The souvenir had some heft to it. She wanted to laugh, but she suppressed the desire. It was an overwhelming urge, bordering on hysterics, until tears welled up in her eyes.

"Why don't you go back to bed?" Ma said, squinting at the clock. "My goodness, three a.m. and you have school tomorrow."

Couldn't Ma forget about school for just once?

"I can't." Jotty rubbed the goose bumps on her arms. "I'm freezing. We need to put something over that window." She doubted she could calm her mind enough to sleep.

Jotty got three large black trash bags and some duct tape from the kitchen.

"Hold the curtains for me." Jotty covered the broken window with the bags and tape.

"That was a good idea. Feels warmer already," Ma said cheerfully.

It wasn't warmer, not really. Jotty looked around. "I'm going to clean the glass."

"Why don't I make some hot chocolate?" Ma asked.

Jotty swept the glass into a pile and put it in the trash before pulling the vacuum from the closet. "I couldn't go back to sleep after this."

"Me neither," Ma said.

Jotty vacuumed up the glass, the machine protesting the hard objects by crunching and sputtering. She felt better with something to do. Her head cleared, and her thoughts were in focus as she picked up all the papers that had blown off the coffee table until she came to a notice from a collection agency with Past Due stamped across the top in red. They were behind in their trailer payments.

A different kind of chill came over her, this one from the inside, icicles jabbing at her. She guessed she had half expected this too. Jotty sank down onto the couch, letting all the papers drop except for the bill. She crumpled the edge in her fist. How would they make it on their own?

"What's the matter?" Ma said, handing Jotty a cup of cocoa.

"This." Jotty shook the letter at Ma. "How are we going to pay?"

Ma's face puckered, and her eyes brimmed with tears. "I don't know, Jotty. Leroy was supposed to make the payments."

"Have you called this company yet?"

"I don't know what to say."

"If you don't say something, Ma, they'll kick us out of the trailer," Jotty said.

"I know, I know. I can only worry about one thing at a time. We've got the window, the lamps..."

"Forget about those things. We don't need a TV or lamps."

"What do I say?"

"Call them tomorrow, explain Leroy is out of work, and set up a payment plan. You can send them part of the money from your socks." Jotty amazed herself sometimes with what came out of her mouth. How had she gotten so smart?

"Do you think that will work?"

"Worth a try. Or I could get a job," Jotty said. Their eyes met. Similar brown-flecked eyes, transmitting silent unspoken thoughts back and forth.

"No," Ma said. "I'll call. How did you get so smart?"

"I learned from you, Ma."

"Not me."

"You're wrong."

They sipped their hot chocolate. Jotty looked out the small door window at the sky growing brighter as the minutes ticked by. An icy-blue arctic mist in the weak winter sun. She felt fidgety, like she needed to get out of the trailer; the sides were closing in on her. She needed to feel the arctic-mist morning around her and breathe in the fresh air.

"I'm going for a ride," Jotty said. It was too early for school and besides, she wanted to take a ride to Rattlesnake and watch the town come awake.

Ma looked outside. "It's freezing out there."

"I'll wear two sweatshirts. I'll be fine."

"What if…"

"Leroy will never climb that far and besides, it's too close. No, I'll bet Leroy is out in the desert far away from town."

"You're probably right."

"I'll take the rifle with me unless you want me to leave it with you?"

Ma leaned away. "I won't use that thing."

Steady Yellow Eyes

Chapter 43

Jotty tucked the rifle under the truck seat and drove through the town. Only an occasional bark from a dog and the howl from a far-off coyote broke the silence. Jotty drove forward, pulled along by an invisible beckoning force. She stopped and looked up, her eyes straining toward Rattlesnake Mountain. She was always attracted to the massive hill, her refuge and inspiration, and she could think about her next move.

The road to the mountain got more rutted and narrow as she drove closer, the truck lurching from side to side, moaning and creaking in protest. She squinted into the headlights to see the way in the gray-blue dawn. The sagebrush-bordered road twinkled with frost.

The road ended as the terrain got wilder, so Jotty stopped, fetched the rifle, and started walking. The wind froze her cheeks; her senses became sharp and clear and one with the wind in her ears. Jotty pushed forward, lungs bursting from the altitude, cold, and exertion. She urged her legs forward, pushing down on her thighs to continue. In a way, she welcomed the dull throb. She was alive, and everything felt possible when she was here. She stumbled over the uneven hard clay and half-buried rocks, but she was determined to watch the sun come up from the boulder just ahead.

Like a cover being lifted, the sky lightened. Tufts of sagebrush and wind-gnarled pine trees came into focus. She smelled the tanginess of the evergreens through the clean air.

The lightened sky allowed her to see the rocks and sticks on the path. If this were a painting, dove would be the perfect backdrop color.

Jotty collapsed against the large boulder and lit a cigarette. She always marveled at her fortitude when she looked back down the hill to where the truck was parked. The summit loomed over her, and she could probably go farther if she wanted. As she smoked, the sky evolved from dove gray and then a soft aquamarine color, Atlantic blue. The sun rose over the side of the mountain.

A flicker of movement from the corner of her eye stopped her hand midair. A mountain lion stood looking at her with steady yellow eyes as if memorizing her features. They were about three truck lengths apart. The rifle was propped against the boulder, but surprisingly she didn't feel panicked, and a surreal calmness washed over her. They looked at each other for a long time before he flicked his tail and disappeared.

She should have been scared of the big cat; they were known to take down deer and even cattle, but it was as if Jotty and the mountain lion had an understanding. For some intuitive reason, she knew the cat wouldn't harm her; they were bound by the shared mountain habitat—she had her place, and he had his.

Jotty leaned back against the boulder and finished her cigarette. A mountain lion definitely belonged in the mural.

Nothing that went on below in Sagebrush mattered up here. The collection letter and the rock through the window seemed ages ago or a bad dream. She tried to concentrate on what to do about those things, but the questions and answers seemed to blow away on the cold morning air.

To her left, she saw a glint, a flash of light. It looked as if someone had started a fire in the desert. She couldn't be sure. She was too far away, but she had seen something out of the ordinary. Leroy's camp? She made a mental note to tell the sheriff about what she'd seen.

She pushed away from boulder and started down the hill, when a truck came into view and parked next to Ma's truck. She stopped and waited.

"Howdy," Tomm called and then waved. His voice echoed off the hard-packed earth as he climbed toward her.

"Fancy meeting you here," she said.

He raised his brows.

"A mountain lion was just over there." She pointed to where the cat had been standing. Her stomach tightened, reliving the encounter. The lion had been right there!

"Weren't you scared? I would be," Tomm said, leaning forward, his eyes wide and unblinking.

172

"Not really. I felt I was watching someone else. I sensed he meant me no harm."

His eyes rested on the rifle. "Would you have used that?"

"If I had to."

She didn't want to shoot the magnificent animal.

"Wow. You're afraid of snakes but not mountain lions?" Tomm asked.

"I just had a knowing. We need a mountain lion in our picture."

He stretched his hands up before looking around. "You're the boss." He stopped and stared into the distance. "Do you see that?"

"What?" she asked.

"Over there. Does that look like a fire to you? Or is it the sun?"

Jotty shaded her eyes. "I saw something there too. My stepfather is hiding in the desert."

"What's he hiding from?"

"The law. Life. His responsibility."

Tomm shaded his eyes and looked harder. "Sure could be a fire. I have binoculars in my truck. Should I get them?"

"If it's not too much trouble."

"No trouble." Tomm jogged down the hill, retrieved the binoculars, and ran back to her side." He was hardly winded from his effort.

He handed her the glasses, and she turned toward the glint. The magnification helped, but she couldn't see a person or a truck, only the glowing. "It's a fire all right." But was it Leroy's fire? Lots of people made fires in the desert, but it would be worth checking out. The sheriff, that was. She didn't relish coming up on Leroy in the middle of nowhere.

She handed the glasses to Tomm. "What do you think?"

"Yup, a fire. What are you going to do?"

"Let the sheriff know."

They stood by the boulder and watched the town awaken. An invisible hand and brush added buttercup yellow to the sky and little by little, everything glowed and brightened. Pink rose spilled over the yellow, a river above them. The sun boldly pushed past the mountain, proclaiming, "I'm here! Let the day begin."

173

"What are you doing here this morning?" she asked.

"I could ask you the same thing," he said. "Sorting things out."

It was nice to share Rattlesnake with someone who enjoyed it as much as she did. Neither Tanya nor Ma wanted to climb the hill. She suddenly wished Tomm was younger. She could easily be attracted to him if he was.

✦ "This is a good place to sort things out," she said.

"I have two children, and I miss them," Tomm said in a quiet voice. She turned to see him swallow before looking away.

"Don't you ever see them?"

Tomm shook his head as the wind ruffled his hair, making the locks rise and fall. "I wish I could say yes. I call, but my ex-wife won't let me speak to them."

Jotty picked her words carefully. "I haven't heard from my dad in about twelve years. He could be dead for all I know. You should try to see your kids."

Awkwardly Tomm put his arm around her shoulders, squeezed gently, and then kissed her cheek clumsily. "Thanks."

Her cheek tingled, but it was a kiss between friends, not lovers. She had never been in love, but she imagined it would be something special.

"I'm glad I came this morning," Tomm said after a long silence. "I needed someone to tell me that."

She continued to watch the sun rise higher.

"What about you?" he asked.

"I have to work things out myself." And as an aside, "If my problems can be worked out at all." But seeing the fire might be one step closer to catching Leroy.

"I'm glad I made the effort to get up early," Tomm said, rubbing his hands together. "Even though I'm freezing!"

"I wish I could snap my fingers and be here. I hate walking up," Jotty said.

"I think that's the best part," he said.

Was that what she liked about the mountain, the difficult part?

"Everything worthwhile takes effort. Being a parent. A marriage. Going to school, I suspect. I think that's why the mountain challenges you." Tomm leaned over to pick up a small speckled rock and tossed it out of view.

Tomm stamped his feet. "I better get going. I need my morning coffee. Do you want anything?" he asked.

"I'll be down soon," she said. She wanted to go higher. Wasn't that always her goal?

Tomm walked silently down the ruts, got into his truck, and drove off, honking once he rounded the corner.

She looked toward the top, took a deep breath, and started up the narrow path through the brush. A roaring sound filled her brain. Her legs protested, but she climbed higher.

The air got colder as she got closer to the summit, and the wind pushed her back. She gritted her teeth and plunged ahead. Did she truly like the extra effort to push herself farther? The answer wasn't a simple yes or no.

Finally, she stopped and surveyed the scene below, locating the boulder where she had started. The cars appeared much smaller now, and even the yellow school bus looked like a Tonka toy.

She held her hair back from the wind's grasp. She had come a long way this morning, but when she looked up, there was still a long way to go.

School was about to start, she imagined, seeing the bus inch along in the distance. She looked up once more before trekking back down. The buzzing in her head vanished, and her thoughts cleared. She would find a way to help Ma and catch Leroy by reporting the possible campfire.

Chapter 44

Jotty stopped at the sheriff's office before going to school. The sign on the door said he was out, and there was a number to call if anyone needed him. She jotted down the number and would call from school.

When she arrived, Jotty stopped in the doorway of the principal's office. The office no longer seemed so distant and unfriendly. The secretary wasn't at her desk, so Jotty look a deep breath and knocked on Clyde's door. Clyde looked up from the paper she was reading and motioned for Jotty to come in.

"You've been hiking?" Clyde stepped from behind her desk and brushed a twig from Jotty's sleeve.

Jotty collapsed into the nearest chair, her legs weak from her extra climb and lack of sleep.

Clyde sat back down behind her desk.

"I went to Rattlesnake Mountain this morning." Jotty moved her head slightly. "I wanted to think."

"It seems like a good place to do that. What did you think about?" Clyde folded her arms on top of her desk, a listening gesture, her nautical-blue eyes intense and probing.

"I need to drop out of school and get a job to help Ma pay the bills."

Clyde shook her head. "You've been saying you wanted to drop out since I met you."

"Things are different now. Leroy lost his job, and Ma's getting overdue bills."

"What about the mural? Your mural?"

"I like working with Tomm, but how will Ma and I make it if I don't work too?"

"There's always a way."

For people like Clyde who had resources and options, maybe. A teen like Jotty didn't have many of those.

"Let's think about this rationally," Clyde said, splaying out her fingers on the desk.

And what was that?

"How?" Jotty asked.

"Let's look at the big picture."

"Like the mural?"

"No, the big picture of your life. High school is a small part of you. You'll have many years to work, but only a short time to graduate and get your diploma."

Jotty nodded.

"What if there was a way for you to work, stay in school, and help your mother?"

"That would be great. Where would I work?"

"On the mural."

"I'm already doing that."

"True and there is a small stipend attached for that. What if I told you we have a workforce grant to help students get jobs and go to college?"

Jotty leaned forward, interested, but she would reserve judgement until after she heard the details.

"What if some of that money went to you?"

"And I wouldn't have to do anything differently?" Jotty asked, her mind racing over possibilities.

"No change whatsoever."

"That would help. What kind of money are you talking about?"

"Around two thousand," Clyde said.

Jotty calculated that would help with the trailer somewhat.

"Is that enough?" Jotty asked.

"It depends on how much your mother owes. Let's look at it another way. Say you do drop out and get a job at the diner. How much would you make an hour?"

"Around three dollars an hour. Double that for tips."

"If you worked thirty hours a week, that would be around a hundred and eighty dollars weekly."

She'd make close to seven hundred a month. It would take her three months to make the two thousand from the grant. She'd be so close to graduation. Would one or two months really matter?

"And I have another idea," Clyde said. "Do you want to hear it?"

Did she?

"Do I?"

"I hope so."

Jotty studied her shoes and picked at the dried sagebrush snagged in her socks as she waited for Clyde to speak. She flicked the twigs into the wastebasket next to Clyde's desk.

"I'd like to do several open houses and invite the public in to see the mural," Clyde said. "Maybe charge a small admission fee. Possibly get some television and newspaper coverage."

"How is that helpful?"

"You and Tomm would need to work those," Clyde said.

"Would we get paid?"

"Something like that."

She frowned. "I'm not asking for charity." Her thoughts went back to car washes and spaghetti dinners to help some hapless person or another. Ma would never go for that.

"Not charity. You'll earn it, believe me. What do you think?" Clyde asked.

She remembered something important she need to do. A flickering flame, a light in the desert.

"I think I need to call the sheriff."

Clyde sat back, surprised. "That's a strange response."

"I think I know where Leroy's been hiding."

"Would you like me to call while you go to class?" Clyde asked.

"Yes, would you? The sheriff would probably respond quicker to your call than mine."

"Sure." Clyde picked up her phone. "And the workforce grant?"

"Yes." She got up, handed Clyde the paper with the phone number. Before reaching the door, she heard Clyde dial the number and ask the sheriff to come to the high school.

Jotty stopped at the entrance to the cafeteria and studied the half-finished mountain in the mural, outlined in coffee brown, and the slope would be buff and sandcastle. When finished, the rocks in bittersweet chocolate and prairie would tower over the cafeteria. The memory of the morning trek so fresh, she could still feel the frost-hardened dirt underneath her feet with her problems swirling away on the high mountain winds.

Part of what she enjoyed about the mountain solitude was being able to turn over each thought like the rocks along the road. She never knew what she'd find underneath—a scorpion in hiding or an arrowhead or just dirt.

The insulation of the mountain continued when the bell sounded for the first class. She followed her fellow classmates much as the wind's path moved around and through obstacles in the way.

"Earth to Jotty," Tanya said, waving her arms.

Jotty smiled and continued on her way to English.

Mrs. Markley greeted her, "Good morning."

Normally she grumbled or grunted a greeting, but she said, "Good morning to you."

It felt good to be a mountain wind as she slid into her seat.

When Jotty was called to the office from Mr. Hornbeck's class, he frowned.

She shook her head slightly, hoping to convey the message she wasn't in trouble. She could continue drawing the grouse. This was another matter entirely. She imagined the sheriff had arrived.

The secretary showed Jotty into the conference room where the sheriff and Clyde were waiting.

"I hear you know where Leroy's camped," the sheriff said, writing on his notepad.

Jotty took the nearest seat. "I was on Rattlesnake this morning and I saw fire to the east."

"Can you show me?"

179

"Sure, if you want to do some hiking." The sheriff's belly hung below his belt. She bet he didn't do much hiking or even walking, for that matter.

"Dr. Benninger? Mind if I take Jotty for a ride?" he asked.

Clyde waved her arms. "Of course. I know this situation has been on her mind."

Their eyes locked for only a second, but they had an understanding. Or was it a new respect?

The sheriff followed Jotty from the conference room. They passed the cafeteria and the mural. "That sure is something," the sheriff said with a soft whistle between his teeth. "My wife's been pestering me to come by. Is it open to the public?"

"The principal wants to have an open house," Jotty said.

"My wife will like that."

Maybe Clyde's idea wasn't so far-fetched.

They got into the patrol car, left school, and headed toward Rattlesnake. The mountain took on a different hue, depending on the time of day. The midmorning colors were taupe, silver sage, and sienna, accented by jack pine. Jotty loved the colors of nature.

They stopped when the road narrowed and got out.

"Where was the fire?" he asked.

"I was up by that boulder." She pointed to her favorite resting spot about halfway up the hill.

"You climbed up there?" he asked, his voice incredulous.

"Sure."

He looked doubtful. "OK, lead the way."

"We need binoculars."

He took them out of the trunk and followed her up the hill.

The sheriff was in worse physical shape than she was. He wheezed as he climbed and stopped to wipe the sweat from his brow. They stopped at her favorite boulder, and she pointed to where she had seen the fire.

Jotty shaded her eyes. The glint was still there. She pointed, and the sheriff used binoculars for a better look.

"Yup, I think you may be right. Definitely a fire. If it is Leroy, there's a reward for his capture, you know."

"A reward?"

"The pit put up five thousand dollars for his capture. He's already cost them fifteen thousand in water and window damage."

"So, if you go and arrest him, I would get five thousand dollars?" she asked. Her breathing stopped in her throat.

"Yup." He hoisted up his uniform and resettled his belt, which was weighed down with his gun and cuffs.

Her heart beat faster. The collection agency would go away. They could eat and even replace the television and buy a new couch. She exhaled. She couldn't imagine $5,000.

"Do you want me to go with you?" she asked, imaging Leroy's face when she stepped out of the sheriff's vehicle.

He cocked his head at her. "Nope, we don't take citizens along when we have arrest warrants. I'll take you back to school first."

She would have liked to see Leroy's reaction when he was arrested. They hiked down the mountain and got into the patrol car.

"Will you let us know when you get him? Ma will be so relieved," Jotty said, when he let her out in front of the school.

"He's a mean, ornery bugger for sure. How your sweet Ma got tangled up with him is beyond me," the sheriff said with a shake of his head before driving away.

And beyond her too.

A Coffee-Brown, Buff, and Sandcastle

Chapter 45

Jotty returned to school in time for lunch and joined Tanya and Sal.

"What happened?" Tanya asked, as they went through the line to get their food. "I saw the sheriff take you away. Did you get arrested?"

Jotty laughed at the absurdity of that comment. "Not arrested. I went with the sheriff to Rattlesnake," Jotty responded.

"Why?"

"I think I may have found Leroy."

"Is he alive or dead?" Tanya asked.

Jotty wished him dead, but no, alive and wreaking havoc on them. "He's alive, I'm afraid."

As they found a place to sit, Jotty half listened to Tanya and Sal, her ears tuning in to the comments about the mural; students liked it. Only Carmen Hernandez said it gave her a headache. People like Carmen gave Jotty a headache.

Grilled cheese sandwiches and watery tomato soup for lunch today, but it would fill Jotty's hollow stomach. They slid into a cafeteria bench. Sal joined them. Buck too. Tanya smiled shyly at him. Jotty tossed her head in disgust. Were things good between Tanya and Buck again?

"Did they capture him?" Sal asked. Sal's father also worked at the gravel pit. Everyone knew Leroy was responsible for vandalizing it.

"I don't know. I haven't heard back from the sheriff," Jotty said before taking a sip of her soup. She glanced at the clock, only about twenty minutes had passed since he dropped her back at school.

Tanya and Sal leaned forward. "Will they lock him up?"

"I hope," Jotty said.

"Can't you call the sheriff?" Tanya asked. "And find out?"

"I'll let you know as soon as I know," Jotty said, looking back at the mural, envisioning a mountain lion crouched by the path, waiting for its next meal. The lion sat patiently, whereas she felt jumpy and off-balance waiting for news of Leroy's capture.

"The sheriff never could find my lost dog," Sal said.

A lost dog and a hiding man were two completely different things. Would they be able to find his camp and arrest him on the spot?

Tanya smiled at her. "It's nice to have you at lunch today," Tanya said, absently brushing away crumbs, taking small bites of her sandwich.

"What did I miss in Mr. Harrison's class this morning?" Jotty asked, taking the last swallow of her soup.

"He told us the story of the pony express. It was once part of Fort Churchill. Oh—" Tanya stopped. "We're going on a field trip in a couple of weeks."

"Where? Bodie again?" Jotty asked, remembering pictures Mr. Harrison had shared of the ghost town.

"No, Fort Churchill."

Mr. Harrison had shown them pictures of the old army fort when they were in the mural planning stages. "Yes," Jotty said slowly. "Mr. Harrison said something about that."

"Your artist guy is going too," Tanya said, giving her a sideways glance.

"He's not my guy."

"Tell us about him," Sal said, leaning her elbows on the table. "Who?"

"The artist."

Jotty looked at her. "Like what?"

"Is he single?"

"Divorced," Jotty said.

"Hmm."

"Two kids. Nice guy. He's Ma's age," Jotty said.

Sal's face changed from being interested to somber. "Too old for me."

Jotty wanted Tomm to reunite with his kids, not get mixed up with Sal in Sagebrush.

The bell sounded, signaling lunch was over. Clyde came in and circulated, reminding students to put away their trash and return their trays. She stopped by Jotty's table.

"Any word from the sheriff?" Jotty asked.

"Nothing."

Was the sheriff incapable of finding him? Or had Leroy been tipped off they were coming after him? Probably the sheriff drove into the desert with sirens blaring and lights flashing. Everyone in the next county could see the him coming.

She wished she could prod the law, make him move quicker. Better yet, she wanted to find Leroy and stop him herself. If only...

Later that same day, the sheriff stopped by their trailer while Jotty and Ma were eating dinner.

"Sorry to interrupt your dinner," he said, refusing Ma's invitation to join them or for a cup of coffee.

"Did you get Leroy?" Jotty asked, excitement crowding in, thinking of the reward money and Leroy's sorry ass looking out of a jail cell.

"When I got there, his fire pit was still smoking, and tire tracks led far out into the desert. He might be gone for good."

"Did you follow him?" Jotty asked.

"Nope. Got another call," the sheriff said. "A pressing matter."

Jotty highly doubted both his statements. She had Leroy's rifle; he'd want it back.

"Let me know if you hear from him," the sheriff said.

They wouldn't hear from him; he'd throw another rock through the window or do something worse.

"We will," Jotty said.

"Maybe he'll leave you folks in peace."

"Let's hope," Ma said without much enthusiasm.

They both knew he'd be back.

"There's the reward money and all..." the sheriff said.

"Yes, we could have used that," Ma said with a tight smile.

He nodded to them.

"Thank you," Ma said, showing him out and locking the door behind him.

"He'll be back," Jotty said.

"I know," Ma said as she sat back at the table. "Do you still have his rifle?"

"Yup."

"Then he'll come back for sure."

She knew that.

He could be anywhere, yet nowhere, hiding in plain sight.

She'd borrow Tomm's binoculars and climb higher on the mountain for another look around. Jotty wanted to catch him so bad she could envision them counting the reward money. Green money for Ma. Green money to live.

Jotty borrowed Tomm's binoculars and began her climb, hoping she could spot Leroy's whereabouts.

The still winter air, calm and cold, hurt her lungs, but still she pushed upward. She stopped at her favorite rock and scanned the surrounding scenery. The barren winter landscape, resembling the gray pictures of the moon, gave nothing away. Everything was hiding from the frost and the cold temperatures.

What was she looking for? A fire, a rusty red truck, Leroy's face plastered on a tree? A bolt of lightning marking his hiding spot? She saw none of those things. She climbed higher and stopped for another look.

Toy-size cars on the main street, wisps of smoke from chimneys, but nothing out of the ordinary. She wanted to catch him so bad, but where was he?

She gave the landscape one last view before climbing down with nothing to show for her effort except chapped lips and thighs aching in protest.

Belgian Chocolate

Chapter 46

Leroy wasn't forgotten, but life and school continued to roll along; a tumbleweed in the wind. The momentum of working on the mural swept Jotty away, but there was always that undying knowing. Knowing Leroy was out there, waiting for them to let their guard down. Even as she worked with Tomm, she felt Leroy's dark, brooding presence. What had they ever done to Leroy that was so terrible? And where had a month gone? Was it hidden behind a boulder, or had it rushed by in plain sight?

The time sped by, marking progress by the evolving mural. Each day something new greeted the returning students: horses on the hill, a coiled snake behind the sagebrush, and a mountain lion partially hidden behind a boulder. Ma's January calendar had over half the days crossed off. They were heading into February.

Now home, after an especially long day of school and painting, Jotty settled back on the couch and closed her eyes, even in her tiredness, she was alert. Is this how Ma felt after her shifts at the diner? Tired but on high alert for Leroy's unpredictable moods? How had Ma handled the fatigue and uncertainty? Jotty vowed then and there she wasn't going to add to Ma's dilemma.

"A penny for your thoughts," Ma said as she joined Jotty on the couch, holding a magazine someone had left behind at Joe's. They didn't really miss the smashed television set.

And she, of course, was sketching and doodling, drawing sage grouse for Mr. Hornbeck. She used Belgian chocolate to outline the birds and wondered what the difference was between plain old chocolate and Belgian chocolate besides a hefty price tag. She put down Belgian and picked up medium sable.

Mr. Hornbeck wanted pictures of the birds in their natural habitat doing what sage grouse did. Apparently, they ate and attracted a mate by making noises with their air sacs and fanning their tails. Then the female raised the chicks with no help from the males. Typical. The grouse lived an endless cycle of birth, growth, decline, repeated over and over in a six-year span if they were lucky to avoid coyotes and other predators.

Ma leaned over and looked at her drawings, a surprised expression on her face. "What are you drawing?"

"Sage grouse for Mr. Hornbeck."

"Interesting," Ma said, opening her magazine.

"Sort of," Jotty said, smoothing down the page of her notebook. Her view of the mountain had changed somewhat. It wasn't just a place for snakes, mountain lions, and wild horses. There were birds and plants of distinction, making it a unique place, an ecosystem all of its own. She had learned that from Mr. Hornbeck.

Ma patted her leg before turning the wrinkled pages of the magazine.

"What was that for?"

"This is nice, just the two of us," Ma said. "You're almost all grown up and won't need me soon."

She'd always need Ma.

"I'll always be there for you, Ma. You know that."

"I know. We'll find a way; we always do."

How had Ma managed to stay with Leroy all these years? Jotty was surprised sometimes at Ma's backbone and fortitude.

"Yes, we will," Jotty said.

"I've never seen you more excited about school," Ma said.

Excited, maybe. Focused and with a purpose, yes. Wanting to get on with her life, of course, but not wanting to leave the mural behind, either. What would future students think of their masterpiece? Would the mural have the same effect on them?

"It's been kind of fun," Jotty said, although fun wasn't exactly what she felt.

"I've never heard you say school was fun before," Ma said.

"No, I guess not."

The stuff she was learning gave her a different view of Sagebrush and Rattlesnake. Mr. Hornbeck had come to Sagebrush specially to study the sage grouse, a unique place where the endangered birds resided. A special place for the birds. Could a mundane place be special? She guessed it could.

Silver, Grays, Whites, and Black

Chapter 47

The next week was the field trip to Fort Churchill—a collaboration between Mr. Harrison and Mr. Hornbeck. Apparently, Fort Churchill was a favorite habitat for the sage grouse. The cold end-of-January weather had endless blue skies and freezing frost at night. They awoke most mornings to the ground sprinkled with sugary crystals that winked in the weak sun before melting.

This morning, they boarded the frost-covered bus for the field trip. The ground twinkled from the evening's light sprinkling of snow. A silver wonderland, Jotty thought, imagining how she would paint the picture if given a chance. Definitely, she'd use a palette of silver, grays, whites, and black to make an abstract picture.

The students' feet churned the frost to muddy slush as they waited to board. Mr. Harrison advised warm clothing for the trip. Mr. Hornbeck had bundled up in a parka, a hat with earflaps, gloves, and a scarf that wound around his neck. He looked like a brown snowman off to explore the Antarctic. Sure, it was cold, but not that cold. Mr. Hornbeck made her laugh sometimes with his East Coast speech patterns and odd way of dressing.

Jotty wore two sweatshirts and a pair of gloves. The right glove was missing the end of the forefinger, and her fingertip peeked out. If she cut the tops off all of them, she could still draw with gloves on. The only problem was the unraveling yarn. If she pulled at it, it got longer, so she tucked it in and tried to leave it alone. She sat on her hands and looked out the window as they left the school.

Tomm sat in front of her, loaded down with pads of paper, a fold-up easel, and colored pencils and pens.

Tanya sat behind her. Tanya was wearing an oversize sweatshirt and a scarf that wound around her neck and shoulders.

Tanya leaned forward and whispered, "Any news on Leroy?"

Although Jotty didn't think finding Leroy was a secret. "Nope. You?"

"We haven't seen him since he borrowed the tent and sleeping bag," Tanya said.

Did that mean he was gone or just moved farther out into the desert?

"Maybe he's gone," Tanya said.

"Maybe," Jotty said, but she didn't think she had seen the last of him.

The trip to the fort took about an hour.

When they arrived, Mr. Harrison passed out information about Fort Churchill. Jotty slowly climbed off the bus. The early morning glow bathed Fort Churchill and the decaying adobe buildings in meadowlark yellow. Everything else glowed in soft chardonnay. She loved the names the paint companies used to describe the colors. She even made up a few of her own, ugly bathroom, sour hurt-your-eyes yellow, and cinderblock gray.

She looked down at the informational paper and reviewed the questions to be answered. Something about the local Indians, pony express, pioneers, and the stage line.

Only partial buildings remained of the fort. All the roofs, doors, and windows were gone; only shells left. The evidence of long-ago inhabitants had vanished except for those in the graveyard.

As Jotty wandered through the ruins, she wondered what the people who had lived here thought about this place. She imagined soldiers and pioneers mingling among the buildings. Did they ever think this fort would end up in ruins, only good for picnicking, camping, and field trips? Is that what could happen to Sagebrush? The school and the mural the only things left? Future visitors looking and marveling at the mural and what it meant. Or why it was painted in the first place.

Tomm had set up his easel and was already sketching in the outline of his picture, and Mr. Harrison, with a huge camera around his neck, was taking pictures and pointing things out to the students. Mr. Hornbeck wandered through the sagebrush, poking in the branches looking for his beloved birds who wintered in the sage or made igloos from the snow—a desert penguin, she thought.

"Help me look for the birds," he asked Jotty.

She shook her information sheet at him. "I've got to do this first." She edged away from him.

The students clustered in small groups, writing and studying the fact sheets. Tanya was working with Sal.

Jotty sat on one of the benches and took out her pad. She wasn't good with drawing people. They were complicated. But she sketched a fairly decent picture of a soldier talking to a pioneer woman with a bonnet on her head.

When she finished, she tucked the pad under her arm and found Tomm. He was sketching the biggest adobe building on the site; he added the missing parts and a tile roof. She nodded at his picture and continued on.

She walked until she came to the cemetery; the path clean and unmarked by footprints. She would be the first person to visit it this morning. A fancy curved arch framed the entrance. Someone had whitewashed the picket fence. She stopped to draw the archway and then ran her hands along the fence. Many people had died at Fort Churchill. The rows of stones and crosses stood as silent sentries over the inhabitants. One tomb was tall and pointed at the top. She idly wondered who this man had been. Obviously, he had some significance because of the size of his stone. She couldn't read all the weathered words. "James...aged thirty-five...loving wife...Sarah...Beloved husband..." He was same age as Ma when he died.

She frowned and closed the double gates carefully behind her. There was a small graveyard in Sagebrush. Some of the kids at school partied there and sat on the stones. They had reported seeing ghosts. Jotty imagined if you drank enough you could probably see anything.

She sat by herself on a bench, tilted her head back, and felt the warmth of the sun. It was good to be away from Sagebrush and wondering about Leroy's whereabouts. But Ma was there. Would he go after Ma while Jotty was away? She doubted it but wasn't sure. She opened her eyes and started filling in her worksheet until she heard a whistle summoning everyone together for lunch. The cafeteria had packed lunches for them, and they gathered around, eating their sandwiches and talking about what they had seen.

Tomm slid in next to her. "I've drawn a couple of pictures we might want to use."

"Me too."

She studied his building while he looked at her cemetery arch. Would Sagebrush be in ruins after 150 years? Would the mural keep history alive with students wondering about what it all meant and who had lived there? Would she be remembered as "Jotty...aged eighteen...painter and daughter of...never forgotten..."

Silver, Grays, Whites, and Black

Chapter 48

Ma and Jotty were plagued by late-night telephone calls now. The ringing phone shattering the silence and scattering their dreams, tumbleweeds in a windstorm.

"Hello?" Ma mumbled into the telephone. "Hello?" Her voice was higher now.

Jotty listened from her bed until she heard Ma put down the receiver.

"A wrong number," Ma said.

Of course it was. Did someone dial the wrong number at the same time each night?

Leroy.

He called at precisely the same time—2:00 a.m. But where did he get the phone? Jotty wondered what time the Half-Moon closed. She would bet her last dollar, if she had one anyway, the tavern closed at that time.

She hatched a plan to be waiting when the Half-Moon closed. But would Ma let her leave in the middle of the night? Probably not.

She had to think of a way to sneak out.

Silver, Grays, Whites, and Black

Chapter 49

The days continued marching forward, the field trip several weeks past, more late-night telephone calls if they didn't take the receiver off the hook. No plan to catch Leroy making the calls from the Half-Moon, either. Life tumbled along, a mind of its own.

Work continued on the mural, one day morphing into another, a pattern without predictability. So when Jotty stopped in the restroom to wash her hands after working with Tomm and found Tanya there, she was surprised at Tanya's hollowed-out figure. They were interrupted by an announcement for the Valentine's Day Dance. The restroom was no longer her sanctuary, but rather a pit stop between classes and the work in the cafeteria.

"Tanya? Are you taking your medicine?" She scanned Tanya's body and took note of her sunken cheekbones.

Tanya studied her dirty tennis shoes. "Well…"

"Did you mother get your medicine?"

"Once she did."

"Do you have any left?" Jotty demanded.

"No. I don't feel too good. I'm not sleeping."

"I can tell. Are you eating?"

"Mostly."

Jotty washed her hands. "Tanya, you have to tell your mother you need your medicine."

"Do I look bad?"

Jotty let out her breath. "You have circles under your eyes, and your cheeks are sunken. No, you look like you haven't eaten in days."

Tanya nodded and studied her sneakers again. "How do I get the money for my medicine? Do you need a helper with the mural? I could wash brushes, whatever."

They needed the money Jotty would make, but she guessed they could spare some for Tanya.

"We don't need any help, but when I get paid I can give some to you."

"When will that be?"

"I guess when we're finished." May or June. "But there's the reward money…"

"For Leroy, right?"

"Yup. I'd like to catch him and get the money for Ma, but I'd always help you, Tanya. You'd tell me if you see him."

"My mother sees him sometimes."

"Where?"

"Hanging around the pit talking to his friends."

Leroy had friends? That was news to Jotty. "Can you look around for me?"

"I have to babysit after school, but I'll try."

Later, as the sun was shrinking and shadows lengthening on the ground, Jotty and Ma sat quietly eating dinner. They shared the small table with the rock Jotty had saved from the window. The rock held the pile of napkins in place.

Ma motioned toward the rock with her fork. "Why did you keep that?"

"I don't ever want to forget," Jotty said.

"You won't."

The ringing telephone interrupted them. She and Ma looked at each other before Ma reached over and picked up the receiver.

"Hello?"

Jotty watched as Ma's face paled.

"Hello, I said."

Jotty snatched the phone. "Come out and fight like a man!" The telephone was quiet. The silence eerie and laced with tension. "We know it's you, Leroy!" And with that she pressed the disconnect button and put the telephone down, the receiver off the hook. There, they wouldn't need to listen to the phone ringing all night long.

"Can I drive the truck into town tonight?" Jotty asked.

"Why?" The color was returning to Ma's sunken cheeks.

"I bet he's using the pay phone behind the Half-Moon to make these calls."

"I don't want you confronting him there," Ma said, putting down her fork and pushing away her plate.

"But why?"

"He may be dangerous."

True, but probably drunk after a few hours sitting at the bar. And she still had his deer rifle.

"Do you have a better way?" Jotty pushed away her half-eaten plate of food too. Suddenly she was full.

"Let the sheriff handle it," Ma said, standing and gathering up the dishes.

"You sit, Ma, I'll take care of the dishes," Jotty said.

The sheriff was handling Leroy with no results. Jotty gathered up the plates, and went to the kitchen to clean up after dinner. She needed a plan. She needed a miracle. She needed…more dish soap as she squirted out the last bit from the container.

Coffee and Cinnamon

Chapter 50

The next day, before school, she stopped by the sheriff's office to talk to whomever was on duty. Sam was there.

"Hey, Sam!" He was sitting at the desk, looking wearily at a stack of papers. The office smelled of fresh brewed coffee. If brown had an aroma, it would be coffee and cinnamon. "I just made a fresh pot. You want some?"

Coffee was tempting. She was tired of waiting and wondering, her sleep restless and confusing.

"Sure."

He poured some in a Styrofoam cup for her. She breathed in the steam; the heat of the coffee warmed her hands.

"What brings you in this morning?" He narrowed his eyes. "Leroy?"

She took a deep breath. "Yes, he's been calling us. I'm sure he's using the pay phone by the Half-Moon."

"Interesting," Sam said. He didn't say he'd try to catch him.

"Do you think you can drive by there tonight? Around two o'clock?"

"Sure, sure."

"Well, thanks, Sam, for your help. And for the coffee."

"Anytime," he said.

She doubted he'd apprehend Leroy, but it was worth a try. She took her coffee and left for school.

Adobe Tan

Chapter 51

In Jotty's estimation, there was never enough time before school to properly work on her part of the mural. It seemed as if she had just gotten started, when it was time to finish and go to class.

"Why so glum?" Tomm asked.

"I hate to leave this." She used the brush tipped with adobe tan as her wand, except none of the Disney magic happened, and she put it in the turpentine.

"Don't worry," he said with a laugh. "It'll be waiting when school is finished."

Of that, Jotty was sure. She climbed off the scaffolding and turned to face their creation. Only partly finished, but still magnificent. The left side, the mountain; and the right, Sagebrush and Fort Churchill.

She left and stopped in the restroom to wash her hands and clean a smudge of dried paint on her cheek. Emmett pushed out a mop and bucket. A Caution Wet Floor sign blocked the doorway.

"Toilet overflowed." He backed away from her.

Jotty saw a flicker of worry in his eyes. He was afraid of her after the exchange over the paint earlier this year.

She felt a stab of remorse about the rough way she had treated him. "Emmett." She took a step closer. "I'm sorry about tripping and accidentally pushing you. It wasn't a good time for me."

"Ah, well…" He adjusted his baseball cap. "That's OK. Haven't seen much of you lately—only the back of you working on that picture."

"What do you think?"

"It's pretty amazing." He grinned, revealing tobacco-stained teeth.

His comment made her feel tingly, and she stood straighter.

"You look good," he said.

She frowned.

"You don't look angry all the time." He pushed back his baseball cap and scratched his balding head. "Sure enough. I think you're growing up."

She didn't know how to respond, so she kept quiet. But secretly she was pleased.

"I saw your stepfather at—" He was interrupted by a figure pushing past them.

"Hey! The floor's wet," Emmett yelled.

Jotty saw Tanya hunched over, grasping her stomach like she was going to be sick.

"Tanya, wait!" she called.

In slow motion, Tanya slipped on the wet floor and landed on her butt.

"Tanya! What's wrong?" Jotty asked.

"Are you OK?" Emmett asked. "I put the sign out and all."

"I feel terrible. I told my mother I was sick, but she just told me to go to school and quit complaining!" She rolled into a ball on the floor. "I think I'm going to die. I feel so bad! Only worse," she said with a wail. "My stepfather kicked me out too. Says I'm too much trouble. What am I going to do?"

Jotty lowered herself to the wet floor to sit beside Tanya. "Don't worry. We'll get you to the doctor. I'm sure you can stay with us." But she didn't know how or when to get Tanya's medicine. She patted Tanya's shoulders. Perhaps Clyde would help. That woman didn't take no for an answer. A pit bull wearing a suit.

"That would be great, but do you have room?" Tanya's face cleared some.

There was the couch as uncomfortable as it was.

Emmett returned with Clyde, who also knelt down beside them and studied Tanya's tear-stained face. "Are you still having problems with your thyroid?"

Tanya dutifully nodded. "I don't feel good, and my stepdad said I was too much trouble with my complaining. He kicked me out." Clyde put her arm around Tanya's shoulders and helped her stand. She fished a clean tissue from her pocket.

Together Jotty and Clyde helped Tanya walk to the office and sit.

"Do you know the name of the medicine?" Clyde asked.

Tanya fished a crumpled paper from her pocket and handed it to Clyde.

Clyde picked up the telephone. "Hello, this is Dr. Benninger from Sagebrush High School. I have a student who needs her thyroid medicine and her family isn't able to get it for her. Can I get it for her?"

Jotty and Tanya held hands while they waited.

Clyde listened and tapped a pencil against her desk planner. "Thank you, I'll be right over."

Clyde looked directly at them. "I'll get your medicine. And secondly, you eating? You look awfully thin to me."

"A little bit. Last night we had soup and crackers."

"That's good."

"Not if you have to share one can with seven people. My mother added two or three cans of water."

"How would you like to stay with me for a bit while we get your weight stabilized and you're taking your medicine. How would that be? I've got an extra bedroom at our place," Clyde said.

Clyde wanted Tanya to move in with her? Jotty had never heard of a principal doing such a thing before. Would Mr. Miller have offered in the same situation? Probably not.

Clyde continued, "My husband's a mining engineer and travels a lot. I'd enjoy your company, and you'd have a place to stay as your body recovers. We've got plenty of room."

Clyde turned to Jotty, "Can you help her get her things, so she can move in after school?"

"I don't know if my stepdad will let me get my things. He said not to come back," Tanya said.

"I'll go with you," Jotty said, sitting up straighter. "We'll get your clothes."

"Thanks, Jotty." Tanya's face cleared and the mottled red blotches faded.

On the outside, Jotty was brave—defiant, fearless, and bold. She didn't know if coping was better Tanya's way or hers.

"Here's an extra key to my trailer." Clyde broke the silence and gave them the address. "I'll be there after I meet with the superintendent, probably around seven. Help yourself to anything in the refrigerator."

After school, Jotty and Tanya took Ma's truck and lurched over the rutted, muddy roads to Tanya's trailer. Jotty gripped the steering wheel to keep from toppling over, and Tanya clutched the door handle as the truck lurched over the uneven road. They didn't talk. The dust from the road rose up around the truck, and they were insulated in the fine gray haze.

Tanya's family lived in a travel trailer miles out of town on a road without a proper name, which meant they had to go to the post office for their mail. Her stepfather leaned some boards against the sides, but Jotty could still see the wheels. They generated their own power, and their water came from a well.

They both sat motionless and quiet after Jotty parked by the front of the trailer. She saw trucks parked nearby, some missing tires, another with the hood open, and one missing a side door.

Jotty got out, looked cautiously around, and asked, "Is he home?"

"No, his truck is gone, but he said not to come back. He called me a parasite," Tanya said, her nostrils flared. "I'm not a parasite."

"Don't pay any attention to what he said. He's just a liquored-up old man. He doesn't know anything," Jotty spat. "Your mother loves you."

Jotty knew all about living with a drunk. It wasn't fun or predictable.

"She loves him more," Tanya added.

Not real love—mostly desperation to survive. Tanya's family was worse off than hers. Tanya's mother worked part-time at the gravel pit, cleaning the offices and toilets, and her stepdad helped when he was sober.

"Come on, let's get your stuff." Tanya trailed behind as Jotty walked up the steps, strode across the metal porch, and opened the warped screen door. "Do I need to knock?"

Tanya shook her head. She looked around. "No one is home. Mom's working again, and my sisters are at Head Start or the after-school program."

Jotty banged open the front door. She hesitated, ears straining for the slightest sound, but only silence filled the trailer, so she stepped in. It smelled of dirty diapers and fried hamburgers.

"Let's hurry while he's gone," Tanya said.

They went directly to Tanya's cramped bedroom, the one she shared with her little sisters.

"Do you have a suitcase?" Jotty asked, looking under piles of clothes, dirty toys, and papers. Tanya shook her head. "Then we'll put your stuff in a garbage bag."

"I'll get some." Tanya returned with two black sacks.

"Those should be good. Hold the bag open and I'll start putting stuff in."

Jotty heard the front door open and close. She froze. Tanya too.

"Hurry," Tanya mouthed.

Jotty stuffed an armload of Tanya's clothes in the bag, her heart hammering, waiting for whoever had come in to confront them. Was it Tanya's mother or her stepfather? Or Leroy?

"What are you doing?" Tanya's stepdad demanded from the doorway.

Jotty's heart lurched and she inhaled until she couldn't take in anymore air. She steadied her breathing and exhaled slowly as she smoothed down the pile of clothes, but anger made her clench the bag in her fists. How come he was so mean? Tanya stood still as a statue at her side.

"What do you think?" Jotty turned to face him. He held a shotgun in the crook of his arm. She wanted to appear nonchalant and cool. "We're getting Tanya's stuff. You kicked her out, remember?" She took a step toward him even though she had the urge to hide.

He smiled, revealing a black tooth. "I told her never to come back." He patted the rifle. "And she's back." He took a small step back.

Jotty forced her legs to move forward again. "She's going to stay with the principal, Dr. Benninger," Jotty said, her eyes narrowing in a challenge.

His face never changed, only a tiny flicker in one eye, but Jotty noticed the small, almost imperceptible step back. "Heard about that new gal principal."

"It's against the law to kick minors out of the house, you know." Jotty took a step forward. She didn't know if that was true or not. "Tanya just wants her stuff. She didn't want to call the sheriff on you, but if we don't get her things, we will."

He spit on the floor. "Take it all. I don't care."

Together they finished loading the rainbow of jeans, T-shirts, and underwear into the bags under his watchful eyes. Jotty glanced at him once, but he remained silently in the doorway.

"Do we have everything?" Jotty asked Tanya.

"I think so." Tanya chewed on her bottom lip and looked around the disheveled room.

"Make sure," he said, spitting again. "Because you ain't comin' back."

Jotty picked up the bags, swung them over her shoulders, and walked to the doorway he was blocking. "Excuse me," she said, holding his glare with her own.

Tanya's stepdad moved out of the way, but he said, "Seen Leroy around. He wants his rifle back."

"I bet," Jotty said, forcing a confident smile on her face, but the sides of her mouth quivered.

"He'll be back for it."

"Good, I'll be waiting," Jotty said.

Tanya's stepdad threw back his head and laughed. He was still laughing as they got to the front door.

Tanya glanced around, picked up a picture of her sisters, and looked lovingly at it. She put it into the bag and followed Jotty to the truck.

The sound of his laughter made Jotty's spine shiver and her hair bristle. He gave her the creeps. They threw Tanya's stuff in the bed of the truck and drove away.

Chapter 52

"I'm glad to be out of there. I didn't know what he would do."
Tanya turned around and looked out the truck's back window. Was she
expecting her stepfather to follow? "I could never have faced him
without you, Jotty."

Jotty's eyes dragged to the rearview mirror; Tanya's trailer was
lost in a gray haze of dust from the dirt road. "It was nothing." But it
had taken several beats for her heart to slow and her breathing to
return to normal.

"Do you think he's seen Leroy in town?" Tanya asked.

"Heck yes. Lots of people have seen him. I'm not afraid of
Leroy." She gulped at her false bravado. Her heart responded with a
quick thump.

"I wish I was more like you." Tanya leaned back and sighed.

Jotty had Leroy's rifle but he was unpredictable and sly. She
first needed to get Tanya settled at Clyde's before she could tackle the
problem of Leroy.

They followed Clyde's directions and drove to her trailer. It
was a double-wide unit with green shutters and a big deck across the
front with built-in benches. The yard had grass and a real cement
driveway.

"Nice place," Tanya said in a breathless, admiring voice.

"Yeah," Jotty said, parking in the drive, not knowing what else
to say. She should have guessed.

"She dresses nice too," Tanya added.

"Let's go in." They got out of the truck, each taking a bag, and
walked to the front door. Tanya fitted the key in the lock, opened it,
and they stepped over the welcome mat into the interior warmed by the
inviting scent of potpourri, wild flowers and a touch of cinnamon.

Tanya walked to the middle of the living room and slowly
turned around. "Will you look at this place? Even smells good."

"Nice." The living room reminded Jotty of the furniture ads she
saw for Montgomery Ward with rooms that were all in coordinated

colors—gray birch, suede, and pine forest. The pillows, rugs, and pictures matched.

Tanya sank down on the couch.

"You're lucky to be staying here," Jotty said. The couch looked new, no sagging or torn cushions. "Let's watch TV until she comes home."

"Do you think we could have a snack?" Tanya asked.

"She said for us to help ourselves."

Together they went into the kitchen and opened the refrigerator. The shelves were orderly and held the usual things: milk, orange juice, cottage cheese, eggs, yogurt and a bowl of apples.

"I'm going to have some yogurt," Tanya said. "You?"

Jotty selected a string cheese.

They turned on the television and snuggled back on the couch. Tanya leaned over and looked at the pictures on the table: Clyde with a dark-haired man, an older couple, and two blond-haired little girls. "These are nice. Why do you suppose Dr. Benninger doesn't have children?"

"Maybe she doesn't want them." Jotty folded her arms and watched the flickering images on the screen.

"Why would you be a principal if you didn't like kids?"

Jotty had a secret theory—to torture and hassle kids, but she had to believe Clyde liked working with students.

"I bet she can't have them. Do you think I'll meet her husband?" Tanya asked.

"I'm sure you will."

"Do you think they hold hands and act romantic?"

"Probably not, Tanya. That's make-believe."

Tanya sighed. "Wouldn't it be nice if that was the way marriage could be?"

Jotty thought back to when Ma first married Leroy. He'd seemed OK then. He'd treated Ma nice for a while, until he started drinking. At least they had eaten more than cereal when Leroy came, but she'd eat cereal forever if he would disappear from their lives. "Yes, that would be nice."

Jotty leaned back and closed her eyes, suddenly tired from the long day and her encounter with Tanya's stepdad. The telephone rang, and she opened her eyes. "I'll get the phone." Out of habit, Jotty reached over and picked it up. "Hello? Hello?"

Only breathing and buzzing. Leroy had found her. How had he tracked her down?

Jotty gripped the receiver—everything stopped. "Leroy, you son of a…"

"Jotty? Is that you?" The static on the telephone faded and Clyde's voice came through.

"I had to put you on hold while I talked to the superintendent. I hope I didn't scare you. You sound frightened," Clyde said.

"I'm not scared." Not anymore, not really. If anything, she felt foolish.

"I'll be right home. Tell Tanya I'm on my way."

Jotty hung up and managed a weak smile. "Only Clyde."

"You had me scared," Tanya said. "I thought you were talking to Leroy."

"He's out there somewhere," Jotty said, pushing aside the curtains and peering into the growing gloom. "Ma's all alone. Maybe I should go get her."

Tanya shivered. "Maybe you should. I'll wait here for Dr. Benninger."

Jotty drove quickly to their trailer. Ma was curled up on the couch, reading a dog-eared magazine. She frowned and arched her brows. "You're home late."

Jotty looked around. Nothing seemed out of place.

"I'm worried about you staying here alone," Jotty said.

"You're worried about me? I was worried when you didn't come home," Ma said.

"I gave Tanya a ride."

"The ride took hours?" Ma put her red, chapped hands on her hips.

Jotty hated looking at Ma's hands.

"We had to get Tanya's stuff." She grabbed Ma's coat from the hook by the door. "I want you to come with me."

"Where?"

"Dr. Clyde...er, Benninger's trailer."

"Really?" Ma looked her over. "OK. You can tell me what's going on with Tanya," Ma zipped her jacket.

They got into Ma's truck and drove back over the uneven roads to Clyde's.

"So what's going on?" Ma asked.

"Tanya's stepdad kicked her out."

"Why?"

"She needs medicine for her thyroid, and her mother won't get it. He doesn't want to spend money on her, I'm guessing."

"That's terrible," Ma said.

"Clyde has extra room and besides, you should see her place, very fancy. Tanya will be better off there."

"That was very nice of her," Ma said.

"That's what I thought. Tanya doesn't need to be in the middle of the Leroy thing."

"Do the phone calls keep you awake?" Ma asked.

"Not really." No use getting Ma more upset than she already was. "I'll be happy when they put him in jail."

Ma patted her hand. "I'm sorry he wakes you up. I hope they catch him soon." Ma stifled a yawn.

Jotty squeezed Ma's chilled fingers. Ma had nothing to be sorry about.

Clyde was home when they returned. Her green sedan was parked in the driveway.

She greeted them at the door. "Tanya told me you were coming. I hope you're hungry. I picked up a pizza."

Jotty's stomach answered with a small flip-flop. She had only eaten the string cheese since lunch.

"This is so nice," Ma said, looking around Clyde's trailer while rubbing her cold hands together.

Clyde said, "Please, sit down. Let's eat before the pizza gets cold."

Ma wiped off the seat of her jeans before she sat on the upholstered chair. Then she squinted at Jotty's clothes before nodding for her to sit also.

Ma turned to Tanya and patted her hand. "How are you doing?"

"I think I feel better even taking only one dose of the medicine."

"That's good."

Jotty smelled the pizza as Clyde put the box and plates on the table. "I made some coffee." She poured steaming liquid into big white mugs and stopped when she got to Jotty. "Do you drink coffee?"

"Coffee's fine, Clyde," Jotty responded without thinking.

"Jotty!" Ma said with a gasp. "Why do you call her Clyde? I'm so sorry, Dr. Benninger."

"That's quite all right," Clyde said, laughing. "That was my college nickname. We called each other by men's names. I was Clyde."

"Why Clyde?" Jotty blurted.

"I had a great-uncle named Clyde. He was my favorite. He drove a big Cadillac with a horn that sounded like bugle taps. My roommate was Sam and my best friend, Pete. Don't ask me why. We just called each other by male names. Sometimes it caused confusion."

She could imagine.

This was a side of Clyde that Jotty had never seen before. Clyde had friends and a personal life. She wasn't just a drill sergeant who ordered everyone around at school.

"I don't care," Ma said. "You're the principal. How disrespectful. And after everything you've done."

"I told her that was my name." She smiled at Jotty. "I want you to call me Clyde." She held up her hand when Ma started to speak. "And what about Jotty's unusual name?"

"I wanted to name her Jody but used two t's instead of a d."

"Oh, interesting. Jotty suits you more than Jody."

"I think so too," Ma said.

Jotty concentrated on her food.

"How's the pizza?" Clyde asked as they silently ate.

208

It was hot, and the cheese dripped off the side, unlike the stuff the cafeteria served with the consistency of rubbery cardboard. Jotty forced herself to eat slowly and not shove it in as fast as she could.

They all nodded and murmured their thanks.

"I'm so grateful to you," Ma said, wiping her mouth. "I told Jotty I wish you'd come years earlier. Mr. Miller let them get away with murder."

"I'm glad we came here too. We've been all over the United States with my husband's job. I connect with the kids in Sagebrush," Clyde said, smiling a genuine smile that made her eyes sparkle. "The school's a big family for me. I can't have children, so all my students are special to me."

Tanya gave Jotty an I told you so look with wide eyes and a slight dip in her chin. They waited, but Clyde didn't continue; she only sipped thoughtfully at her coffee.

Tanya yawned and sagged down in her chair.

"Why don't you get ready for bed—you look tired," Clyde said.

"I am a little," Tanya said, struggling to stand.

"Second bedroom on the right," Clyde directed.

"I'll help you, Tanya," Jotty said.

Ma looked at her watch. "We'll put this stuff away, and then we should go. Dr. Benninger must want to relax."

Tanya washed up in the hall bathroom while Jotty found her pajamas in the tangled mix of clothes in the garbage bag. Tanya would have to sort through this tomorrow.

When Tanya was settled in the bed, Jotty went back to the dining room. The table was cleaned, and Ma had on her coat.

"Thank you for the pizza, Dr. Benn—"

Clyde cut her off. "Oh no, none of that. I want you to call me Clyde." She patted Jotty's arm. "Gives me a good feeling."

"Thank you for everything," Ma said. "You've done so much for the school this year."

"Let's go, Ma," Jotty said, tugging on her sleeve.

When they got into the truck, Ma said, "I don't care what she tells you; don't call her Clyde. She's a beautiful, dignified woman with a heart of gold. Clyde sounds so crude."

"Whatever makes you happy, Ma." Jotty yawned, making her jaw crack. Getting to bed would feel good.

Ma folded her arms and settled back into the torn seat covering.

They drove home without a word between them. The air coming in from the crack in the window was clean and sharp, the kind Jotty could smell.

Chocolate Brownie and Salmon-Scale Blue

Chapter 53

The telephone shattered the silence of the early evening. Ma wasn't home yet from the dinner shift. Jotty struggled off the couch, put down her peanut butter and jelly sandwich, and groped for the receiver. "Hello."

"I want to kill you, you bitch." The voice was muffled, but Jotty knew Leroy's voice on the telephone. His anger transmitted through the receiver.

"I'll bet you would," she said with a shaky laugh. She was glad he couldn't see her hands tremble.

"You've got my rifle, you spoiled brat," he grumbled.

"Yeah. I do. You want it back?" she taunted.

"I'm going to come over there and get it!"

"Good, I'll be waiting!" she said with false bravado. The line went dead. Her heart beat loudly, and she steadied her breath. He was still in the area. She doubted he would call long-distance.

Ma returned home when Jotty was still holding the telephone, frozen in place, her thoughts going a mile a minute. "Who are you talking to?"

Should she worry Ma? She responded with, "Tanya. Do you want to see her?" She felt the urge to leave the trailer, avoid a confrontation with Leroy.

Since getting on medicine and eating better, Tanya looked healthier and wanted to go home. Why? Jotty wondered. She secretly hoped Tanya could stay with Clyde forever.

"Of course," Ma said, putting her coat back on.

Together they drove to Clyde's trailer, the type of place she wanted to buy for Ma someday.

Tanya, propped up on pillows in Clyde's guest room, was doing homework.

Of course, Clyde would insist she did her schoolwork.

Tanya closed the book with a snap. They pulled chairs to the side of the bed.

"Where's Dr. Benninger?" Ma asked, looking around.

"At a school board meeting," Tanya said.

Jotty motioned toward the government book on the bed.

Tanya gave her a one-shoulder shrug. "Something to do. I want to keep my grades up. Dr. Benninger said I might be able to get a scholarship for college."

"You want to go to college?" Jotty asked.

"I'll have to if I'm going to be a teacher."

A teacher, that was new. "You want to be a teacher?"

"Yeah, I like little kids," Tanya said.

Tanya helped with her four younger sisters.

Jotty wasn't sure what to say. She looked down at her knees and picked at a spot of dried paint, the chocolate brownie color they had used to paint some of the mural buildings. And the salmon-scale blue. Her jeans were a roadmap of hues from the picture, the more recent colors bolder than those faded from the washing machine.

Ma said, "I think you'd make a wonderful teacher."

"You do?" Tanya asked.

"Yes."

"Some of these things have a way of working themselves out," Ma said.

"Like what?" Jotty asked, wondering what Ma was referring to.

"Your birthday is next week, Jotty, and you're still in school," Ma said.

She would have to mention that. Get her dig in. She glared at Ma.

Tanya laughed. "You two are so funny! I wish my mom and I could joke. She's so serious."

Ma nodded. "She has more responsibilities than I do."

Tanya pushed the pillow into place behind her back and sat straighter. "I really like it here, but I miss my mom too. Not my stepdad, but my sisters and my mom."

"When are you going back?" Jotty asked.

"As soon as my mom says I can. She has to ask my stepdad."

Ma stood. "We just came by to say hi. We haven't had dinner yet. We should be going. Jotty?"

212

"Right."

As they drove home, Rattlesnake Mountain loomed black against the night sky. The town was quiet, and the only lights glowed softly from windows. Jotty's mind was quiet too, anxious to eat and go to bed.

But as they got closer to the trailer, they saw red curls.

"I wonder what that could be," Ma said, leaning forward.

"A fire." The realization hit Jotty as soon as she said the words.

"A trailer's on fire!" Ma gasped. "Drive faster. I hope it's not ours!"

But Jotty knew it would be theirs.

Jotty accelerated toward the fire. The truck drunkenly lurched forward, gravel spitting from the rear wheels. They raced ahead and skidded to a stop at the side of the road. Flames darted in and out of the front window, eating away at the black plastic from the broken window.

"I'll get the hose," Jotty yelled.

"No!" Ma grabbed her arm. "Go for help."

In the distance, they heard the faint whine of a siren. Help was on the way.

Jotty ran to the back of the trailer and hooked up the hose. The heat surrounded her, making breathing difficult, as if she had her face inside an oven. The hose, stiff and unwieldy from the cold, refused to move. Jotty jerked with all her strength, dragged it to the front, and turned on the nozzle. At first, nothing happened. She shook the nozzle, trying to dislodge the water. Eventually water snaked through the hose and squirted out.

She took a deep breath as she sprayed water into the front window. Her lungs felt as if they would burst for lack of fresh air. The water didn't seem to help. The siren got louder.

Finally, the fire truck stopped next to Jotty. Volunteer firemen jumped down and pulled thick hoses from their truck. Jotty dropped hers and ran back to Ma. Gasping for air, she doubled over to cough out the smoke. Ma stood rigid and straight by the truck, her eyes never leaving the trailer. Jotty put her arms around Ma as they watched, with Ma sagging more and more into her arms.

Jotty looked at her watch, only half an hour had passed before the flames were extinguished.

A fireman came over. "We got here just in time. Your quick thinking and that garden hose saved the trailer. Any longer and the whole thing would have gone up," he said, lifting his arms.

They got the picture. Ma sagged completely against Jotty, going soft and spongy. "I think my husband did this. He's been out to get us," she said with a strangled sob.

"We need to call the sheriff again," Jotty said, more as a mental note to herself than to Ma.

As if on cue, the sheriff turned into their drive, red and yellow lights flashing, and behind him, Clyde's green sedan.

One of the firemen went inside and called out, "Not much damage. Mainly water. Someone started the front curtains on fire."

The sheriff came toward them, followed by Clyde in a suit and heels. What was she doing here?

As if knowing, Clyde said, "I was coming home from the meeting when I saw the fire truck and followed, hoping it wasn't a home of one of our students."

Which it was.

The fireman said, "You shouldn't stay here tonight. There may still be hot spots. Do you have someplace else to go? We can call the Red Cross for you."

"They can stay with me if they don't mind the pull-out couch," Clyde said.

"I hate to impose..." Jotty saw Ma working her jaw, vacillating. "Thank you, Dr. Benninger."

"My husband is working in the field for the next two weeks. Besides, Tanya's there, and she would enjoy having company. I'm extremely busy at school."

Jotty mulled this over. Keeping away from Leroy might be good and frustrate him to no end. Yes, staying with Clyde would be fine.

After answering the sheriff's questions and reporting Leroy's calls and threats, they got back into the truck for the short drive to Clyde's. Jotty reached under the seat for the rifle. Her fingers caressed the cold, hard, reassuring steel barrel. That's what Leroy wanted. She'd give him something—a bullet right between the eyes.

She'd have to be on guard. He seemed to be everywhere and nowhere at the same time. He needed to be caught. Why hadn't Sam waited for him when the bar closed? What other pressing police business could be happening at two o'clock in the morning?

Grainy Gray-Black

Chapter 54

Jotty and Ma had been at Clyde's trailer for two days. They shared the fold-down bed in the living room while the window in their own trailer was fixed and the interior dried out from the water.

Ma breathed quietly as Jotty stared at the ceiling, unable to sleep.

Every time sleep came closer, her thoughts chased the blissful darkness away. Slowly, everything turned a grainy gray-black, and she could make out shapes. She turned over and closed her eyes. But her thoughts came one after another: Leroy's calls and threats, the fire, and the finish of the mural, followed by an open house to showcase their work. It had been a very strange year. Tomorrow she would turn eighteen and had no plans to leave school. All she wanted was to finish the mural and graduate.

"Are you awake?" Ma mumbled, rubbing her eyes.

"Sorry, I didn't mean to wake you. I've been thinking."

"We all have a lot on our minds," Ma said.

Jotty turned over.

"Thinking about your birthday?" Ma said softly. "Seems yesterday I was eighteen. I was so full of plans."

"What were they?" Jotty asked.

"I don't know…"

"Ma…"

"I wanted to be a nurse."

"You still can," Jotty said.

"I'd have to finish school first," Ma said.

"They've got programs to help you finish," Jotty said.

"Maybe."

"If I can graduate, then you can at least think about finishing too." Jotty turned to face her, but Ma was quiet.

"Did you ever figure life would be so difficult? Living in Sagebrush. Wondering what Leroy would do next?" The darkness made Jotty's thoughts clear and sharp, nothing grainy or out of focus.

She pictured Leroy hurting Ma and then shooting him. The thought punched her gut—Leroy dead on the floor. Could she shoot him? Really shoot him? It was one thing to watch the drama on television, but in real life, it was forever.

Ma cleared her throat. "I wanted things that I read about or saw in movies. I guess I thought in some ways my life would be similar to television."

"The Designing Woman show?"

"No, that's too over the top for me. I'd just like furniture that isn't broken. I don't care if it matches."

Jotty couldn't see Ma in one of the Designing Women rooms, but she could see her in a place like Clyde's. Nice, but not outrageous.

Then after a pause, Ma continued, "I hope Leroy will leave us alone. We can make it if we cut corners. Get by until…"

Leroy wasn't going to leave them alone. He wanted his rifle, and he was as stubborn as a mule when he'd been drinking. No, that wasn't true. He was stubborn all the time. Besides, Jotty wanted the reward money for helping to catch him. They wouldn't need to worry if they had the reward.

"I don't want anything to spoil your graduation," Ma said.

"I'll finish," Jotty said, quietly.

"You better," Ma's voice caught.

"What will there be for me after high school?" Jotty didn't want to live in a trailer and be married to someone who treated her badly.

"College?" Ma asked.

"Never given it much thought." Not in the daylight, only at night in her secret fantasies.

"That's for Roger. He gets all As without trying. He'll get off the res and away froSagebrush and be a doctor or something. I'll be stuck here forever."

"Tanya mentioned college," Ma said.

"Do you think she was serious?" Jotty asked.

"I hope she is. I hope you'll both go. You don't try in school, but still you pass," Ma said.

"School's easy." The teachers passed her on so they wouldn't need to deal with her again.

Jotty couldn't imagine more school. Mr. Harrison's class made the fifty minutes interesting. If they could all be that engaging, then maybe. Or Mr. Hornbeck's course on Nevada birds and habitat. They transmitted their excitement for their subjects unlike Mrs. Markley, who taught from habit, not really relating to her students.

Ma added, "I hear college is different. One of the truckers who eats at Joe's went to college. You pick and choose classes according to your major."

Jotty was quiet. "What is a major?"

"It's what you're studying—business or nursing. But if you're happy staying in Sagebrush, then that's fine by me."

A low blow. "Ma!"

"Well then, you'll have to go to school if you want to leave."

Jotty shook her head, rustling the pillow. "I know I have to leave, but I want you to come with me."

Ma found Jotty's hand under the blanket and squeezed it. "That would be nice."

"I want to paint and be an artist, but I don't want to take jobs in the middle of nowhere."

"The mural's wonderful. Everyone's heard about it at Joe's."

"How many people will know about the mural in ten years? Who comes to Sagebrush?" A mural should be looked at and enjoyed, not locked away in a cafeteria in a tiny town with a small high school.

"You'll know the mural's here. You're the most important thing in the world to me." Ma grasped her hand again. Jotty felt her mother's scratchy, sandpapery skin.

"I know, Ma." Jotty untangled her hand. "I want you to have a nice house to live in. Look at this place—but in a bigger town with lots to do." With an art gallery even.

"You always seem to find something to keep yourself occupied. I think that's one of the reasons you're such a good artist." Ma stifled a yawn. "You've had lots of time to practice. We never know why things happen, but I believe there's a reason."

Jotty mulled over Ma's logic, and then she asked, "Why did you move to Sagebrush?" Ma was from Reno.

"Your father loved the mountains and the open feeling. He didn't care for the cramped feeling in the city. He wanted to hunt. So we came here. We wanted to do things our own way. Not like our parents."

"Did you have me then?"

"I was expecting you."

Jotty swallowed hard, shut her eyes, and asked, "How come you split up?"

Ma was quiet, and at first Jotty thought she was sleeping, but her eyes were open, shining circles in the dark.

"We grew up," she said, taking Jotty's hand again. "I was only eighteen when we got married. We couldn't see anything, except ourselves. We wanted each other, and when I got pregnant, we felt the only thing to do was to get married. We grew up fast and then grew apart. The marriage was a mistake from the very beginning."

"Was I a mistake?"

"No, never. You're the best thing to happen to me," Ma said. Jotty believed her.

"Dad went away when I was about five," Jotty whispered.

"He stayed as long as he could. He loved you. I knew he was unhappy. I was unhappy. He stayed because of you."

"He sure doesn't act loving," Jotty said.

"I think sometimes people are embarrassed when too much time goes by and they haven't called. I don't know why he dropped out of your life. You were important to him. I think he forgot about us because of the pain. He's probably started a new life," Ma said.

"I don't know how anyone could forget a little kid who loved them," Jotty said.

"People do what they have to so they can survive. Forget things even." Ma stifled another yawn and said, "We'd better get some sleep. We'll talk more tomorrow." Then she turned over and snored softly.

At first Jotty had ached with hurt when Dad ignored her. She would climb as high up the mountain as she could and cry. Now she felt numb. She had built a wall around that part of her life.

She closed her eyes, the darkness washing over and through her, easing away into sleep. A couple of hours of rest were better than nothing.

Chapter 55

The next day, Jotty and Ma went to see their trailer. They walked up the steps and were greeted by a huge fan drying out the carpeting and furniture. The entire place reeked of something burning in the oven.

Jotty touched the carpet, still damp, but not soaked from the fire hoses. "I think it will still be a couple of days before we can come back."

Ma touched the couch. "Hmm. This is still wet too." Ma scanned the room, appraising it, before saying, "I don't understand why the sheriff can't catch him. Everyone at Joe's tells me they've seen him," Ma said, worry lacing her words.

"They probably don't care," Jotty said as they locked the front door and got back into the truck for the drive back to Clyde's.

As they left, Jotty turned toward the side window and squinted into the glare. Outside the sun hung low in the sky, and orange flooded the desert, bathed in bronze-coin gold. An illusion only, Jotty thought sadly.

"That's their job," Ma said.

"If he set fire to the gravel pit, they'd find him."

"Perhaps," Ma said.

They drove silently to Clyde's and pulled into the drive. "I was hoping we'd be able to go home for your birthday."

Jotty enjoyed staying at Clyde's. There were no telephone calls, and Ma seemed to relax and eat better. Her cheeks didn't cave in as much. She lost her weary, fearful eyes. Tanya too.

"That's OK, Ma. It's OK here."

"I didn't think you got along with Dr. Benninger."

Truthfully, Clyde had grown on her, little by little. She was good to Tanya.

Later the same day, as they all finished eating the dinner Ma had prepared for them, the telephone rang.

"Probably my husband. He's somewhere in Idaho." Clyde picked up the receiver. "Hello." She narrowed her eyes. "Who is this?"

Jotty froze. Was it Leroy?

"You can't go around threatening people," Clyde said with a rising voice.

Leroy. The hair on the back of Jotty's neck rose. Ma's eyes were wide and staring. Tanya's too.

"I'm calling the sheriff!" Clyde replaced the receiver on the stand. She turned toward the startled group at the table, her face mad. "That's the worst part of my job."

How had Leroy managed to find them at Clyde's? Jotty's stomach constricted. Her happy, warm feeling evaporated.

"What did he say?" Jotty asked.

"He was disgusting. I won't repeat it. I think I know who it might be."

She said he, confirming Jotty's suspicions.

"I get crank calls all the time; goes with the job," Clyde said, coming back to the table.

Was it Leroy? Or someone else?

Spruce Green and Tahoe Blue

Chapter 57

The day of Jotty's birthday, she drove Ma to work and then went to school.

"Not a very nice day for your birthday," Ma said as Jotty stopped the truck for her to exit."

It figured. "It might change." Nevada weather was unpredictable in the spring.

"I hope so. Happy birthday," Ma said.

"Thanks." She didn't know what to think of this milestone event. Happy or sad? She felt just as she had yesterday, worried about Leroy and making ends meet. Now she had choices, but did she really have choices?

Jotty pulled away from the curb and headed toward school all the while squinting at the leaden-gray morning—not light and translucent, but a deep gray from the mountaintop up, not a sliver of blue to be seen. March weather was unpredictable; bright with sunshine one day and the next, overcast and dreary. She turned into the school parking lot, parked, and went in to begin the morning mural work. The school was warm and bathed in the glow of the overhead lights. The cafeteria workers were putting out food and drinks for breakfast, and Tomm was hard at work.

The mountain was almost finished, but not finished. A mountain was never complete, evolving daily. And she guessed that summed up being an adult. She wasn't quite finished growing up.

"Good morning!" Tomm said as Jotty got ready for the day.

"Ditto!"

He laughed.

Jotty began shading the pathway. Using various shades of tans and browns for the features, she put the finishing touches on the rattlesnake, coiled as if to strike, and the fang-bearing mountain lion. The paint was numbered, not named. She liked when paint had names she could remember. A number was forgettable, much like eighteen. It wasn't a memorable number yet with nothing to distinguish it from seventeen.

No, she wanted this picture to be memorable for all those who looked at it. Taffy versus tan held more meaning, Tan was forgettable, whereas taffy made her mouth water, and she smiled.

"You're smiling this morning," Tomm said, stopping to reload his brush.

"Am I?"

"You certainly are."

"Thinking about the numbers for these colors. I don't like not knowing the names."

Tomm scratched his chin, leaving a streak of brown.

"You've got mocha chocolate brown on your chin!"

He laughed and held out the hem of his T-shirt. "And what's this color?"

"Definitely spruce green and Tahoe blue."

Sal came into the cafeteria and yelled, "Happy birthday, Jotty!"

Tomm turned to her. "It's your birthday today?"

"Does it show? I'm finally eighteen, but I don't feel any different."

"Probably not. Aging isn't fun or exciting when you get older," he said.

"I thought I'd suddenly be an adult," she said with a laugh.

He grinned back at her. "I remember feeling the same way when I turned eighteen. I could vote, legally smoke, and get a tattoo." He shook his head. "I didn't do any of those things. I was going to get my girlfriend's name tattooed on my arm. Good thing I couldn't afford it, or I'd be regretting it, especially since we broke up soon after."

None of those things sounded appealing to her, either.

"Anything special you want to do?" he asked.

"I thought about dropping out of school."

He gave her an astonished, incredulous look. "Graduation is only a couple of months away."

Jotty didn't answer right away. Instead, she surveyed the mural, looking at what was left to paint. "I'm not thinking about it now," she said.

"Good. I need you to help me finish this."

They were interrupted by Clyde saying, "I have a draft of an article the newspaper is going to run about the mural and open houses." She put something on the table and left.

"What do you think about the open house?" Clyde's suggestion of an open house for the public to view the mural had gotten pushed aside by the more mundane aspects of her life: a fire, broken windows, and threatening telephone calls.

"I've shown some of my work before. It's kind of nerve-racking to have people talking and judging your masterpiece."

"Do they say bad things?"

"There's a critic in every crowd. A vocal one," he added.

So true. Jotty had been one of them. She guessed she could swallow her pride and try to take it without getting mad.

"Just follow my lead," he said. "You respond by saying, 'That's an interesting observation,' or something like that. 'You have a good eye. Ever think about being an artist?' They usually say, 'No, too much work.' Then you know you have 'em. And they usually shut up."

She laughed. "I'll have to remember that."

The bell sounded and Jotty climbed down. She stopped briefly to look at the paper Clyde had left before going to wash her hands before class. She went into the girls' restroom. As she ran the water over her fingers and watched the mocha-brown swirl down the drain, she smelled the sleeve of her shirt. Even after two washings, it smelled smoky. Would they ever get the smell out?

"Jotty Alfarnso to the office," the intercom announced.

She frowned as she headed toward the front of the school. School hadn't even started for the day, and already she was in trouble?

Clyde met her by the door. "I saw someone trying to break into the truck you've been driving to school. Could it be your stepfather?"

Leroy, still on the loose, appeared here and there around town, never staying long before vanishing.

"Give me a description," Clyde said.

225

Jotty hated to even think about him, but she replied, "Fat, pig-faced, always wears a greasy baseball hat, and has dirty-yellow hair." She held her breath as if describing him would make him appear.

"That describes the person I saw. He was trying to break the window with a board. I yelled, and he ran off. He got into a rusty reddish pickup with one hubcap on the driver's side and drove away," Clyde said.

He was getting bolder, even coming to the school. He must be desperate for his rifle.

"Are you sure you're safe at your trailer if he's still around?"

Should she tell Clyde about the rifle? She shrugged.

"I'll need to file a police report on the incident," Clyde said.

"If you think it will help," Jotty said.

Clyde narrowed her eyes. "Why did you say that?"

"We've been filing complaints against him for years, but nothing happens."

"This was on school property."

What was the difference? The school was important, but their individual problems weren't?

Jotty followed Clyde to the parking lot and to Ma's battered truck. "Do you see any other damage?" Clyde asked.

Another scratch in the door. The window had a jagged crack from the board. It was hard to tell if there was new damage. The truck was a total wreck. "Just the window," Jotty said.

Clyde turned on her heel and marched back to the school, and Jotty followed.

Had Leroy remembered it was her birthday today? The scumbag even tried to sabotage that.

But the day of Jotty's birthday got better. After school, the war council was convened, Jotty thought with a giggle in her head. Not exactly a war council, but all the important people for the mural: Tomm, Mr. Harrison, Mr. Hornbeck, Clyde, and Jotty. They were clustered around a cafeteria table together to plan their upcoming open house.

Jotty surveyed their odd group. Before she had been the only nonadult in the tribe. But today she was an adult. She straightened her

226

spine and took a deep breath. What no fireworks? No flashing signs? Was she supposed to feel any different?

She pulled her thoughts back to the strategy session, leaning forward to concentrate.

"I'd like to have a table with information about the sage grouse," Mr. Hornbeck said.

Clyde wrote down his idea.

"Refreshments definitely," Clyde said.

"Mr. Harrison, will you speak? Tomm? Jotty?"

Speak? Her? Jotty swallowed. "What would I have to say?"

"A bit about yourself and how you started drawing and painting the local mountain."

"I guess I could say something."

Emmett walked in with his broom, stopping before the picture, scratching his head. He turned to see them studying him and gave them a sheepish smile. "I like this picture," he said.

"Do you see anything missing?" Clyde asked.

He adjusted his cap back on his head, settling it more firmly. "What about the coyotes? They've been here much longer than the horses."

Jotty had seen the coyotes sitting along the ridge, watching her, appearing the size of a medium dog.

"We can add a coyote to the ridge," she offered.

"That would be good," Emmett said, putting the broom in motion and sweeping back and forth over the floor.

Tomm cleared his throat and said, "When are we thinking about having an open house for the mural?" That was the underlying question. When—and would they be finished in time?

Clyde passed around a calendar with school activities printed in red. "We should avoid weekends when we have a track meet or baseball game."

Jotty squinted at the squares, activities, and dates. She had never attended a track meet or a baseball game. Were they fun? Had she missed too much?

Mr. Hornbeck cleared his throat. "The fifteenth doesn't work for me. We're counting sage grouse that day, aren't we, Jotty?"

She rolled her eyes, but smiled at him. "Yes, the grouse must be counted." She groused to herself, making her smile bigger and Clyde's concerned frown deeper.

"Very important," Mr. Hornbeck said.

Clyde put an X through that date. "So we're limited to the eleventh and the twenty-second. Any objections to those dates?"

"None," murmured voices around the table.

Clyde put her palms on the table and stood. "It's settled then, the eleventh, with the twenty-second as a backup or an additional day if we have a good turnout on the eleventh. I'll put this information in the newspaper and call the radio and television stations."

"And us?" Mr. Harrison asked.

"Decide what you'll say, and make any handouts you may think are helpful."

"What about us?" Tomm asked.

"You'll need to describe the process, the meaning of the mural, and how it was conceived. And of course, finish it or at least have ninety percent completed."

Tomm frowned at Jotty as if concentrating hard. "It'll get done," she said.

"I know, I know," he said. "You need to talk about the mountain. Your mountain."

Hardly. She wasn't Rattlesnake Mountain by any stretch of the imagination, but she felt a sense of pride at the comparison. The next time she climbed it, would she feel adult pride? Or would everything still be the same?

Later at Clyde's they celebrated Jotty's birthday with a cake Ma had made at Joe's. Ma shyly drew out two bulky presents. Tanya gave her a rectangular box, and from Clyde there was a large gaily wrapped gift—all covered in bright paper. Ma usually never wrapped anything, giving her whatever it was without all the trimmings.

"A special birthday," Ma said, clasping her hands. "You're eighteen." As if no one else knew she was an adult.

Clyde didn't mention that Leroy had come to the school earlier, and Jotty was glad for that. Today felt more like a week, so many things had happened in a rush. Ma would only fret and fuss and be worried if she knew. Jotty had pushed Leroy's visit deep into her head where no one could see. There would be time later to share that information and not spoil the night.

"Aren't you going to open your presents?" Tanya asked. "Mine first." Tanya's color had returned to her cheeks. She looked better since taking medicine and eating more nutritious meals. She blossomed under Clyde's care. It was too bad Tanya wanted to go home. This was a better place for her.

Jotty unfastened the paper, careful not to tear it. Inside were two paintbrushes. The professional kind Tomm used. "Thanks," she said breathlessly. She ran her fingers over the soft, smooth bristles, imagining dipping them into paint and gliding them across the scene.

"Dr. Benninger ordered them."

Jotty turned them over in her hands. They were firm but flexible and held their shape. Her lines would be precise and professional.

Ma gave her a new T-shirt, the color of melon, and a package of socks. Practical gifts.

The big box from Clyde sat on the table. "Go ahead," Clyde said, pushing it toward Jotty.

The box held a new set of paints complete with acrylic tubes, watercolors, pencils, oils, and an instruction booklet. The acrylics had names: azure, cerulean, scarlet, lime, bottle green, buttery, dusk, russet, leaden, and steely. When opened completely, it held one hundred and twenty-five colors.

This was too much. It was wonderful. Jotty swallowed as she looked over the unopened tubes. If she closed her eyes she could almost smell the oil and pigments. Her best memories involved paint.

Ma touched her hand. "Don't you like it?"

Jotty looked up and blinked; everything was wavy. The paints swam.

"No, it's so nice. I don't deserve this." She sniffed and swiped at her eyes before pushing it back to Clyde. "It's too much."

"No, I think it's just right," Clyde said.

"But I wasn't very nice at the beginning of the year." Jotty's voice got smaller.

"So we got off on the wrong foot. It's all behind us now," Clyde said, pushing the box back to her. "I'll tell you what. You can paint me a picture. Something with the mountain in the background. My husband and I never know how long we'll be in one place. I can take it when we leave."

Clyde leaving?

"Jotty?" Ma said, frowning.

"Thank you."

Jotty wanted to grab the paints and hug them. She couldn't wait until she was alone so she could caress each one and look at the book. She didn't want anyone else to touch them before her, but Tanya picked up the tubes and squinted at them. Jotty had the urge to snatch them back and replace them in their holder, but she didn't; she wouldn't. Tanya was curious only. Jotty guessed she should have been flattered by her interest.

"Strange names for the colors," Tanya said. "What about just plain blue or red?"

Blue and red didn't evoke the emotions Jotty felt when she thought of azure. It was a deep blue with a hint of lavender that reminded her of a clean mountain stream, the colors changing as the water swirled with the current and danced around rocks and logs. No, blue didn't conjure up those images. She gave Tanya a small tight smile.

Tanya grimaced and put the paints back.

"Cake everyone?" Ma asked. "This is one of Joe's special concoctions."

"Yes, cake!"

Ma produced a cake with pale buttercup-yellow frosting. Jotty hated to mar the perfection of the cake by eating it. But that was the idea, right?

Urban Gray

Chapter 58

The day after her birthday, Jotty and Ma moved back into their trailer. Jotty sniffed. "It still smells of burned macaroni and cheese."

"Why macaroni and cheese?" Ma asked, setting down her bag of clothes.

"Don't you remember when I left it on the burner and forgot about it?" Jotty stepped onto the cleaned carpets, the industrial-size fans gone.

"Oh, yes, the alarm went off," Ma said, surveying the room and touching the newly installed front window.

"We had to throw it away, pan and all."

"We tried and tried but could never get the smell out. It was ages before we didn't notice it anymore." Ma poked around the kitchen.

Jotty went into her bedroom, calling over her shoulder, "I'm not sure we'll ever get rid of this smell." Burned rubber and synthetic material, with chemicals for good measure. Her bedroom was much as she had left it, unmade bed and some dirty socks rolled up in the corner. She closed the door so Ma wouldn't see the mess.

"What do you want for dinner?" Ma asked, putting on her work apron. She was working the dinner shift.

Jotty looked in the cupboard. Macaroni and cheese. She smelled the box; it too reeked of fire.

Ma laughed. "If you burn that, we'll never know!"

Jotty opened the refrigerator that didn't smell like smoke, but of something rotten. She searched for the culprit. An onion sprouting legs and turning the color of diesel oil.

"Have you found anything?"

"Hot dogs and mac and cheese," Jotty said.

Jotty made her meal and didn't burn anything, and Ma caught a ride to work with Joe.

After eating, Jotty sat at the dining room table and turned over the rock Leroy had thrown through the window months ago. It was heavy and almost smooth on one side, a rock that had been busted in two. She wasn't sure of its exact size, maybe six inches by eight or nine inches; big enough to paint the mountain, a few horses, and a mountain lion.

She laid her new art set before her. There were no directions for rock painting, but she figured the acrylics should adhere and cover the surface. The flat side would be the trail to the top and the rounded side, the blue outline of the Truckee River with miniature ponies.

She began by mixing coffee and linen to get the shade for the mountain. As she painted the rock, the telephone rang. Ma was still at work. She put down her brush and picked up the telephone. Heavy breathing. She knew instantly who it was, but instead of being scared, she was mad. Mad that he was still bothering them. Couldn't he just leave them alone?

"You're not fooling anyone, Leroy. We know it's you. Why don't you come out and fight? Be a man!"

No response.

"You're a coward."

Click.

She replaced the receiver and went back to painting the rock. As she worked, her mind thought about all the things worrying her. Of course, money was always at the forefront: how to pay their bills and keep the trailer. She guessed lack of money would always be first if they stayed in Sagebrush.

She placed the rock on a newspaper to dry. She picked up azure and cerulean and mixed dots of each together. They were too intense for the sky. She added a dab of white and swirled them together. The result was the perfect combination for the Nevada sky, the color of the state flag, she realized.

The telephone interrupted her thoughts again.

She grabbed it. "Quit playing games with us, Leroy! Did you hear me?"

"Jotty. It's me. Ma. I'll be home later than expected. Joe will give me a ride."

Oops. "Sorry, Ma, I thought you were a crank caller."

"You thought I was Leroy. Did he call tonight?"

"No." A fat white lie.

Leroy was close to a pay phone someplace. Probably in town. Should she drive around and look for him?

"I'll be home close to nine."

She hung up the telephone before slipping out of the trailer and into Ma's truck. She drove through Sagebrush. Most of the other cars were going the opposite way, leaving the gravel pit for their homes. A steady stream of cars snaked down Main Street. Jotty pulled into the alley behind Joe's, the Half-Moon Tavern, and the antique shop. She got out and crept to the side where she knew there was a pay phone and saw the back of a pickup truck. A rusty red pickup. Leroy was in the bar. She hurried back to her truck and drove forward. Could she shoot him if she confronted him?

Leroy stumbled around the corner just as she reached his truck. When Leroy saw her, he had that deer-in-the-headlights look before scrunching his brows together in a scowl. She recognized that look too.

He jumped into his truck and gunned the engine, fishtailing out of the alley. With her heart hammering loudly, she followed, leaning forward to grab his rifle. He sped around the corner with her on his tail.

With tires screeching, Leroy cut into traffic. Horns blared at his near miss. His last hubcap rolled drunkenly around before being flattened by the other cars. Jotty stopped and let the cars go by. Damn! She wouldn't catch him now. Slowly her breathing returned to normal.

When traffic cleared, she drove to the edge of town, near the road that led to where Tanya's family lived. It was getting dark, but she thought she saw a cloud of dust. It would be foolish to chase him through the desert.

She stopped and rolled down the window. Cold air surrounded her as she listened. She heard the traffic in town, but nothing in the desert. All was still and quiet. She had lost him. But maybe he'd think twice about using that pay phone again. But worse, she wouldn't be able to collect on the five-thousand-dollar reward money. Damn, the money would have solved a bunch of problems. He'd try to retrieve his rifle again; she was sure of it. She'd have to be on her guard.

233

Jotty rolled up the window, put the truck in reverse, turned around, and drove home to work on her rock as she waited for Ma.

Mayflower Blue

Chapter 59

Leroy had vanished, and that was good for now. But when the mural and open house were finished, Jotty wanted to catch him and collect the reward. But first things first. She occupied her mind with the mural and the open house. They worked longer each night to get most of it finished. Those weeks passed quickly. Her birthday had been six weeks ago. How come time used to tick by slowly, but now it was a locomotive barreling down the track?

So today, on the Saturday morning of the open house, before Jotty showered and dressed, Ma came in and handed her a package.

"What's this?"

"A new T-shirt so you look nice."

Jotty removed the shirt, shook out its creases, and held it up. "You gave me a new shirt for my birthday." She had saved that "new smell" shirt for just such an occasion; besides, it was the only clothing she owned that didn't smell of smoke or have paint stains.

"Well, here's another one. Blue is your color."

She put on the new shirt—mayflower blue—and modeled for Ma.

"Are you sure, Ma, you won't go with me?"

Ma put down her cup and pushed back the curtains, assessing the day's potential. Jotty saw a clear spring sky, the color of her new shirt. The bleached clouds blended almost perfectly with the mayflower blue.

Ma dropped the curtain. "I'm going to help Joe. He figures business will be brisk, with people coming to the school to see the mural."

"As long as you're at work and not here alone." Jotty used her best stare on Ma.

"He won't come in broad daylight," Ma said.

235

"He came to the school on my birthday." She had meant to tell Ma earlier, but forgot in the excitement to finish the mural before the open house.

"He did?" Ma's eyes opened wide, the white part around the pupils the most prominent. "He's getting bolder."

She shouldn't have told Ma. The incident had been many weeks ago. Now Ma would worry. "Clyde chased him away."

"You need to be careful," Ma said, echoing Clyde's sentiments. Ma clenched Jotty's arm, too upset to even yell at her for calling Dr. Benninger "Clyde."

"I will. Nothing will happen today. A busload of art students from the university will be at school," Jotty said proudly.

"That's good. There will be lots of people around," Ma said, as if reassuring herself.

"Do you need a ride to Joe's?" Jotty asked.

"No, he'll pick me up. He knows we only have one vehicle now."

Jotty kissed Ma goodbye and drove to school.

She wasn't worried about herself, only Ma. Would Leroy come to school in the middle of the open house? She pursed her lips. Probably not. He wasn't that stupid.

She and Tomm had worked late into the night to finish. To the naked eye, the mural was finished, but it wasn't really.

So now, Tomm folded the tarps and put away all their supplies in Emmett's custodial closet, Mr. Harrison ran off fact sheets on the copy machine, and Jotty helped move the paint cans into the hall. When finished, she leaned against a cafeteria table. The television station from Reno was setting up lights and cameras, lugging in trunks, equipment, and cables. Tanya was there with Clyde.

Tanya's stay with Clyde had been good. Too bad Tanya couldn't live with her forever. Jotty even saw Clyde give her a hug. Tanya probably didn't get too many of those at home.

Tanya glowed as she helped in the office, answering the telephone that rang constantly since they got there.

Jotty left the office, walked into the cafeteria, and studied the mural. She closed her eyes, opened them, and tried to view the mural without bias. She had worked so close, for so long; she hardly saw it in its finished state. They had each worked on the individual elements, but now it all flowed together and told the story of Sagebrush.

What would the university students think? She tried to see the picture the way they would for the first time.

At the far-right end, in the forefront, was a small wooden schoolhouse with uneven wooden plank walls and a lopsided sign that read Sagebrush Grammer School. Children dressed in old-fashioned clothes played with balls and dolls in the school yard. Mr. Harrison had given them a black-and-white photo of children wearing similar clothing.

Fort Churchill stood in the background, smoke curling into the air from their campfires. Most importantly, behind everything was Rattlesnake Mountain, dotted by a few wild pintos. Mr. Harrison's tribute. The mountain lion glared from behind a boulder, and a rattler poised to strike. The coyote sentries looked down from their perch at the top of the mountain. And of course, a covey of grouse clustered at the bottom. She couldn't forget to add them after counting them for Mr. Hornbeck. Little by little, she had grown fond of the feathered fowl.

The rest of the mural was of downtown Sagebrush: a general store, saloon, two other old-fashioned buildings with ranchers, merchants, townspeople, soldiers, and miners milling about in the street and on the wooden sidewalks. A stagecoach was leaving town.

The wooden sidewalks were gone now, but some of the original buildings remained. The mercantile now housed the antiques shop. Sagebrush looked more alive and exciting during the 1800s than now.

Jotty looked down at her new shirt. Damn, did she have paint on it already? One of the cans must be leaking. She went into the hall to clean her shirt and check the cans.

In the bathroom she dabbed at the spot with a paper towel. Next, she lifted and looked under each paint can. The adobe, #9472, was the leaking color.

She heard hesitant footsteps behind her, probably Mr. Harrison or Tomm.

"Got ya!

An arm grabbed around Jotty's neck and a hand clamped over her mouth before she could scream. Her nostrils flared. She'd recognize that smell of stale sweat, smoke, and beer anywhere. Leroy. She struggled to get away from him, shaking her head from side to side. His hands gripped her tightly, his forefinger pressing on her windpipe, making breathing difficult.

Her surprise led to anger. Red boiling emotion and a feeling of overwhelming strength.

Jotty kicked Leroy's shin, and he released her. She whirled to face him.

"You bitch." He rubbed his leg as they eyed each other. "Where's my rifle?"

"I sold it." Jotty watched his face change from contempt to amazement and back to contempt.

They circled each other like feral cats, looking for the advantage, hissing and bristling.   "You had no right!" He lunged for her. His face distorted, making his puffed-up bread-dough features run into each other.

Jotty sidestepped him. Leroy had been drinking, which made him mean, but clumsy.

Leroy breathed heavily, winded.

She grinned at him. "I want to blow you away for what you did to Ma and the trailer."

Leroy jumped at her. She hadn't expected him to be so quick. He grabbed her hair and jerked her sideways. Pain ripped her skull as she fell. Her elbow slammed into the floor but she managed to roll to one side and spotted the paint cans. She grabbed the nearest one as Leroy dived after her. Anger surged through her as she tasted salty blood on her lip. With Herculean strength, she hoisted the can and smashed it down on Leroy's head and neck. He looked startled as he screamed, falling face-first, his nose hitting the floor with a dull thud.

Jotty lifted the can again, watching for movement, but he remained still.

"Jotty? I heard a noise. What's going on?" Tomm came around the corner and stopped. "Who's that?"

238

"My stepfather."

"Oh, yeah, Mr. Football." A fitting title for Leroy, along with drunkard and mean-spirited.

"Yup, hit him on the head with a paint can."

"Those are heavy." Tomm picked up the can and moved his arm up and down as if weighing the contents. He wore a shirt and tie today. He looked very nice.

"I know," she said with a shaky laugh. "He deserved what he got; he's been beating on my mother for years."

Tomm turned Leroy over and felt his neck. "He's still alive."

That was good. He could rot in prison for all she cared. Blood oozed from his nose, and saliva ran down the side of his mouth, but his chest moved rhythmically up and down.

"He'll live, but he'll think he's got a massive hangover," Tomm said.

"Won't be the first time," Jotty said, wiping her hands on the back of her jeans. She wanted to scrub off the stench Leroy left. Did she have blood on her new shirt?

"Do you want me to call the sheriff for you?" he asked.

"S...sure." Her voice shook and wavered, and all her strength drained away.

Clyde came down the hall, stopping when she saw the body, and then hurrying toward them. "Is everyone OK?" She stopped just short of Leroy's body. "I think that's the man I saw in the parking lot!"

"My stepfather," Jotty said.

Mr. Harrison hurried toward them too. He had on his Indian headdress. "Whoa. Who's that?" He was followed by Mr. Hornbeck. Somehow, they become good friends through the mural process.

"My stepfather tried to choke me." Tiredness came over Jotty and she slumped down against the wall.

Clyde took her arm and pulled her into the cafeteria and onto a chair. "You're as pale as a ghost." She examined Jotty's neck.

"I'm...I'm fine," Jotty said, struggling out of the chair, but her neck felt bruised and warm.

Clyde shook her head in disbelief. "Sit down."

Jotty sat.

Tomm came in with a wet towel. "Here, wipe your face. You'll feel better."

The water felt good on her forehead and cheeks. She tasted blood in her mouth and ran her tongue over the inside of her cut lip.

"I'll call an ambulance." Clyde looked at her watch. "I hope they hurry. We open in an hour. I don't want anything to spoil this." She walked rapidly to her office.

Jotty listened to a loud hammering on the front door, but closed her eyes and breathed deeply. She sensed Tomm hovering.

"I'm OK," she said.

"Just making sure," he replied.

She opened her eyes and listened to the voices in the hall. The sheriff came toward her. "I understand Leroy tried to choke you."

She nodded and showed him her neck.

"It's a bit red. You OK?" he asked.

"I'm fine now." She got up and said, "He's in the hallway."

Together they walked over to Leroy's inert form.

"How did you manage to knock him out?" the sheriff asked, holding a toothpick between his teeth.

"I hit him with that paint can," Jotty said. Adobe tan to the rescue.

They listened as the banging on the front door started again.

"You have quite a crowd out there. A tour bus pulled in after me," the sheriff said.

How many people were there?

The sheriff frowned as he studied Leroy. "The slippery weasel won't know what hit him. With his record, he'll have quite a long time to think about it though. And you, young lady, have earned yourself the reward."

She gulped. Five thousand dollars. She couldn't imagine that sum of money. The phone calls and deep breathing would stop now. Ma could live in peace. They could live quietly just the two of them.

The banging on the doors intensified as the ambulance and EMTs arrived.

One first looked at Jotty's neck. "Are you in pain?"

And the other at Leroy.

240

"No, I'm fine."

"If you're not, you should see the doctor."

"Just take him away." She waved her arms over Leroy. They hoisted Leroy onto a gurney and took him off to the closest medical care facility, and then the sheriff would take him to jail.

The sheriff said, "Give me half an hour for statements, and then I'll get out of here." He listened to the banging at the front door. "They're anxious to get in, and I can understand why." He whistled through his teeth. "That's some picture. My wife wants to come by to see it too."" "I'm glad we have a lot of people here," Clyde said briskly. "The more the better."

Jotty thought of Leroy. The more the better minus the one in the ambulance. They should have charged him the admission fee, she thought as she rubbed her neck. She never wanted to see him again.

Adobe Tan

Chapter 60

The sheriff finished taking statements and left. Clyde unlocked the doors, and the art students thronged in, exclaiming about the ambulance and the sheriff.

"He fainted at the sight of the picture," Jotty said. She cracked herself up sometimes.

The art student studied her before grinning. "You're teasing, right?" They were about the same age. "Hey! You're the high school girl, who helped paint this, aren't you?" the university student continued as if Jotty had answered her. "This is amazing. The whole story about you and this picture is inspiring. We couldn't wait to meet you."

No one had ever wanted to meet her before.

Clyde had made calls to the local paper and radio stations. Jotty's picture had appeared in the local newspaper and afterward, Ma had been inundated with questions at Joe's. This was bigger than she could have imagined.

Clyde motioned her toward the area in front of the mural and showed her how to use the microphone. "Just press this button to talk like this. Testing." Clyde's voice bounced around the cafeteria.

Jotty frowned.

"Talk slowly and you'll be fine. Why don't you circulate for a bit?" Clyde said.

Suddenly feeling shy, she looked around. She didn't need to circulate, the crowd surrounded her. They asked questions in rapid-fire tempo, pointing and gesturing toward the mural.

"Why did you add that?"

"I—" She was interrupted.

"Are there really mountain lions here?"

"Yes, but—" Another interruption.

"Have you seen horses?"

Jotty didn't bother trying to answer the questions and instead nodded her head.

"What type of paint did you use to get that effect?"

"You're really good. How long have you been painting?"

"Since I was little," Jotty said. She couldn't remember a time when she hadn't been drawing or coloring pictures.

The cafeteria was packed with students, and the camera crew filmed the entire event. It was hard to gauge how many people were there—maybe three hundred? The story was to be on the six o'clock news.

The cafeteria staff had baked sheets of cookies and made vats of sugary fruit punch to be served to the guests. Mr. Harrison, wearing his Indian headdress, passed out brochures and information. He looked every bit the part of a chief. Mr. Hornbeck carried a stuffed sage grouse. What a pair they were. The crowd surrounded them too.

Clyde motioned Jotty over to her side and spoke into the microphone, addressing the crowd. "Thank you all for coming today. Many of you have already met her, but I want to introduce you to the girl who suggested the mural and our artist in residence, Jotty Alfarnso and Tomm Claybanks. They have painted a truly inspirational piece for Sagebrush High School."

The audience clapped. Jotty nodded, but kept her head down. A prickle of tears threatened to escape. She didn't cry very often.

There was the sound of buzzing bees from the crowd.

Clyde waited. "It's magnificent, don't you think?"

More buzzing, murmuring, and clapping. Someone whistled.

Jotty stood silently watching their reactions. Her eyes darted around the room. Her gaze stopped on one face or another, curious about the people in attendance, randomly searching out acceptance. She stopped on a familiar face, Emmett, the school custodian, the person who kept painting over her other murals. He had his hair slicked back. He smiled broadly at her. She grinned back. Her heart swelled. They were clapping for her, for all of them.

Clyde continued speaking, first introducing Tomm. "Mr. Tomm Claybanks. Do you want to tell them what this has meant to you?'

He stepped to the mic. "This is a dream-come-true project for me. The school and citizens of Sagebrush have been very welcoming.

I'm especially glad to have worked with Jotty and Mr. Harrison and Mr. Hornbeck. I didn't realize this small school had such wonderful, knowledgeable teachers. And Jotty is the most talented young artist I've ever worked with." He turned to her and motioned her closer.

She moved to the mic and stood by Tomm's side, shoulder to shoulder. It seemed natural after months of working together.

"Do you want to say anything?" Clyde asked.

"Me? No." She hated talking in front of people and leaned away from the microphone.

Several people laughed and she shrugged.

"I now present Mr. Harrison, our social studies teacher and local historian. Or should I say chief?"

Mr. Harrison, resplendent in his headdress of feathers, took the mic. "The history of this tiny town is anything but small." His voice commanded attention. The room was quiet as he spoke. "Sagebrush was a railway hub during the great migration west. During the silver strike in Virginia City, much of the ore came through Sagebrush. Most of the mines are long closed, but Sagebrush is still here. The mural shows a bit of how it looked during the mining period. You can see it was a thriving and busy place." He paused so they could look at the mural.

"These two," he said, gesturing toward Jotty and Tomm, "took my suggestions, looked at my old pictures, toured Fort Churchill with me, and came up with this mural, a testament to the rich history of Sagebrush. I think they did a wonderful job, don't you?"

Clyde next motioned for Mr. Hornbeck. He took the stage and said, "Not only is this area rich in history, it is also part of the sage grouse's natural habitat. They are protected birds and only nest in certain parts of the western United States. Because of my—or rather, our studies—they will be around for many years."

The applause was loud and long. Again, the tears pricked at the corner of her eyes. Jotty blinked rapidly before giving the audience a small, shy smile.

Clyde finished with, "I'm sure you want to talk to them, all of them, and ask questions."

Clyde turned off the microphone and let the crowd swarm around Tomm and Jotty. The questions came fast.

"Why paint Rattlesnake Mountain?" one asked.

Jotty found her voice. "There's not much around Sagebrush that's awesome. I think Rattlesnake Mountain's beautiful even in an ugly way." She spoke from the heart.

The crowd murmured in agreement.

"Why do you think the mountain is called Rattlesnake?"

"I've seen rattlers there before." OK, not true. She saw one dead rattler and possibly another slither into the sagebrush, but they didn't need to know that. What if the mountain suddenly got so popular she couldn't go there and continue to enjoy its peace and quiet?

"You've seen the rattlesnakes?" someone asked.

"Yes, several big ones. They lie on the path where it's warm." Maybe that would keep the sightseers away.

"Tomm? How was it to work with a high school student?"

Tomm answered, "She's a pretty amazing high school student. I don't remember acting that grown-up when I was her age. She helped paint the mural so when people look at it, they aren't just seeing the images but are transported back in time. They feel the wind in their hair, the dirt under their boots, and they see the beauty in ordinary things. I can almost smell the sagebrush, can't you?" A low buzz of agreement. "She has quite a talent. And an eye for color and proportion. A unique person."

"Jotty? Are you going to art school?" someone asked.

She paused for moment before answering. In the dark, at night, she thought about art school, but she always got hung up on the paying for it part.

"Yes," she replied, a little surprised at how easily her answer slipped out.

"What about Crandall?" That was their art school. She hadn't even known it existed until a few weeks ago.

"Sure." Had she really said that? A warm feeling came over her, an unexpected emotion.

"We have a good school!"

"We could use someone with your talent for our art shows and displays around campus," another added.

Flashes of pictures, her pictures, exploded in her head. She could almost see them on the walls. What a feeling!

When the questions finished, Jotty took a glass of punch. She drank thirstily and then cleared her throat. Her throat felt raw from answering questions and talking over the undercurrent of voices.

"Why don't you come for a visit?" the art professor from Crandall asked, striding to the table for a last cookie and drink. He handed Jotty a brochure. "Take a look. We'll mail you an admissions packet."

Visit them? She folded the brochure and tucked it in her back pocket.

"Maybe," she answered slowly. "I don't get to Reno very often." Could they manage a trip in Ma's old truck? Jotty's head whirled with the possibilities as the Crandall students filed out to their bus. With the refreshments gone, people slowly drifted away.

When the time was up and only a few people remained, Clyde took the microphone and said, "We want to thank all of you for coming today."

When the last visitor left, they collapsed together at a table. All the refreshments were gone; the only evidence remaining were scattered crumbs and a splash of red.

Clyde pushed the cash box to the middle of the table. "Shall we count our till?"

They each took a pile of bills and checks. "Let's sort it in piles of one hundred dollars."

She followed Clyde's lead and first sorted by denominations, ones, fives, tens, and twenties. There was a check for $500 from the Crandall School. Jotty gulped. She had never seen a check for that much before. When she finished counting, she had over $600 in her pile. In total, they made almost a thousand dollars. She could hardly believe the amount. They were having another open house in two weeks. Would the same number of people attend that one?

But best of all, Leroy was locked away, and the reward money was hers.

"I think we need a second open house," Clyde said. "Everyone up for two weeks from today?"

There was agreement from everyone.

The second open house was as busy as the first. People came from as far away as Reno, Virginia City, and Fallon. Ma went to the second open house.

"I had no idea! Oh, my goodness!" Ma said, clasping her hands to her cheeks. "It's so big! No wonder it took all these months to finish."

This open house was also bittersweet. Sweet because of all the people who attended, but bitter because it was also Tomm's last week. He was leaving Tuesday for another project. The school was having an assembly on Monday to thank him.

Jotty didn't want to tell Tomm goodbye, but she knew she needed to be there. He was a friend, and she would miss him.

On Monday morning she went first to the cafeteria, but he wasn't there. A few students were eating breakfast. Tanya waved her over.

"Hey!"

"Hey, yourself." She hadn't seen much of Tanya since the first open house. Tanya had moved home to help her mother. But because of Clyde, Tanya's thyroid problems had stabilized, and she even wanted to go to college. Their senior year had swirled away, smoke on a windy day—urban steel or foggy mist?

Would Tanya make a good teacher? Jotty flipped back through the names and faces of her favorite teachers, mainly from elementary school. Yes, Tanya would be a good primary teacher.

Tomm walked by. He had on his shirt and tie again for the assembly. She waved to him and followed him to a far corner.

"I wanted to tell you goodbye," she said, feeling shy.

"Me too, but I don't really want to tell you goodbye," he said. He stood before her, his hands clasped together, his head tilted down, studying the floor.

She nodded, her throat threatening to close from the overwhelming emotion she felt. "I can't believe we're done. It's hard saying goodbye to a friend." How would she feel when Tanya left for college? Probably the same—sad and happy all at once—an indescribable scrambled feeling.

"I know."

"I heard that the Hawaiians say 'aloha,' which means hello and goodbye," he said. "Maybe we should say that instead?"

"Aloha." An unfamiliar word, but it flowed over her tongue. "So you're leaving tomorrow?" She moved the toe of her sneaker back and forth.

"Yes, going back to Reno."

"Is that good?" His ex-wife and kids were there. Would he be able to see them?

"I have another mural to paint for a bank. You should stop by and see me," he said.

"Maybe I will." Crandall was in Reno, and Tomm would be there too. They stood awkwardly.

"I'm going to miss seeing you, Harrison, and Hornbeck every day," Tomm said.

"We made a good team." They stood quietly and looked at the mural. Jotty felt protected somehow from the noise all around them as students filed in for school. Neither wanted to say the last word.

He cleared his throat. "I'm meeting with a lawyer on Wednesday to see if I can visit my kids. I miss them."

Tomm's kids needed to see him.

He continued, "You made me realize what they might be feeling. Even though I don't want to face my ex-wife, I'd do anything to see them again. Including going to court if I have to."

The bell sounded. They both stiffened. She needed to go to class. "I'll see you at the assembly."

"Keep in touch." He squeezed her hand and gave her a card.

She looked away, afraid she might cry.

"Maybe we can team up again," he said.

"That would be great," she said, not turning to look at him.

"My address and number in Reno."

She put the card in her pocket.

"Aloha.

Foggy Mist

Chapter 61

After the assembly and Tomm's departure, school felt flat and lifeless. Jotty contented herself by working on the rock she was painting for Clyde. The rock transformed into a mini-version of the mountain and its inhabitants. It kept her hands and mind busy.

Jotty sat in their quiet trailer and painted. Ma was still at work. Jotty put the final touches on the rock, setting it aside to dry. Ma came in from work. She smiled. "You got a telephone call at Joe's."

"At Joe's?"

Ma dug around in her pocket and pulled out a small neatly folded square of paper. She squinted at her writing. "A Mr. Carl Jones from a new cat food company."

"Cat food? We don't own a cat." The feral cats that lived on the fringe of the trailer park didn't count as pets, did they?

"The company is building a processing plant between Sagebrush and Reno and they want you to paint pictures on the side of the building."

She didn't draw cats. She drew scenery and horses and mountain lions. A cat was just a smaller version of a mountain lion, wasn't it?

"Oh, and something came in the mail for you."

Jotty frowned. "What?" She rarely got anything in their post office box.

"This." Ma handed her a large manila envelope. "From a school."

Jotty opened it and studied the brick building on the front. The Crandall School of Art.

"You're a pretty popular girl now."

She didn't feel particularly popular. She wasn't on student council or the dance team. She'd never had a date in her life.

"Call Mr. Jones back. I want to hear what he says." Ma nudged her.

"Isn't it too late?"

Ma looked at the clock. "You're right; they're probably closed for the day. Call in the morning."

The next morning, right at eight o'clock, Jotty dialed the number and asked for Mr. Jones.

"Hello, this Jotty Alfarnso from Sagebrush."

A pause.

"The artist?" she said.

"Oh yes, thank you for returning my call." Ma huddled close, her ear by the receiver.

"We're building the new cat food company, and we heard about your mural. You were recommended by Tomm Claybanks. Would you be willing to do another mural?"

"I'll…" Ma poked her. "Uh…Sure."

"We'll pay for your supplies and paints and anything else you want. Would twenty-five hundred dollars be adequate for your services?"

"I…I think so." A whirlwind of words, pictures, and emotions swirled through her head. That was a lot of money. "I'll have to figure that out." The cost of paint, gas, brushes to sort through. There would be wonderful paints and supplies, and someone else was going to pay for it. She wanted to shout and pump her fist in the air.

"You call me back with a list of things you'll need, and we can talk more. I'm going to take a drive over to Sagebrush to see your work."

A bigwig wanted to see her work. "Thank you."

Ma grabbed Jotty around the waist when she hung up. "Jotty! That's a lot of money!"

It was a lot of money. Jotty grinned back at her. The mural money and the reward money meant she could think about Crandall. Really think about it, not just in her dreams.

Foggy Mist

Chapter 62

The rock Leroy had thrown through their window became a
miniature of the mountain for Clyde. Jotty had finished it and let it dry
completely.

As Jotty rearranged the items in her backpack, Ma looked at
the rock and frowned. "This is interesting."

"It's for Clyde."

Ma frowned, but didn't correct her. "A graduation present?"

A going-away present.

There were only about two weeks left of school. The mural was
finished, and it felt strange to ride the bus again, to get into a different
routine. She wanted Clyde to have the rock before the school year
ended. She hoped to slip away from the school when they graduated
and not make a fuss.

Once at school, she went into the office, hoping Clyde was
there.

"Jotty?"

"Here." She thrust the rock in Clyde's hands. "I painted
something for you."

Clyde gasped. "That's heavy!" She studied the scene on the
rock. "This is wonderful. For me?"

"Yes." They stood awkwardly looking at each other. Not the
same sizing-up look Jotty remembered from the beginning of the year.
An understanding look between friends who had witnessed something
life changing.

Clyde turned it over in her hands. "This is wonderful. I'll
treasure it forever. Thank you for everything."

She guessed she should have thanked Clyde too. Maybe later
she could say those words. Did the Hawaiians have a musical-
sounding word like aloha for thank you?

"Aloha."

Clyde laughed, "A funny thing to say!"

"Hello and goodbye."

And thank you thrown in for good measure. They stood awkwardly for several more seconds before Clyde's telephone rang and she returned to her desk. Jotty looked around the office before leaving and stopping at the cafeteria doorway. She wished she could be a little mouse next year and see the faces of the new freshmen. Would they feel the same excitement when they looked at the mural?

This chapter of her life was over. She was painting another mural. She'd be drawing cats, not mountains. That was OK too. It meant jobs for the Sagebrush people. Her artwork would be visible from the highway.

She had practiced drawing cats in various poses: sleeping, playing with a ball, and sitting on a perch. All different colors of cats, multihued cats of buff, caramel, truffle, bronze, and midnight. She sat outside their trailer and watched the feral cats run in and out of the sagebrush. They gradually got used to her sitting there and even took a few tentative steps in her direction. If they got close, and she held her hand out, and they hissed at her. They were the opposite of Tanya's cats that napped in the sunshine and purred when petted.

The strokes involved with painting cats felt strange, mountain slopes were broad. With cats, it was more detail oriented. She had to purse her lips, concentrate, and will her hands to slow down and paint the distinct lines and features. Whiskers were far different than painting a boulder or clump of sagebrush. She'd get used to it. She could make the change, she decided.

Strawberry Roan

Chapter 62

On Saturday morning at the end of May, Jotty packed her backpack with a sandwich, an apple, and a jug of water.

"Where are you going?" Ma asked.

"To take a hike."

Ma looked out at the sun blazing up the sky.

"It's going to be a hot one today," Ma said. "Mid-eighties. Do you want a hat?"

"No hat." She wanted to have the sun warm her face. "I might even climb to the top today."

"You've been saying that ever since you were a little girl," Ma said, putting away the jar of peanut butter Jotty had taken out of the cupboard.

"It's always good to have a goal."

Ma studied her face. What was she looking for? Jotty didn't know. But finally satisfied with whatever she saw, she nodded at Jotty.

"Couldn't you make filling out that application your goal?" Ma said.

"Ma!" The application to Crandall Art School was tucked in her backpack. She wanted to read it over without Ma standing over her shoulder making suggestions and comments.

The mountain always helped her prioritize things. It wasn't on a time schedule; it moved at its own pace.

She drove to the mountain, hitched the backpack over her shoulders, and started her climb.

The sun warmed the back of Jotty's neck. As she climbed, rivulets of sweat trickled down her temples. Maybe she should have taken a hat.

She stopped and turned back. She half expected to see Tomm's truck come into view. He was in Reno, hopefully seeing his kids. She didn't see any other cars this morning. She turned back to the task at hand.

The higher she climbed, the drier her mouth became. She swallowed over and over, but the dusty grit remained. Still she pushed upward, passing small spindly pine trees and variously colored clumps of sagebrush.

In the late spring/early summer, sagebrush bloomed purple, green, and yellow, making some people sneeze, but giving a little color to the caramel desert. Jotty stopped and fished out her water. She took several long swallows before wiping her eyes. She had never been this high on Rattlesnake Mountain. This was new territory for her. She wanted to get to the top, but her legs shook, and she was afraid they'd collapse under her. She sank down on the dusty path and leaned back against another large boulder. A new vantage for her that afforded her a different view entirely. She wished she had known before what she could see from this height.

Jotty shaded her eyes and looked down at the tiny, still town. From here, the trailers didn't seem so battered and sad. They were even pretty with the pine trees bordering them and the late-spring sky surrounding everything in gold brilliance.

Jotty pulled out her sketch pad and colored pencils. She drew a cat pouncing and another napping in the sun. Satisfied with her efforts, she closed the pad and took out the envelope from Crandall. Slowly she took out the sheets.

What was the worst thing that could happen if she applied? Rejection. She guessed she could handle that. She had known rejection before. Rejection from teachers who didn't understand, Leroy, her own father, and herself. She had rejected the notion she was a worthy person.

But now she realized, by her racing heart, how much she wanted to attend Crandall. This was a way out of Sagebrush. She was finally getting her wish, but she felt unsure and a bit scared.

Something nudged her arm. The strawberry-roan-colored horse sneaked up on her and now stood watching her. Jotty had been concentrating so hard she hadn't seen or heard the horse approaching. The roan continued to smell Jotty's sleeve and backpack searching for treats.

Jotty tentatively patted the soft inquisitive nose. She had never tried to touch her before. But the mare had thrust her Belgian-chocolate velvety nose against Jotty's sleeve as she blew out grassy puffs of air. "I'm sorry, girl; I don't have anything for you."

The horse did not move away, but continued to smell her hair, shoulder, and backpack. It was then that Jotty remembered the apple. Slowly, so as not to disturb her visitor, she pulled the fruit from her bag and offered it to the horse.

Daintily, the roan took the apple from Jotty's fingers. In one crunch, the apple was gone. They looked at each other for a long while. The roan's brown eyes were limitless and accepting. "I wish I had more for you," Jotty said.

As if understanding, the roan turned, swished her tail and slowly climbed in a zigzag pattern back to the rest of the herd. The band watched from a distance, some nibbling at the sagebrush and some watching intently. The lone stallion whinnied and tossed his head. Jotty wished she had something for all of them.

The herd then turned and made their way around to the side of the hill with the river. She watched until the last horse disappeared from view.

Jotty smiled as she shaded her eyes and looked at the summit. She wouldn't get there today, but that was OK. But as Ma reminded her, she'd been trying to climb to the top all her life. She got a bit farther each time. There was always tomorrow or the next day. Next time. Next time, she'd climb to the very top.

*****

Sue C. Dugan is an author living in Northern Nevada with her husband, dog, and cat. She likes nothing more than to walk the hills behind her house with her trusty companion and walking partner, Hailey. Together they have encountered coyotes, Golden Eagles, wild horses, hawks, snakes, and tarantulas. To call Nevada beautiful is an understatement—it is a hidden-spectacular gem.